Abby started across the hall

She whispered a silent prayer as she slipped the key into the lock. It fit, and they stepped into a short corridor painted institutional green.

The unit was much smaller than the main psychiatric ward. As Abby remembered, only a handful of disturbed patients were housed in the half-dozen rooms that lined the corridor. Room 315 was the first door on the right. As soon as they stepped inside, Abby knew something was terribly wrong. The room smelled fetid and the man-size form on the bed was draped from head to toe with a white sheet.

"Oh, my God! Steve!" Abby gasped.

There was no response from the bed, just the finality of death.

Dear Reader,

We're delighted to bring you Rebecca York's first Harlequin Intrigue. After innumerable books, rave reviews and bestsellerdom, she has turned her talents to creating an exciting new ongoing series for Intrigue—43 LIGHT STREET.

It looks like a charming old building near the renovated Baltimore waterfront, but inside 43 Light Street lurks danger...and romance.

In this, and future 43 LIGHT STREET books, Rebecca York spins spine-tingling thrillers, eerie psychological suspense and good ol' adventure stories—all laced with the passion and romance that you expect from a Harlequin.

Rebecca York is the pseudonym of two Maryland writers—Ruth Glick and Eileen Buckholtz. Longtime lovers of romance and mystery, they have penned mainstream psychological thrillers as Samantha Chase, a young-adult series under their real names, romances as Amanda Lee, and, of course, an award-winning suspense series, Peregrine Connection, under Rebecca York.

We hope you'll enjoy this and all the upcoming titles in their newest series—43 LIGHT STREET. Be sure to look for the 43 LIGHT STREET logo to identify the future books.

Sincerely,

Debra Matteucci
Senior Editor and Editorial Coordinator

Life Line

Rebecca York

Harlequin Books

TORONTO • NEW YORK • LONDON
AMSTERDAM • PARIS • SYDNEY • HAMBURG
STOCKHOLM • ATHENS • TOKYO • MILAN

Harlequin Intrigue edition published August 1990

ISBN 0-373-22143-6

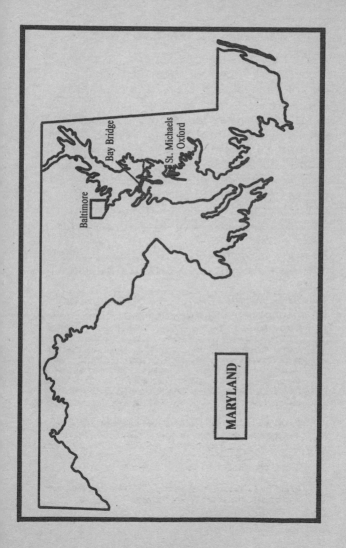

MARYLAND

CAST OF CHARACTERS

Abby Franklin—Her career as a psychologist meant everything, but she risked her reputation—and her life—for a man who didn't want her help.

Steve Claiborne—Dangerous, disturbing and determined to cut through the web of lies that surrounded his sister.

Frances Backman—A local girl who'd come a long way from her humble beginnings.

Cecile Claiborne—Rich man's bored wife— or the lynch pin in a dangerous conspiracy?

Derrick Claiborne—Did he really act in his sister's best interests?

Sharon Claiborne—Her desperate plea for help drew Abby into a storm of peril and betrayal.

Adam Goodwin—Money was the bottom line for this slick insurance salesman.

Ezra Hornby—Desperate to keep the Lazarus Rescue Mission alive.

Donald Kellog—World-famous surgeon on the cutting edge.

George Napier—Was he really as crazy as he sounded?

Jo O'Malley—This private detective taught Abby a trick or two.

Miles Skinner—Did he stand to gain from Sharon's death?

Melissa Wexler—A gifted little girl who never met a puzzle she couldn't solve.

Jonathan Wyndham—Chief of Staff at the Sterling Clinic.

Chapter One

"They're going to kill me. Pleeeease, you've got to save me."

Reaching for the phone at six in the morning had been reflex. Now the urgency in the voice on the other end of the line catapulted Abby Franklin to instant wakefulness as effectively as a cup of bitter coffee.

"Who is this?"

A high-pitched sob echoed in her ear.

"It's all right," Abby soothed. "Just tell me what's wrong."

"My head. Ooooo, my head." It was a woman's voice—distorted by pain and fear.

"Are you hurt? Have you been in an accident?"

"It's splitting in half." The words were punctuated with a tortured groan. "Ahhhh—"

Abby could feel the waves of anguish radiating through the phone lines. As a psychologist, she knew the best way to respond was with a mixture of comfort and authority. Still, it was hard to keep her own voice steady. "You have to tell me what's wrong."

"Oh, Lord. The spiders. Horrible little spiders are crawling out."

Who was she talking to? As Abby snapped on the bedside light, her green eyes squinted in momentary pain. It sounded as if the caller was a patient in the middle of a psychotic break. Or someone on a bad drug trip. But who? The voice wasn't recognizable from her current caseload.

"Oh, please. Make it stop."

Careful, Abby cautioned herself. Say the wrong thing and she'll hang up. "I know the spiders seem terribly real," she murmured reassuringly. "But you have to believe me. It's just an hallucination."

"Noooo—"

"I can help you." Abby prayed she was getting through. "Just tell me who you are."

"Why should I?"

"Please."

There was a long pause, and Abby held her breath, her knuckles white as she clenched the receiver.

"This is Sharon," the woman finally said.

The words were slurred, and the tormented voice didn't match the Sharon she remembered. "Sharon Claiborne?"

"Yessss." Before Abby could respond, the woman hurried on. "Oh, God. My head. It hurts so much. The spiders—"

"Sharon, where—?"

The line clicked and then buzzed.

"Sharon...Sharon..." She shouted, knowing instinctively that it wasn't any use. The young woman had hung up. Abby leaped out of bed and, heart pounding, sprinted down the hall to the spare bedroom that she used as a den. Her phone directory was where she always kept it—at the center back of her teak desk. Flipping through the entries, she located the card with Sharon Claiborne's name. After she dialed, the phone rang twice, and she stood with every muscle rigid as she waited.

When the telephone company's prerecorded message clicked in, her body sagged. "We're sorry. The number you have dialed is not in service."

Did she have the wrong number? Quickly she tried information, but their listing was the same as the one on her card.

Abby slumped back into the desk chair and ran shaky fingers through her dark hair. The call had rattled her badly. Sharon was out there somewhere—in trouble. What in the name of God had gone wrong?

Therapists weren't supposed to get emotionally involved with their patients, but Sharon Claiborne had touched Abby deeply. She'd been so defeated when she'd first come in for counseling almost three years ago. In the middle of a messy divorce, Sharon hadn't trusted her own judgment. But as the two of them had sorted through the young woman's tangled emotions, she'd pulled herself back together with a minimum of help. Abby had always thought of Sharon as one of her success stories. A few minutes ago she'd sounded like a lost soul calling for help from the depths of hell.

Suddenly realizing she was shivering in the early morning chill, Abby crossed her arms and rubbed the goose bumps that had sprung up on her skin. Even when she'd slipped a long velour robe over her cotton gown, she still felt chilled to the bone. Out the window, the red glow of the Domino Sugar sign across the marina caught her attention in the gray dawn light. Abby stared at its eerie reflection in the water of the Inner Harbor as she tried to think logically.

She could call the police. But what could she tell them? A name. A telephone diagnosis. No real facts. If only she had access to Sharon's records. But they were down at her office. Closing her eyes, she massaged the throbbing spot at the bridge of her nose and strained to remember forgotten details. Sharon came from old Baltimore money. And she'd taken back her maiden name when she'd gotten divorced.

She could contact her parents. No. They were dead. The personal data was coming back. Sharon had two brothers. One of them wasn't going to be much help. He'd dropped out of the family business and gone off to the Far East—or somewhere. But the other brother and his wife had still been in the area two years ago.

Abby pulled out the phone book and ran her fingers down the column of Claibornes. There were a couple dozen entries, but only one in the Greensprings area where Sharon's brother lived. Derrick Claiborne. That sounded right.

But what if she had the wrong person? He was going to be pretty annoyed about getting a call at six in the morning.

Then she remembered the anguished voice of her former patient and shuddered. *They're going to kill me. Pleeeease, you've got to save me.*

Making the call turned out to be another exercise in frustration. Again she didn't reach an actual human being.

"Hello. This is Derrick Claiborne. I'm sorry, we can't come to the phone right now. But if you leave your name and number, we'll get back to you as soon as possible."

Abby sighed and left both her home and office number. At the end of the message she added, "I need to talk to you as soon as possible about your sister, Sharon. I think she's in some kind of trouble."

She didn't have a prayer of going back to sleep. Instead she headed for the shower. She had a full schedule—patients in the morning and her weekly teaching stint at Goucher College in the afternoon. But if she got to the office early, she could scan Sharon's file. Maybe she'd find something useful.

STEVE CLAIBORNE TURNED as the sari-clad servant ushered a visitor onto the wide veranda of his mansion house in Jamshedpur, India.

For a moment the two expatriots regarded each other. It was Clive Johnson who broke the silence first. "Steve, old chap. I've got a job I think you'll be interested in."

Steve stretched out lean legs covered by cotton twill slacks and propped his hip comfortably against the railing. He was a tall man, a couple of inches over six feet, but his rangy build and fine-tuned muscles gave him the agility of a Bengal tiger.

A scar jagging into the sun-streaked hair at his temple testified to the fact that he'd once been too brash, too bold and too reckless for his own good. Now he had a better-honed survival instinct.

Blue eyes as appraising as an expert poker player's studied Clive Johnson from under partially lowered lids. In response the short, stocky man swallowed and thrust his hands into his pockets.

"A job?" Steve laughed ironically. "I just finished repairing all the bullet holes in my plane from doing you that last favor."

"I swear, Claiborne. This is different. It's not running guns to the Afghan rebels."

Steve looked back through the French doors at the cool, dark interior of his colonial manor house. Inside, Mira was setting the table with white linen and gleaming crystal. In the kitchen the cook was fixing *kamargah*—lamb in spicy butter sauce—for dinner.

He'd left a life of luxury back home in Baltimore to come out here and freight cargo around the Far East. And he'd done pretty well on his own, even if he hadn't picked the world's most stable—or safest—occupation. But he'd made his choices a long time ago.

Sometimes a high level of risk was the price of the lifestyle he'd carved out for himself. Hell, if he were honest, he'd admit risk was part of the attraction. Every minute had a special zest when you lived on the edge of danger. "Okay, I'm listening."

"This job's a piece of cake. A pickup in Hong Kong and a drop in Islamabad."

"That's a long round trip. What's your client paying?"

"Sixty thousand. Plus expenses."

Steve whistled through strong, square teeth. "What am I carrying, plutonium for a secret Pakistani nuclear reactor?"

Johnson laughed. "Nothing like that, my dear fellow. Believe it or not, this is a mission of mercy. There's a businessman in the capital whose son needs a kidney transplant. The international medical organization the father's been working through has finally found a donor in Hong Kong."

"If the guy's working with an international medical organization, why does he need a free-lance pilot to make the delivery?"

"By the time they get through all the red tape it's going to take to get that kidney out of Hong Kong legally, the boy will be dead."

The hard kernel at the center of Steve Claiborne softened. A father who'd bend the law to save his son. What was it like to have a parent who cared that much? He didn't know. But suddenly he realized he wanted to help the man. "Okay, what's the deal?" he asked gruffly.

"Half the money up front. And you leave tonight."

"Pretty short notice. I don't know whether I can get the plane checked over in time."

"It has to be tonight."

Steve sighed. It was a good thing he hadn't gotten up early this morning. "All right. Tell your client he's got himself a pilot."

An hour later Steve was deep into preparations at the small airfield where he kept his plane. Which was why he missed the message that arrived that evening from his sister, Sharon.

THE RED BRICK, turn-of-the-century building that housed Abby's office was at 43 Light Street. If inanimate objects had personalities, this one would be a faded grand dame with a few lingering pretensions to elegance. Inside, she boasted black-and-white marble floors, commodious closets and an antediluvian plumbing system that delivered hot water only when the spirit moved it.

The quirky, retired shipyard mechanic in charge of keeping the boiler fired up and all the other parts in reasonable order was named Lou Rossini. He also trapped the mice that invaded the basement in winter, gave unsolicited advice to tenants and mopped the floors. Abby found him doing just that when she pulled open one of the heavy brass doors.

"Hey, I just got that clean. You're gonna track it all up," he called out, then greeted her. "You never get here this early. None of the tenants does." Lou sloshed his mop into the bucket of dirty water and winced.

Despite her lack of sleep and subsequent anxiety, Abby didn't take offense at the gruff salutation. "Your lumbago bothering you again?" she asked.

"Some."

"I was reading about a new backache clinic they're starting at Hopkins. Maybe they can help you."

"Hopkins. Yeah, maybe. Thanks for the tip, Doc."

"Sure." There was no use explaining again to Lou that she was a psychologist, not a medical doctor. He'd never grasped the distinction.

Abby's suite was on the fifth floor at the back of the building. Inside, she'd played up the carved oak woodwork and ten-foot ceilings with period pieces she'd found in antique shops.

She usually breezed right past the prints on the walls of traditional Baltimore scenes—the Walters Art Gallery juxtaposed with street vendors selling fruit and vegetables from horse-drawn carts. Today she stopped and stared at a picture of red brick row houses with gleaming marble steps, remembering that Sharon had moved to a restored Federal Hill row house after her divorce. Had she given the place up?

Why was her phone disconnected?

Skipping her usual cup of tea, she dialed the number again—with the same results. Sighing, she went to her files and pulled the young woman's records. Bringing them back to one of the easy chairs that faced the sofa, she sat down and began to read. But her carefully penned notes didn't give her a clue about what had happened last night.

At eight-fifty Abby still hadn't heard from Derrick Claiborne, so she called his office. A secretary informed her in a pleasant but very firm voice that Mr. Claiborne was in a meeting and couldn't be disturbed, but Abby was welcome to leave her name and number. She did, reiterating the urgency. It was frustrating that she couldn't do anything more right now, but her first patient, Mr. Fletcher, was due any minute, and he'd be terribly upset if she wasn't ready right on time.

At precisely nine a sad-eyed man with longish hair hanging over his ears opened the outer office door. An actuary at the Social Security Administration, Mr. Fletcher had a meticulous personality that seemed to be well suited to his work. But gradually he'd become increasingly upset by even minor variations in his daily routine. At the same time his life had become filled with elaborate rituals—most of which were designed to protect him against germs. Finally his supervisor had suggested a psychological evaluation.

Abby knew he'd used a premoistened towelette to wipe his hands after pressing the elevator buttons and that he had grasped the doorknob through a handkerchief.

As she stepped into the waiting room, she smiled encouragingly. "Good morning, Mr. Fletcher."

"Good morning." As always he reached into his carryall and pulled out several airline-style seat protectors, which he carefully spread on the back and arms of his chair before sitting down. As always Abby wondered what he'd do if his car broke down and he had to set foot in a taxi—or on a bus, God forbid.

For the next fifty minutes Abby did her best to concentrate on his problems. But she simply couldn't resist glancing at the Claiborne file still sitting in her out basket.

It was the same with Mrs. Shrewsberry at ten. Somehow the matron's neurotic complaints about the inattention of her grown children didn't have the compelling urgency of Sharon's terror over the phone last night. But

Abby's professionalism carried her through, and by the end of the session she'd gotten the woman thinking about volunteering in the school literacy program as an alternative focus for her energies.

When the morning schedule was completed, Abby anxiously checked with her answering service. No calls from Sharon—or her brother. What was wrong with the man? Hadn't he gotten her messages? Or didn't he care about his sister?

With her lips pressed together in a thin line, she checked Derrick's office address—Hunt Valley. Not exactly on her way to Goucher College. But if she grabbed a carton of yogurt for lunch, she could stop and see him before her one-thirty seminar on mental illness in modern society.

Abby drove north along York Road, noting that the scenery switched abruptly from residential to industrial park as she approached Hunt Valley. Claiborne Associates was in a chrome-and-glass structure that also housed a stock brokerage firm and a computer service bureau.

Stepping into the Claiborne executive suite was like being enfolded in money. Three-inch-thick carpet. Rosewood furniture. And a Ben Shahn original on the grasscloth-covered wall behind the reception desk. Abby recognized all the accoutrements.

"Do you have an appointment?" The nameplate on the chic redhead's desk said Miss Barnett.

"No."

"I'm sorry, but—"

Abby rarely pulled rank. Now she wished she'd worn a power suit instead of the aqua cotton sweater and skirt she'd chosen this morning. However, she drew herself up to her full five-foot-five height and gave the secretary her most assertive stare. "I am Dr. Abigail Franklin. I phoned Mr. Claiborne this morning about an emergency call I received from his sister who is a former patient of mine. If Mr. Claiborne is unable to speak to me, I will feel compelled to take the matter to the police."

Miss Barnett's demeanor changed instantly. "If you'll just have a seat, I'll find out if Mr. Claiborne can squeeze you in."

"Thank you."

Abby had barely settled herself on the gray leather sectional couch when the secretary was back. "Come this way."

The inner sanctum was even more luxurious than the outer office. Derrick Claiborne's desktop was cut from a single slab of black onyx. His executive chair looked to be imported Italian glove leather. And there was a swimming-pool size conference table that would have filled most rooms; it took up only a tiny corner of the suite.

The man himself completed the picture of executive success. Abby decided at once that he certainly didn't project the same image as his sister. Sharon's eyes had been softly focused. Her brother's were appraising.

He stood up briefly when Abby came in, and she could see that he was tall with the kind of build that came from working out faithfully at the gym two or three times a week. A designer suit spanned broad shoulders. And his graying hair was carefully combed to the side to hide the thinning top.

Abby's analytical mind made a quick assessment. High energy, power and ruthlessness were the words that leaped to her mind as she regarded the president of Claiborne Associates.

Under the circumstances, his voice was surprisingly subdued. "Dr. Franklin. I'm a little perplexed about your message."

"I was hoping you'd call me back."

"Believe me, I was planning to, but a crisis developed this morning and I was the only one who could straighten things out."

Without being invited, Abby had taken a seat. "But your sister's health and safety—"

"Have taken top priority."

"I beg your pardon?"

For the first time Claiborne looked uncomfortable. "Dr. Franklin, I'm afraid this is a very delicate matter. As I recall, you're the psychologist Sharon saw after she and Miles broke up."

"That's right. But your sister phoned me at six o'clock this morning. She seemed to be in extreme distress." Abby hesitated when she saw the lines in Claiborne's forehead wrinkle. But she had to make him understand just how serious this was. "She was terribly disoriented as though she might be on drugs. I tried to get her to tell me where she was, but she hung up. When I called her number, it had been disconnected. My only alternative was to phone you."

"Yes, well, I do understand. But, uh—" His hands were steepled in front of him on the desktop. "Dr. Franklin, my sister was calling you from a hospital. She had a nervous breakdown recently."

Abby couldn't suppress a look of dismay. "She did? I wouldn't have thought that Sharon—"

"We were just as stunned as you." He cleared his throat. "She's been in psychiatric care for the past few weeks."

"She sounded so upset and so anxious to talk to me. Maybe I could help. Where is she being treated?"

"I appreciate your solicitude, but I'm sure you understand why the family wants to keep this episode quiet."

"Mr. Claiborne, mental illness doesn't carry the stigma it once did."

"Yes, well, Sharon didn't want anyone to know what had happened."

"But she phoned me."

He shook his head. "I'm afraid she's lost touch with reality. What I can't understand is how the staff allowed her to make the call. With what I'm paying per month, I could have sent her on a world cruise," he murmured, and then looked as if he wished he'd kept that last comment to himself.

Despite last night's exchange, it was still difficult to believe that a basically sound young woman had gone off the deep end. "Is this drug-related?"

"I really don't feel I can violate my sister's privacy."

Abby struggled with a feeling of helplessness. It was as if she'd stepped into the middle of someone else's bad dream. "Well, if there's anything I can do—"

"I assure you, Sharon is getting the very best of psychiatric care." His tone of voice made it clear that the interview was over.

A few minutes later Abby found herself in the parking lot again. Derrick Claiborne had told her that everything possible was being done for Sharon. But had he checked the hospital's credentials before committing his sister? With anyone else she would have asked, but pushing the matter any further with the president of Claiborne Associates was tantamount to questioning the man's judgment. And he obviously didn't respond well to criticism.

She was a logical, organized person. The mystery of Sharon's call was cleared up and she should be relieved, Abby told herself. Yet as she got into her car she felt uncomfortably short of breath. *What's wrong with you?* she asked herself. *Sharon's not wandering around the city sick and terrified.* But she had sounded so alone—and so desperately frightened. As Abby nosed her car back onto York Road, her hands clenched painfully on the steering wheel. She'd done everything she could—or everything she should—hadn't she? Then why did that strangled call for help last night keep echoing in her mind like the cry of a soul in torment?

Chapter Two

Abby tried to put her worry into perspective over the next week. There was really nothing she could do. Derrick Claiborne had made it clear that her help wasn't wanted or needed, and Sharon hadn't phoned her back. Perhaps she'd just been in the middle of a bad episode, and now things were under control.

Abby's strategy was to keep busy. After work she walked to the Lexington and Eastern markets to buy groceries from the produce and seafood vendors. And one evening she wandered over to the aquarium to watch the beluga whales play ball. But she couldn't distract herself for long. Anxiety kept nagging at the edge of her consciousness like a subliminal message on a motivational tape.

The whole thing just didn't quite make sense. Every time Abby thought about her former patient, a chill swept across her skin just the way it had that first night. Sharon had been a fighter. And she'd been so determined to put her life back together. What had thrown her so badly now?

As she was locking her office Wednesday evening, Jo O'Malley stopped her. "Hey, don't leave yet," her friend called out. "You owe me a buck fifty."

"I do?"

Abby walked back toward the other woman's office. Stenciled in gold on the frosted glass panel of the door were the words O'Malley and O'Malley, Private Investigators. However, since her husband had been killed in the line of duty three years ago, Jo had been going it alone. As the redheaded gamine had explained to Abby when they'd first met, having a man around the office—even if in name only—gave the clients a feeling of confidence.

"A package came for you last week, and I've been trying to remember to give it to you," Jo explained as she rummaged in the closet. "I know I put it somewhere."

"I hope it wasn't Columbia River salmon."

"It was mailed in Baltimore."

Abby watched the pint-size woman move two-foot stacks of phone books and folders and mused that she was stronger than she looked. The package in question finally surfaced on the windowsill near an overgrown spider plant.

"Aha! I found it."

"New filing system?" Abby would never have been able to function in the midst of such disorganization. But she wasn't one to impose her methods on others.

"No. I knew I'd remember to tell you when I watered the plants. The problem was, you weren't around then."

"That makes some sort of sense. Which means I must be in trouble." Abby's lips quirked upward. Jo could usually make her smile. Her gaze shifted to the square parcel. It was wrapped in plain brown paper, and there was no return address—which gave Abby a strange feeling. With the mail the way it was these days, who could assume a package was going to get where it was going? "I wonder what this is?"

"It's not your birthday."

"And I don't remember ordering anything."

"If you had, there'd be a label."

Abby tore off the wrap. Inside was a cardboard grocery box swathed in layer upon layer of wide masking tape. It wasn't a neat job. The binding was bunched and twisted.

"Frankenstein wrap and mail service," Jo speculated.

Abby started to shrug, but the gesture turned into a little shiver. Jo must have felt it, too. "There isn't...uh—anyone who has it in for you?" she questioned.

"You mean like an escaped mental patient?"

"You said it, not me."

"I don't think any of my patients have secret grudges." Abby picked up the box and gave it a little shake. There was no sound from inside. "Got a pair of scissors?"

"Sure." It took Jo a moment to find them. Decisively Abby began to cut through the strands that held the box like a fly in a spiderweb. Several minutes later she got down to the cardboard. Both women unconsciously held their breath as Abby lifted the top flaps.

"Look at that!" Jo exclaimed as Abby pulled out an exquisite Oriental box. Across the top were intricate ivory inlaid dragons. Flowers and peacocks decorated the sides. The handles were burnished brass. "It's beautiful."

Abby searched for a card. There wasn't one. "Who could have sent it?"

Jo examined the workmanship. "This didn't come from Hong Kong Discount Importers. Could that accountant you've been dating have sent it?"

"Jack and I haven't seen each other in a while."

"I'm sorry."

"Don't be." Abby switched her attention back to the box. "Besides, this wouldn't have been his style—either the wrapping job or the gift. This thing must have cost a fortune."

"Then maybe you have a secret admirer."

"Oh, come on." Holding up the chest, Abby looked for hinges or a catch. There didn't appear to be a way of getting inside. "Do you think this could be a puzzle box? I had one when I was a kid. But it wasn't anywhere near as fancy as this."

"See if you can get it open."

"I'm trying." Intrigued, Abby shook the mystery gift again and thought she detected a muffled rattle. When she ran her finger over the elaborate design, she felt a hairline seam in the wood. "Damn. This thing is really put together for keeps. But I'll bet there's a certain sequence of pressure points that makes the top spring up or something."

"Yeah, but you could spend months getting the right combination of moves." Jo peered at her friend. "I don't suppose you want to try a crowbar."

Abby shuddered. Destroying something that beautiful was downright criminal. "No, I think I'll take it to an expert."

FELLS POINT WAS one of the few places in Baltimore where trendy night spots coexisted with run-down bars, and yuppies brushed shoulders with blue-collar workers.

It was also a place where no one gave a second glance to an oddly matched couple sharing a dimly lit booth in the Rockfish Tank, one of the seedier bars.

They were a very odd couple, indeed. One was dressed in faded jeans and had short, spiky hair. The other wore an impeccably tailored business suit. They were both edgy and trying to look cool.

"You were right about the computer. Here are the diskettes." The burglar set a plastic box on the planked pine between them.

The one in the suit pulled the box across the table, flipped the lid and riffled through the contents. "Good."

"You owe me five hundred dollars."

"This is only part of the job. Where's the puzzle box?"

"It was at her house last week. Now it's gone."

The face across the table paled. "What do you mean, *gone*?"

"I tore the blasted place apart. It just wasn't there."

"You idiot! You know I can't have the police involved. It's not supposed to look like a robbery."

The young punk took a swallow of beer. "Relax. I was real careful. I set everything back just the way it was. There isn't a spoon in the kitchen drawer out of place. Nobody's gonna know I was even there."

"You're absolutely sure the box is missing?"

"Yeah."

Across the table a pair of eyes turned steely. "If I find out you're not being straight with me, you're wasted."

"I wouldn't be stupid enough to give you any trouble. Honest."

THE PUZZLE EXPERT Abby had in mind was nine-year-old Melissa Wexler, who lived in a condominium one floor up from her own apartment. Labeled gifted and talented at age three, the youngster had an insatiable natural curiosity. Abby had helped the family channel Melissa's inquisitiveness and had gotten the little girl into a special program at the Maryland Science Center.

"Dr. Franklin!" the youngster exclaimed. "You're just in time to see my new car. Could you move your legs a little bit wider?"

Abby had gotten used to strange requests from Melissa. She planted her shoes a foot apart and waited. Seconds later a shiny red race car zipped between her feet and out into the hall.

"Where'd you get that?"

Melissa shook her blond curls. "The body's only a kit. But I wired the radio control stuff myself."

"I'm impressed."

The little girl gave her a blow-by-blow description of how she'd assembled the car. Then she noticed the box. "That thing's pretty. What is it?"

Abby set the chest on the living-room table. "I have the feeling it's a puzzle. But I can't open it."

"I'm good at puzzles."

"That's why I thought of you. Give me a call if you figure the box out. Or if you give up."

"I never give up."

After chatting for a few more minutes, Abby went back to her own apartment to fix dinner. She knew a lot of women living alone who just pulled a package out of the freezer. But cooking was something she enjoyed. So she made a point of taking the time to prepare something fairly elaborate several times a week. Tonight she was having crab and pasta salad. While she waited for the fettuccine to cook, she opened the *Evening Sun* and leaned over the dinette table as she flipped the pages. After scanning the headline news, she turned to the entertainment section. If there was something interesting at the Charles, maybe Jo would go with her this weekend. The movie theater was right near a mystery bookstore her friend liked so much—the Butler Did It. Jo had a thing for stories about spunky women detectives, a predilection Abby found amusing.

She was still grinning as she started to thumb past the obituaries—until a name leaped off the page at her. Her hands went rigid, and she sucked in a startled breath. Sharon Claiborne.

There was no picture. Maybe it was someone else. *God, let it be someone else.* A pulse began to pound in her temple as she scanned the entry. "Twenty-seven years old...beloved sister of Derrick and Stephen Claiborne..." All at once her knees started to shake and she sank onto a dinette chair.

No! Silently Abby denied the tragedy. But she couldn't deny the reality. Since talking to Derrick she'd kept telling herself that everything was under control. Sharon was in a hospital. She was being treated. What had gone wrong?

On the stove the pasta boiled over, but Abby didn't even notice through the film of tears that misted her eyes.

BMWS AND MERCEDES-BENZES lined the narrow lanes of the Dulaney Valley Cemetery. Had Baltimore Society come to say goodbye to Sharon? Or were they here out of respect for her brother?

The azaleas were drooping with their last blossoms, and a fine drizzle dampened the mourners. Not wanting to intrude on the family's privacy, Abby stood under a black umbrella across from the canopy that had been set up at the gravesite. She'd felt compelled to come to the funeral. If she and Sharon had met under other circumstances, they could have been friends. Instead, Sharon had been one of her first patients. And her sense of satisfaction in helping the young woman turn her life around had confirmed Abby's conviction that she'd entered the right profession.

Now Sharon was dead, and she couldn't help feeling a deep sense of personal loss like a heavy black cloak weighing down her shoulders. God, what a waste. Why did something like this have to happen?

Tears blurred Abby's vision, and she struggled to bring back her sense of equilibrium. Fumbling in her purse for a tissue, she wiped her cheeks. It took several moments to get herself under control.

Afraid to risk any more runaway emotions, she looked across at the mourners. Derrick and his wife were dressed in black. The man on their right wore boots, gray slacks and a rumpled navy blazer that looked as if it had traveled halfway around the world crammed in a duffel bag. Even if he hadn't been standing somewhat apart, he wouldn't have looked as if he belonged with the mourners. Steve, the other brother. Of the two, he seemed to be the more affected.

As the minister's words of comfort rolled over the assemblage, Abby scanned the other well-bred faces. She recognized several state senators, a representative from the governor's office and Jonathan Wyndham, the chief of staff from the Sterling Clinic, one of Baltimore's most prestigious private hospitals. Which ones had known Sharon personally? Which ones would miss her?

Her gaze was drawn back to the two brothers. There was a strong family resemblance—the same strong chin, the same bladelike nose. Yet Derrick was obviously the senior. While his thinning hair was shot with gray, Steve's was thick and sun-streaked. Even in mourning the older Claiborne projected the polished and confident image of a man used to commanding corporate boardrooms. Steve had no less presence, but he had obviously chosen to make his mark in a much less civilized arena. The adjectives that leaped to mind when she looked at him were untamed, dangerous, aggressive.

Like a wild animal suddenly aware of a hunter invading his territory, his head jerked up. Across Sharon's grave his keen eyes went right to Abby and drilled into her. They were light and as bleak as an arctic landscape. For an unguarded moment she caught his pain—and also his anger. She shivered and quickly broke the eye contact. This wasn't someone she'd want to have for an enemy, she thought instinctively.

The minister concluded the service and looked up. "The family has asked me to invite everyone back to the house this afternoon," he said.

The crowd broke into little groups. Some returned immediately to their cars, while others stood talking in low voices.

A short woman with gray hair worn in tightly wound finger curls touched Abby's arm. "There are so few young people here. Were you one of Sharon's friends, dear?"

Abby looked down into the wrinkled face. The eyes were red and watery—both from age and grief. "Sharon was my patient. But, yes, I was her friend, too."

"You're not Dr. Franklin, are you?"

"Why, yes, I am. How did you know?"

"I'm Sharon's Aunt Sophie. She visited me in Chicago a couple of years ago when she was having such a bad time after the divorce. She spoke very highly of you."

"I liked Sharon a lot. And I admired her inner strength."

"I did, too. That's why I can't believe what happened."

"I haven't heard the whole story."

"She killed herself."

Abby sucked in a knife-sharp breath. "Oh, no."

"Drugs. She was on drugs and they—" The old woman swayed unsteadily, and Abby reached out with a supporting arm. At the same time a middle-aged man appeared at her elbow.

"Let me help you to the car, Aunt Sophie."

"That's all right, Freddy. I'll go with this nice young woman." She turned to Abby. "I'm not imposing, am I?"

"Of course not." Abby had debated about going back to the house. She'd wanted to offer her condolences, but she'd wondered if Derrick would feel she was intruding. Now she had a good reason for satisfying her own emotional needs.

"I still can't believe it," Sophie repeated in a bewildered voice as they made their way slowly down the gravel path. Abby voiced her agreement. This just wasn't like the Sharon Claiborne she'd treated two years ago. But then, things could change—especially when drugs were involved.

ABBY HAD NO WAY OF KNOWING, but it was as interesting to note who'd stayed away from Sharon's funeral as who had come.

Ezra Hornby, a small man with salt-and-pepper hair, a bulbous nose and the pragmatism of an underdog's campaign manager, was one Baltimorean who'd skipped the service. This morning his eyes were closed as he knelt in prayer. No small sacrifice considering the arthritis in his knees.

Poor Sharon Claiborne. Her goodness would transcend her mortal existence. He was sorry about the passing of her soul. Of any soul, for that matter. But sometimes God moved in mysterious ways.

Souls were his business. He reclaimed them from the back alleys and sidewalks of Highlandtown at the Lazarus Rescue Mission on Eastern Avenue.

Give a man a square meal, a place to flop and as much spiritual nourishment as he could absorb. Then perhaps you had a chance to dry him out, help him find a job and make him a productive member of the community.

The trouble was, all that took money—more than the social service system could supply. Over the past thirty years he'd done his share of scrambling for funding. Money was a powerful force—for good or evil. Long ago he'd decided that it was what you did with it, not where it came from, that made the difference in the end.

After leaving the small chapel, he limped down the hall to his office. The walls behind the shabby desk were full of framed, warmly inscribed photographs of Ezra with everyone from Frank Sinatra and Lucille Ball to Betty Ford and Spiro Agnew, the former Baltimore County politician who'd risen so high and then fallen so far.

On the wall by the door were the plaques of appreciation. There wasn't one for Sharon. Not yet. But she'd done so much for the mission. It was too bad she'd never know how important her final contribution had been. In a few months he'd have to think of a suitable memorial for her.

IT WAS A THIRTY-MINUTE RIDE to the Claiborne residence. The house turned out to be a Southern-style mansion set on twenty acres of well-manicured property in Greensprings Valley. Abby knew the area well. She'd been raised in an equally expensive but not quite so pretentious home just a few miles down the road. But she hadn't kept up with the neighborhood comings and goings since her parents had retired to Florida.

Inside, a crowd of twenty or thirty men and women fitted easily into the spacious, decorator-appointed rooms. Silver trays had been set out on the broad Chippendale dining-room table. Abby recognized the pricey little sandwiches and pastries from a local gourmet shop.

"Can I get you something?" Abby asked Aunt Sophie.

"That would be so kind, dear."

After settling the old woman on a velvet couch, Abby went to fill a plate for her. As she circled the table, she heard her name and looked up. Dr. Jonathan Wyndham, the chief of staff at the Sterling Clinic, was making his way toward her.

"I haven't seen you since your parents defected to warmer climes."

"How are you doing?"

"Fine, except that I miss your father at our Saturday morning golf foursomes. He was the only one who regularly scored higher than me."

Abby laughed.

"How is the old duffer?"

"He's fine, too. You ought to see the golf courses down in Boca Raton. And Mom loves the area, too. It's got the world's most exclusive shopping mall."

"I didn't know you were acquainted with Sharon," Wyndham remarked.

"Actually, she was one of my patients."

The physician looked surprised. "But you weren't on the authorized list."

"Sharon was at the Sterling Clinic?"

"Didn't you know? What a terrible tragedy," he murmured. "I hate to lose a patient like that."

"Yes. Can you tell me what exactly happened?"

"We're still investigating."

After a bit more polite conversation, Abby excused herself to take the plate of food back to Aunt Sophie. The old woman was talking to Derrick's wife, Cecile.

The hostess had shed her black jacket and gloves. The designer dress underneath was cut to show her fashionably thin figure to best advantage. Around her neck was a clustered diamond pendant the size of a quarter.

"So thoughtful of you to come back to the house. Aunt Sophie's been telling me what good care you've been taking of her." Although the words were spoken softly, there was an edge of tension in the voice. But then who wouldn't be under stress after a suicide in the family? There was always so much guilt burdening the loved ones left behind.

"It was no trouble."

"I know you must be busy. Don't feel that you have to stay on Sophie's account."

"You're right. I'm going to have to be leaving soon. But I did want to tell you how sorry I was to hear about Sharon."

"It helps to know that a lot of people cared."

As Cecile moved on to another group, Sophie pursed her lips. "She and Sharon never did like each other."

"Sometimes that makes the guilt worse," Abby told her.

"Guilt is one emotion that woman doesn't allow herself."

"Oh?"

"With Sharon gone there's one less person drawing from the family trust fund."

"But surely—"

Abby's protest was interrupted by a gritty voice. "What are you doing, Aunt Sophie, giving away all the family secrets?"

She knew who had spoken before she looked up. Steve Clairborne might be talking to his aunt, but he was looking accusingly at Abby. Up close she noted that his eyes were blue—and just as icy as they'd been at the cemetery.

The old lady's cheeks colored. "Now, Stephen, mind your manners. Have you met Dr. Franklin?"

He raised an inquisitive eyebrow, drawing her gaze to a jagged scar that disappeared into his hairline. Probably he ran with a rough crowd where disagreements were negotiated with weapons instead of words.

"Dr. Franklin?"

"Abby Franklin was Sharon's psychologist."

"Then she did a damn lousy job." The words echoed in the room, and Abby felt the hair on the back of her neck bristle. In her peripheral vision she saw several people glance inquisitively in their direction.

The unfair accusation, not the scrutiny, made her face go pale. "I treated Sharon several years ago. I wasn't involved—" She cut off the sentence abruptly as last week's early-morning telephone call leaped into her mind like a goblin waiting in the dark.

"You're a fine one to talk, Stephen Claiborne," his aunt scolded. "You've spent the past eight years in the Far East doing God knows what."

He ignored the old woman's outburst. In fact, his assessing eyes never left Abby's face. Only force of will kept her from taking an involuntary step backward. Whatever other talents he possessed, the man was a master of intimidation.

"You might as well come clean with me, Dr. Franklin. I know you're trying to hide something, and I'm damn well going to get to the bottom of it." As he spoke, his glance flicked to Cecile and then back to Abby. "Are you working with her? Is that it?"

"What are you talking about?"

Instead of answering, he reached out and clamped his fingers around her wrist. They were warm and strong and rough with the touch of a man who didn't make his living pushing papers.

Abby jerked in reaction. "What are you doing?" she managed in a tone that had suddenly become thready.

"Lying has an elevating effect on the pulse." The timbre of his voice had changed subtly, too.

Abby's poise was rarely shaken in public situations, even when dealing with patients who were out of control. Now she exhaled quickly, vividly aware of the blood pounding in her artery where Steve's fingers pressed against her skin. It took every bit of savoir faire she possessed to call his bluff. "So does the survival instinct."

He knew exactly how to hold her without hurting her. His grip wasn't painful, but it bound her as effectively as a handcuff. There was no question of snatching her arm away without making a scene. Instead, she forced herself to meet his gaze and was gratified to see that he didn't look as self-possessed as he had before.

"Believe me, I'm just as mystified as you about what went wrong with Sharon," she insisted.

"Sure you are, doc."

It was on the tip of her tongue to go ahead and tell him about the call so that he'd know she wasn't hiding anything deceitful. But why did she have to justify herself in the face of his back-alley tactics? She'd already talked to Derrick. He could fill in his brother if he wanted to.

"You'll have to excuse the family's lack of decorum. Funerals can be so trying." Aunt Sophie broke into the private confrontation, and Abby realized she'd forgotten all about the old woman—and everyone else in the room.

Steve's grip loosened and he lowered his eyes as if he'd suddenly regretted his impulsive behavior. Abby pulled her hand away, slipping unconsciously from primitive reaction to civilized manners. "A family crisis can unbalance even the most stable," she observed quietly. She could have added the word *man* to the end of the sentence, but she didn't quite dare.

Abby and the old woman exchanged a few more polite remarks. Then, without giving Steve Claiborne another glance, she made her exit. As she closed the front door and stepped off the portico, she noted that the morning's light drizzle had turned to a steady downpour.

She dashed for her car, slammed the door behind her and sat dripping in the front seat as she thought about the Claibornes. Sharon. Derrick. Cecile. Steve. It struck her that they were like the cast of characters in a Eugene O'Neill play rife with subtle undertones and not-so-subtle antagonisms carefully spelled out at the beginning. But by the third act you'd discover that everything you thought you knew about them was only one version of the truth.

Abby brushed a trickle of rainwater off her cheek and sighed. The trouble was, this wasn't a play. It was real life. Sharon was dead, and Abby wanted desperately to understand what had happened to her former patient.

Chapter Three

Abby thought about going straight back to her office and digging out the tapes she and Sharon had made. It wasn't just that Steve Claiborne had accused her of not handling the case right. Even though he'd been wrong about the time frame, she wanted to satisfy herself that there hadn't been any clues back then that Sharon was thinking about committing suicide.

But as she drove back to the city, her energy seemed to drain away. Perhaps it was the emotional encounter with the Claibornes. Perhaps it was just that she'd been keeping such a hectic schedule. What Abby ended up doing was going back to her apartment and crawling into bed. To her surprise she didn't wake up until seven the next morning. She felt guilty about sleeping away the rest of the day, but at least she was feeling physically better.

Monday was always busy, so she didn't have a chance to get out Sharon's records until five. As soon as her last patient left, Abby locked her outer waiting room door and got out her recorder, half a dozen tapes and Sharon's files. Somewhere along the line the drive to comprehend what had happened had taken on an urgency that she didn't fully understand. It was partly her own need to find out why she'd failed with Sharon and partly the bond the two of them had forged. Intertwined with that was the desire to prove to Steve that he was wrong about her. She didn't like the mix, but she was going to have to work through the feelings just the way she advised her patients when they were having conflicts.

She kicked off her shoes and shrugged out of her suit jacket. It was almost dinnertime and her stomach was rumbling, so she got out the last carton from her cache of gourmet yogurt in the small refrigerator in the bathroom. Damson plum, one of her favorites.

After she settled herself on the love seat, she took a spoonful. But as soon as the tape began to play, her stomach knotted and she set the yogurt down. Somehow, hearing Sharon's voice had taken her appetite away.

"Do you mind if I record our session?"

There was a hesitant laugh. "Nobody else is going to hear this—right?"

"It's strictly confidential."

"I've never been to a shrink before."

"Everybody's nervous the first time. Just try to relax and tell me about what's bothering you."

Hesitatingly at first and then with more intensity, Sharon had started to talk about her disintegrating marriage. That had taken up most of the first session.

"I didn't really think telling you this stuff would make me feel better. But it does," Sharon confided fifty minutes later.

"Shall we set up a schedule of appointments, then?"

"Yes."

The familiar voice brought back Abby's memories in sharp detail. She hadn't recalled it wrong. Sharon really had turned her life around, and she'd had so much to live for. Why had she gotten involved with drugs? Why had she taken her life?

Picking up the young woman's folder from the table beside the couch, Abby thumbed through some of the notes she'd made. Then she inserted the next tape into the machine.

The folder lay open in Abby's lap as she listened to an account of Sharon's family life. Despite the Claibornes' wealth, the young woman had come from a disadvantaged background. Emotionally disadvantaged. She'd forgotten that Sharon and Steve were the children of their father's second marriage. Derrick, who'd been away at prep school and college while they were growing up, was from the first marriage and hadn't had much in common with his younger siblings.

"Maybe that's why Steve didn't want to go into the family business," Sharon speculated. "By the time he dropped out of Harvard Business School, Dad had retired and Derrick was running the show."

"Were you and Steve close?"

"He was the only one I could count on. Mom was into the golf lesson and garden party scene. But no wonder. Dad was so busy making money that he was hardly ever home before we were in bed for the evening. They rarely connected with each other, either. It was more like a corporate merger than a marriage."

There was more. Abby pushed the pause button on the tape player, remembering some of her original conclusions. Sharon had been compelled to search for the warmth and love she hadn't gotten from her parents. Unfortunately her upbringing had made her a poor judge of husband material. Abby switched the machine back to play.

Sharon went on to share one of her most painful memories about Steve. "I was in my first year at Cornell and having a hard time adjusting to studying when he called up and said he wanted to talk to me. I was so excited about seeing him. I took him to my favorite campus hangout. We talked about how hard it was your first semester in college, and I was feeling so much better. Then he dropped the bombshell. He was going away. Leaving the country. I couldn't believe it and asked him why. He said he was tired of trying to live up to somebody else's expectations for his life.''

"How did you feel?''

"Sick. Devastated. I'd always assumed I could count on him to be there for me." She was silent for a minute. "I think I started looking for a replacement. Someone I could transfer my attention to. Unfortunately it turned out to be Miles Skinner, the jerk I married.''

"So the disastrous marriage was all the hard-hearted brother's fault." The condemning comment didn't come from the tape recorder on the table next to Abby. It came from the tall, inscrutable figure blocking the doorway. Steve Claiborne. Abby's mouth went dry.

At his sister's funeral he'd made an attempt at looking civilized. Today he'd simply pulled on well-worn jeans and a white T-shirt topped by an Eisenhower jacket. Along with his hard face, scar, and lean, muscular body, the outfit gave him the tough-guy appearance of a street thug.

Abby made an attempt to swallow past the sandpaper in her throat. She'd been so intent on the tape that she hadn't heard him enter. Apparently he could move as silently as fog when he chose to. "How did you get in here?''

"That lock on your door wouldn't keep a pickpocket out of an evening purse. I recommend getting it changed.''

She felt her face heat. "You have incredible nerve breaking into my office."

He shrugged. It was an acknowledgement, not an apology.

His eyes flicked down to her stocking feet and then to the jacket tossed across the back of the chair. All at once she was conscious of her own vulnerability and wished she hadn't made herself quite so comfortable.

Steve didn't make any threatening moves, but she was acutely aware of the way he stood blocking the only exit to the room. It was late. There was probably no one else left in the building. And she was alone with a man who'd come very close to threatening her yesterday—and hadn't cared whether a roomful of people heard.

She forced her gaze to meet his. This was *her* office, a place where she was the one in control, even with patients in a good deal of emotional distress. Yet she couldn't really convince herself that past experience had any bearing on the present situation. Steve Claiborne was too much of an unknown quantity.

Her training warned her to stay calm. Casually her eyes flicked to the phone.

"Don't try it."

Abby took a deep breath and let it out slowly. "What do you want?"

"Those tapes, for starters."

"They're confidential."

He laughed harshly. "Sharon's not going to care now."

"How much have you already heard?"

"Not enough to figure out what's going on. And believe me, I'm going to." Brusquely he strode across the room, ejected the tape from the player, snatched up the others and slipped them into the pocket of his leather jacket. Next he grabbed for the folder in her lap.

Abby's fingers closed protectively around the file. But it was like getting caught in a tug-of-war with RoboCop. He pulled her to a standing position, clamped her arms to her sides with one of his and lifted the records out of her hand.

"If you think you can wrestle with me and win, you ought to have your head examined, Dr. Franklin."

Tucking the folder under his arm, he turned and stalked toward the door. Abby was about to tell him he might not like what he was going to hear on the tapes when she changed her mind. Whatever advice she offered would just be taken wrong.

"You can't get away with this," she warned instead.

"Who's going to stop me?"

"The police," Abby shot back.

"Listen, lady, I've gotten the better of cops in hell-holes like Phnom Penh and Da Nang. The Charm City brigade just doesn't make me sweat."

"In Baltimore you can't buy your way out of trouble."

He laughed. "You can always buy your way out of trouble." With that he turned and disappeared through the door.

Abby sat on the sofa shaking—as much with anger as with fright. She forced herself to take several measured, steadying breaths. Finally the pounding of her heart subsided to a normal pace. Claiborne might not be intimidated by the police, but he'd have some explaining to do if they picked him up with her tapes and confidential patient files. On the other hand, by the time the police got here, he'd undoubtedly be long gone, and she didn't have a clue about where he was staying.

STEVE CLAIBORNE SLAMMED the door of his Corsica. After settling himself behind the wheel, he dumped the pile of tapes into the passenger seat. Then his eyes lit on the fancy stereo system that had come with his rent-a-car upgrade. It was equipped with a cassette player. Might as well start running through the sessions between Sharon and Dr. Franklin.

Once out of the garage, he picked up a cassette with an October date two years ago. But he was strangely reluctant to slip it into the recorder. He'd told the lady shrink that confidentiality wasn't an issue. Now he had a strong sense that he was about to violate his sister's privacy.

Then he shrugged. As he'd pointed out, Sharon was dead. And he had a primal urge to put his hands around the neck of whoever was responsible. Sharon's sessions with Dr. Franklin could hold the clue he needed.

Pulling to a stop at a red light, he pushed in the tape, and his sister began to speak. At first he was so caught up in the sound of her voice that he didn't really pay attention to the words.

"...stray kitten home and was hiding it in my bedroom closet. Steve and I were sneaking it food. But then the maid caught on to what we were doing and finked on us. Mother threw a fit, had the animal control people take Taffy away and locked me..."

The van behind Steve honked and his foot jumped on the gas pedal. Once he'd gotten into the sense of what Sharon was saying, he'd started listening so intently that he hadn't realized the light had turned green. He'd steeled himself to never hearing from his sister again. Now it was almost as if she were here in the car talking with him. Except that he wanted her to respond to his voice—not Dr. Franklin's.

The Corsica shot forward, and he lost several moments of the monologue while he negotiated a turn that took him up Charles Street.

"...found me on the porch roof trying to climb down a rope made out of sheets. After he dragged me back inside, he let me cry about Taffy and then he took me down to Baskin-Robbins and bought me a double scoop of Rocky Road."

Steve sucked in a sharp breath. Unbidden, the terror of seeing his little sister dangling from the end of that sheet washed over him. He'd forgotten about the incident. No, he admitted, he'd blocked it out, just as he'd blocked out so many early memories. All at once he realized the episode must have been etched in Sharon's memory.

He'd been heading back to his hotel. Now he realized that he was way past the turn. Instead of circling back, he continued north. The tape whirred and Sharon's soft voice continued to fill the car.

Each childhood story she shared with the psychologist jogged his own memories. Some of the recollections made him smile; others brought a grimace to his features. Several times he almost reached out to snap the tape off. But then he pulled back his hand. He had to know. He had to understand.

If some of the early accounts were grim, it was the more recent events that made him feel as if a piece of barbed wire were twisting in his guts. He'd told himself he and Sharon were both tough. Suddenly he understood that only he had grown a leathery, cynical hide. Sharon hadn't dealt with life the way he had. Making the relationship with her husband, Miles Skinner, work had been more vital to her sense of self-worth than he'd realized.

"If anybody from my family had given me some support when I saw things going down the tubes, I guess I wouldn't have ended up coming to you," Sharon was saying. "Derrick was all wrapped up in his business. And Steve was on the other side of the world."

"How did that make you feel?" Abby interjected.

"I expected it from Derrick. But I'm still angry at Steve. Doesn't he know how much I need him?"

"No. I didn't know," Steve whispered. But it was too late. He didn't realize he was trying to see through a film of moisture until he had to pump the brake to avoid hitting a truck that had stopped abruptly in front of him.

He pulled onto a side street and sat for several minutes until his emotions were under control. Then he glanced up at the street sign to see where he was. Sighing, he turned around and headed back to the city. The first thing he needed to do was buy a recorder so that he could play the rest of the tapes in his room. Then he had to put himself through the torture of finding out what his sister really thought about him.

MILES SKINNER'S normal business day was from noon to nine so that he could catch the lunchtime browsers and the yuppies who liked to drop by after dinner to see his latest acquisitions. He'd just opened up when the bell above the door of his shop off Howard Street jingled.

He looked up from the table in the back that served as a little workshop. "Can I help you?"

"Maybe."

It was then that Miles recognized the tall man sauntering down the aisle toward him. The antique dealer's face turned from ruddy to ashen, and his hand stopped in midstroke on the silver coffeepot he was polishing. For a moment he pictured himself beating it out the back door. Instead, he decided to tough it out. With Sharon pushing daisies, there wasn't a damn thing her brother could prove.

"Steve."

He ignored the attempt at friendliness. "Skinner."

Steve cocked a quizzical eyebrow as he looked around the small shop at the shelves of artfully arranged cut glass, brass and ornate silver. If he'd had to guess what kind of occupation Sharon's ex-husband would have ended up in, it wouldn't have been selling heirlooms from old estates. Used cars, maybe. But then, on the other hand, why not? The antique business was another situation where smooth talking and easy charm counted for a lot. After the things he'd heard Sharon say last night, he could just picture Miles cozying up to people when they were vulnerable, and carting away the family treasures. Buying sterling at electroplate prices, then selling it to urban homesteaders looking for a touch of charm.

"What brings you here?"

Steve forced his voice to remain even. "I thought we could talk about Sharon. I expected to see you at her funeral."

"Yeah. Well, I was real sorry to hear about what happened. But I figured I'd be about as welcome as a fox at a chicken convention."

"I wouldn't have stopped you from coming to pay your respects." *Only because I hadn't heard the tapes yet or done any checking in Sharon's neighborhood.*

"Whatever Sharon and I had was over a long time ago."

"Was it?"

"Get to the point."

Steve hesitated for a moment. This was the second time in as many days that he was playing the heavy. However, the end justified the means. "I want you to understand that I know there's something funny about the way Sharon died. And if you had anything to do with it, I'm going to make sure you live to regret the day you ever tricked my sister into marrying you."

Sweat broke out on Miles's forehead. "Hey, I swear I haven't laid eyes on her since we signed the divorce papers."

Steve stared at the antique dealer. There was nothing overtly threatening about the stare. It just went on and on without wavering.

Miles licked his lips. "Okay, I did stop by her house about a month ago."

"You almost bumped into one of her neighbors."

"I just wanted to ask her for some money. I swear that was all."

"Are you the one who ripped out her phone lines?"

"Not me. Honest." Under Steve's scrutiny, Miles's hands started to tremble. "Listen, I did hear she was dating some guy," he offered.

"Who?"

"An insurance salesman."

"Does he have a name?"

"Adam, uh, Goodman or something like that."

"Any idea where I can find him?"

"Around. You can never be sure where he's going to light. But I'll keep my ear to the ground. Tell me where you're staying in case I scare anything up."

Steve considered his options. Right now no one knew where to find him—not even his dear brother and sister-in-law. That gave him a certain degree of safety. But he didn't have the time or the patience to let things drag on or the time to quiz everyone Sharon knew. However, there was a way to hurry things along. If you dangled a tasty morsel in front of a cobra, sooner or later it was going to strike. The trick was making sure it didn't bury its fangs in the back of his neck. Reaching into his pocket for a pen, he scribbled a phone number on one of Miles's business cards. "I'm at the Hampton Hotel."

"I'll call you if I hear anything."

"I'd appreciate that."

Steve turned and left the shop. Miles waited several minutes to make sure he wasn't going to return. His hands were still clammy as he thumbed through his address book and dialed a number. But he couldn't pass up the opportunity to kill two birds with one stone.

"Hello."

"This is Miles Skinner."

"Has Steve been around to see you?"

"Yes."

"And?"

"I found out where he's staying."

"Where?"

"You know, I've had a request from a buyer for a Wedgwood clock like the one in your library."

There was a muttered expletive on the other end of the line.

"Do you want to deal or don't you?"

"Yes."

"Suppose I stop by after I close the shop this evening."

"Come to the back door."

ABBY HAD SPENT a restless night, her thoughts filled with the Claibornes—especially Steve. The man was harsh, abrupt, intimidating. But ludicrous as it seemed, she couldn't help feeling sorry for him.

She came from a warm, loving family that had given her the support she needed to go out and make the most of her potential. What would it be like to be raised by parents so caught up in their own petty lives that they hardly spared a thought for you? And when they did they held you up to standards impossible to meet.

It had made Sharon yearn for warmth and closeness. Apparently it had done just the opposite to Steve. There was a hard shell around the man through which only Sharon had penetrated. Even though they hadn't been in contact much over the past few years, her death had knocked the props out from under him. Somehow knowing she was there had added ballast to his life. Now he was suffering with remorse because he'd taken the relationship for granted. The trouble was, Abby was caught in the double-barreled crossfire of his anguish. And that was a dangerous place to be.

Could she help him find out what had happened to his sister, even though he didn't want her help? Why did she care? An idea came to Abby in the middle of the night. She rarely used her staff privileges at the Sterling Clinic. But there was no reason why she couldn't stop by and ask to see Sharon's records. She told herself it was to settle her own doubts about her former patient. She silently acknowledged it was as much for Steve's sake as hers.

Abby's one o'clock patient canceled at the last minute, and she didn't have another appointment until three, so she walked back to her condo, got her car out of the garage and drove to Mount Washington, a section of the city where rambling old houses sat well back from the tree-lined street.

Twenty minutes later she turned in between gray stone gateposts and made her way through the well-manicured grounds of the Sterling Clinic. The hospital itself was an imposing stone building with two massive wings angled away from a central portico that housed the administrative offices.

Abby left her car in the staff lot and had just stepped into the drive when an ambulance came screaming around the corner, sirens blazing. She jumped back, feeling the vibrations shake her body.

The doors swung open even before the vehicle pulled to a stop in front of the emergency entrance. Uniformed attendants jumped out and rushed a limp form on a stretcher into the building.

Her glimpse of the life-and-death drama was over in a few seconds. She could only imagine what was going on in the emergency room as she made her way toward the front entrance. It looked as if the staff were making an almost superhuman effort to save the patient's life. Had they done as much for Sharon?

A guard checked her ID and opened the door to the office complex. As she approached the executive suite, a distinguished-looking man came out and turned in her direction. She recognized him immediately. It was Dr. Donald Kellogg, one of the country's best known surgeons. She'd read in the *Baltimore Sun* that he'd become associated with the hospital network that had recently purchased Sterling. The physician stopped and stared at her.

"Don't I know you, young lady?"

"I'm Abby Franklin, sir. You were kind enough to give me an interview for one of my graduate papers."

"Of course. What brings you here?"

"I wanted to see the records of a former patient, Sharon Claiborne."

"Claiborne. Oh, yes, I know about the case. Terrible tragedy. There's going to be—" Before he could finish the sentence the loudspeaker system blared.

"Dr. Kellogg to the emergency room. Dr. Kellogg to the emergency room."

"Sorry."

"I understand." Abby was speaking to his back. He was already on his way down the hall.

After watching him disappear into the elevator, Abby proceeded to the records office around the corner. As she pushed open the door, she thought about the system the hospital used. Access to the records was restricted. You put in your request at the counter and waited for one of the aides to bring out the folder.

Abby wrote Sharon's name on a slip of paper, signed her own name and handed the form to a stocky woman in a green uniform.

"I'll be right with you." The aide disappeared into the back room. She was gone for a long time. When she returned, her hands were empty, and there was a guarded look on her face. "I'm sorry. That file is unavailable."

"Why?"

"I don't know. I just work here. When there's a red seal on a file, I can't pull it."

Abby tried to keep the disappointment out of her voice. "But I treated the patient a couple of years ago. Isn't there any way I can see her records? Could I go back there and take a look for myself?"

"No one's allowed in the back without authorization. You can leave a request and you'll be notified if the restriction is lifted."

"But—"

"Sorry. I'm only doing my job."

Frustration churned in Abby's stomach as she left the office, yet she understood the clinic's position. Probably they were conducting an investigation and wanted to make sure that the records were intact. But what harm could it do if she just had a quick look? Maybe if she appealed to Dr. Wyndham, he'd make an exception.

SHE DIDN'T NOTICE a door close quietly as she made her way quickly down the hall. Behind it, a pair of eyebrows was drawn together in worry. Things had been complicated enough last week. This was the final straw.

Steve Claiborne was sniffing around town like a Doberman on the trail of fresh blood. Now Abby Franklin had shown up asking questions. The watcher drew in a shaky breath and exhaled. It was just damn rotten luck that Dr. Franklin had treated Sharon Claiborne a couple of years ago. Now she was sticking her nose in where it didn't belong. And there was too much at stake to allow her to uncover the truth.

Thank God she'd already been identified as a risk so that they could start working on the problem. The others were going to be glad that somebody had already taken the initiative on this one.

"HELLO, DARLING."

"Hello." Cecile Claiborne's reply was stiff and automatic. There had been a time when a call from her lover had made her heart pound with excitement. Now it pounded with fear.

It had all started off so innocently at the country club six months ago. She'd been relaxing in the bar after three invigorating sets of tennis, and a new friend of Derrick's had joined her. He'd been charming, attentive and sexy in the way of men with power, exactly the qualities that had attracted her to Derrick fifteen years ago. The problem was that once her husband had been sure of his acquisition, he had become more interested in boardrooms than bedrooms. The corporate mergers took long hours of careful planning and cunning strategy. For Derrick, the sexual encounters were just a way of dissipating tension. They took ten minutes if she was lucky. Five if he had an early meeting.

It wasn't her fault. She'd gone the whole route. Quiet little dinners on the servants' night off, sexy nightgowns and disgusting porn movies on the VCR. The movies had caught his attention for a while. But heightening Derrick's excitement didn't make him any more responsive to his wife's needs.

So she hadn't felt guilty about discreetly satisfying her craving for tenderness with other men. Until six months ago, every partner she'd picked had been flattered to be the object of Cecile Claiborne's affection. But with her current lover everything had changed. Instead of being the partner in control, she found herself the one being controlled.

"What do you want this time?" she asked the man on the other end of the line.

"I have a little project for you."

"I'm not taking on any more of your projects."

"Don't be so hasty." There was just enough threat in the voice to make her shiver. "I have a nice little package with your husband's name on it. Federal Express can have it on his desk tomorrow morning."

"You wouldn't dare." It was hard to keep her voice steady. Once an element of risk had only added a bit of spice to the relationship. But when she'd realized she was risking everything, her life had become a nightmare.

"Of course I would."

She sat down on the damask coverlet of her queen-size bed. "He'd be angry at you, too."

"He needs me."

The implication was that Derrick didn't need Cecile. Someone else would fill the role of Mrs. Claiborne just as well.

"What do you want me to do?"

"That's better." There was a long moment of silence as he let her sweat. Finally he murmured, "I want you to make a date with Adam Goodwin. In one of those out-of-the-way places where you like to have lunch."

"Why?"

"Just do it."

The other end of the line went dead, and she slammed the receiver back into its ornate gold cradle. But anger didn't stop her teeth from chattering as she flopped back against the pillows and pressed the heels of her hands against her eyes.

Chapter Four

Jonathan Wyndham had been too busy to speak with Abby. Back in the lobby of 43 Light Street she was still so preoccupied with the problem of getting Sharon's records that she almost bumped into Jo O'Malley and Laura Roswell. Her two friends were standing by one of the Ionic columns that flanked the doorway.

"Lost in thought?" Jo asked.

Abby shook her head apologetically. "Sorry."

"Did you forget something?" Laura added. She was a lawyer whose office was also in the building. Frequently the three women helped out with one another's cases. Abby had been an expert witness for Laura a number of times, Jo had done some of the lawyer's legwork and Laura had advised the two other women on legal points.

"Forget something?"

"Lunch," Laura clarified. A classic blonde with wavy shoulder-length hair and clear blue eyes, she was one of the building's more recent tenants. After law school she'd signed on with a large Baltimore firm, but her interest in custody cases and children's and women's rights hadn't brought in the big bucks that would have guaranteed her a partnership. And her philosphy didn't really fit in with the firm's. So she'd struck out on her own. She was still enjoying the exhilaration of building her practice through her own efforts. "Remember our date to celebrate the settlement on the Stansfield case?" she asked.

Abby's face filled with chagrin. "Oh, no. I stood you two up."

"Something more important?" Jo asked.

"That case I was talking to you about last week. Sharon Claiborne. I wanted to get a look at her records, but the Sterling Clinic has them off-limits." Quickly she filled Laura in on the details.

"Is it legal for them to restrict the records if I have staff privileges?" Abby asked.

"I think so. Unless you want to try for a court order. You'd probably have to have proof that there was some indication of malpractice."

Abby sighed. "Sounds like a Catch-22."

"The laws are so strict that soon you won't be able to apply for a dog license without getting a preregistration permit first," Jo quipped, but there was an edge of disgust in her voice.

The other two women laughed. "And you'd find a way around it," Laura said. "Probably by having your own form printed up."

Just then Lou Rossini, the building superintendent, rounded the corner. Instead of his usual gray overalls he was dressed in a plaid sport coat and green polyester slacks. It was his good-luck racetrack outfit.

"Glad to see you're feeling better," Abby observed.

"Yeah. Thanks."

"Off to Pimlico?" Jo inquired.

"Got a hot tip. Baby's Breath in the fifth. If you ladies want, I'll cut you in on the action."

Abby and Laura shook their heads, but Jo pulled out two dollars. When Lou had departed, Abby gave her friend an inquisitive look.

"I figure with Lou's connections it's less of a long shot than the lottery. Besides, I want him to fix the window that's stuck in my office. So it's a better investment than you think." She pushed the button for the elevator.

"Whatever works," Abby agreed.

"Do you want me to see what I can dig up on the Sterling Clinic?" Jo asked.

"Sure." One thing Abby had learned, if you could get Jo O'Malley interested in a case, she was like a dog with a burglar by the ankle. She wouldn't let go until she'd shaken the family silver out of his pockets.

As they rode up to their respective offices, Abby apologized one more time, then she turned to Laura and added, "Are you and Bill going out to dinner to celebrate your victory?" Bill was Dr. William Avery, the internist Laura had married while she was still in law school.

The blonde's face took on a resigned look. "I don't think so. He hasn't been real interested in my work lately."

"How come?" Jo asked.

Laura shrugged. "I think he's just wound up with his practice."

Abby detected more in the reply than Laura had spelled out. But she'd learned it was best never to volunteer professional advice to friends.

Fifteen minutes later she was back at work—counseling a seventeen-year-old girl who'd been a straight A student until her parents had gotten divorced. More disturbing than her lack of interest in school was the eating disorder that had become the focus of her attention. It was difficult getting Cindy to talk about her feelings, but by the end of the session Abby felt she'd made some real progress.

She was just writing some notes in Cindy's file when there was a knock at the outer office door. Abby glanced at her watch. She didn't have another appointment until five. It was a new patient. Someone named George Napier. Could he have gotten the time mixed up?

As she entered the waiting room, Abby could see the silhouette of a tall male figure through the frosted glass. His hand was poised to knock again when she opened the door and found herself confronting Steve Claiborne. She couldn't exactly say they were standing face-to-face. He was about eight inches taller than she was, and her line of sight was about level with his broad shoulders. Quickly she raised her eyes.

The last time he'd come here he'd been hostile. Now there was an unreadable expression in his blue eyes. Involuntarily she took a small step back.

Steve shifted his weight from one foot to the other, suddenly wishing he hadn't let an impulse carry him to Abby Franklin's door. Hell, he should have mailed the damn tapes back to her with a note. But it was too late to retreat now. "Can I come in?"

"That depends," she answered cautiously. "What do you want?"

He didn't blame her for the wariness, not after the way he'd come on like a heavy in a gangster movie the last time he'd been here. "This isn't particularly easy for me." He cleared his throat.

Abby's brows raised slightly.

"I guess I came to apologize for acting like an ass yesterday." He gestured with his right hand, and she saw he was holding a small shopping bag. "I brought the tapes back."

"Oh." She ushered him inside.

Steve closed the door quietly and stood looking around the waiting room as if he were taking in the comfortable sofas and antique oak furnishings for the first time. Finally, acknowledging that he was stalling, he lifted his eyes to Abby's. "I'm not used to admitting I'm wrong. But I could tell from the tapes that you and Sharon had a good relationship. You were helping her."

"But you wouldn't take my word for it."

"If you take a stranger's word, you're a fool. Possibly a dead fool."

There weren't many people who lived by his kind of creed, Abby mused. The harsh words gave her a bit more insight into Steve Claiborne's personality. The man was a loner, and he didn't give his trust easily. It was probably a waste of effort to try and forge any sort of understanding with him. But he'd decided to apologize for his previous behavior, after all.

"Why don't you come into the office and sit down?" she heard herself suggesting with some degree of surprise. "I was just about to have a cup of tea. Do you want some?"

"Do you have coffee?"

"Instant. How do you like it?"

"Black."

When Abby turned back from the electric teapot with two cups, Steve was sitting on one of her couches, his long legs stretched out and crossed at the ankles. Despite the casual pose he didn't look relaxed.

Abby set his coffee cup on the end table and settled onto the other couch. Steve took a swallow of the hot coffee. "Is this where you and Sharon talked?"

"Uh-huh."

For several moments they were both silent. Abby picked up her teacup and held it between her palms. Either he was going to leave in the next few minutes, or perhaps she could convert him into an ally. She didn't know why that had suddenly become important, but it had.

"Steve," Abby murmured, "I know Sharon's death—" she searched for the right words "—really hit you hard."

"How do you know?"

"Partly because of the way you've been acting."

"I see. Are you going to start probing my psyche, Dr. Franklin?"

"No. I'm just trying to communicate with you." She paused to let that sink in. "Sharon's death really upset me, too," she added in a low voice, hoping she could make him understand what she was feeling. "She was one of my first patients. Even though you're supposed to be detached, I felt very close to her."

Steve's shoulders were rigid. Across the small room Abby heard him draw in a deep breath and let it out slowly. "The hell of it is," he muttered, "I feel responsible for what happened. Sharon had written me a letter saying she needed my help. But I was away on an assignment. When I got back, she was already dead."

"It wasn't your fault."

"She was my *sister*! She was the only one in the family I gave a—I cared about."

"You weren't responsible for her actions." Even as she said the words to Steve, Abby realized that she was also speaking to her own guilt. For days she'd been telling herself she'd done her best. The hard part was believing that it was true. "You're not the only one she tried to reach out to. Did your brother tell you about Sharon calling me?'' she asked.

Steve's brows knit together. ''No! When?''

Abby hurried on with an explanation. ''Sharon phoned me at home about a week before she died. She was very upset.''

''Then why in the name of God didn't you do something?'' Leaping out of his seat, he crossed the room and grabbed her shoulders. His fingers dug into her flesh, and she gasped.

''I'm sorry.'' His hands dropped to his sides, but they were balled into fists.

Abby pressed her lips together before she spoke. ''Steve, don't you think I tried? She was disoriented, hallucinating. I kept begging her to tell me what was wrong. When I tried to find out where she was, she hung up.''

He uttered a curse.

''Her number was out of service. I called Derrick. All I got was a recording. So I went to see him the next day. He assured me she was in the hospital and getting the best possible care. When I opened the paper and saw her obituary, I . . . I . . .'' Her voice trailed off.

Steve pounded his fist against his palm. ''I've quizzed Derrick half a dozen times and I can't shake his story. He told me she was in the disturbed ward, which means she should have been under close observation. So how did she get to a phone? And how did she kill herself?''

''Steve, I've been trying to figure it out, too. I've got staff privileges at the Sterling Clinic, so I thought I could get a look at her records. But when I went over there this afternoon, I found out they've slapped a restriction on them.''

''What are they trying to hide?''

"I don't know. Maybe a nurse forgot to lock a door. Maybe somebody left her alone when they shouldn't have. They claim they're in the middle of an investigation."

"They're stonewalling."

"Or they're going to issue a report."

He sank down heavily on the sofa beside her.

Abby studied his face, aware that she was seeing a very different side of Steve Claiborne. The psychologist in her noted that his expression held a mixture of frustration and anxiety and a certain wariness that made her want to help him. The woman in her noted with a small jolt that she found his deep blue eyes and rugged features very appealing. Her gaze was drawn to the scar on his forehead, and she caught herself before she could reach out to trace it with her finger. When she'd first seen him standing on the other side of Sharon's grave, she'd thought of it as a visible sign of the kind of violent life he'd chosen. Now she silently acknowledged that he might not have had so many choices. Maybe the scar was really a symbol of the wounds he'd suffered.

"Could I ask you some questions? I mean, about Sharon." The words were so low that she had to strain to hear him.

"I'll tell you anything I can," she answered, looking down at his strong hands as he clasped them tightly around a jean-clad knee.

"Those tapes, they're from your early sessions with her?"

"Yes."

"She sounded pretty upset."

"She was. Breaking up with Miles destroyed her self-confidence."

"How was she later?"

"A lot stronger. A lot more sure of herself."

"Did you solve all her problems?"

"*I* didn't solve her problems. She did the hard work by herself." Abby took a sip of tea as she paused to consider. If Sharon were still alive, they'd never be having this discussion. But Sharon was dead. "She was still looking for a man she could love. She'd made that her major goal. I tried to help her understand that she had to let relationships develop and grow naturally. I'm not sure she knew how to do that."

"Yeah, I know. But deep down she was a survivor."

"Yes."

"Maybe I'm way off base. Maybe I can't see the truth. I need to understand what happened. Do you think she was in such bad shape that she should have been hospitalized or that she would have killed herself?"

Abby heard the anguish in his voice. Instinctively she reached out and covered his large hand with her smaller one. She felt his muscles tense, but he didn't pull away. They sat in silence, sharing the physical contact.

Steve was surprised to realize that he wanted to turn his palm up and knit his fingers with Abby's, but he didn't do it. More than that, her openness made him want to let out some of the pain he'd bottled up inside. But he didn't do that, either. He'd gotten by on his own emotional resources for a long time. There wasn't any reason to stop now.

Casting around for a more neutral line of thought, his eyes focused on the small gold pendant around her neck. But after a moment he realized he wasn't really looking at the piece of jewelry. He was thinking about the way it lay in the hollow of her throat and how soft and creamy her skin looked. His gaze flicked upward and rested on her lips. They were slightly parted—the bottom one fuller than the top and sensually inviting.

His gaze jerked away but didn't leave her face. He saw that her eyes were downcast. For the first time he noticed that her lashes were dark and silky. Then he became aware of how warm and gentle her hand felt where it rested on top of his.

Why was he focusing on such intimate details?

Silently he acknowledged that he found Abby Franklin very attractive. But so what? There was an infinity of things he didn't know about the woman, he told himself sharply. Just because she was a turn-on didn't mean he could trust her.

"Steve, tell me how you're feeling."

Had she read his mind? He moved his hand from under hers. For just a moment her fingers pressed against his thigh. Then she snatched her hand back.

"I'm not used to talking about how I feel."

"Sometimes it's hard to open up." Abby fought to keep a tremor out of her voice. Sitting like this with him was having an unexpected effect on her equilibrium. "But it helps. I was shocked to hear Sharon was in the hospital—and even more shocked when I found out she was dead."

"Then you don't think she killed herself?"

"I hadn't seen her for two years. I just don't know for sure."

"I was hoping you could give me some answers."

"I wish I could." All at once she realized that they'd been together in her office for almost an hour. "I have a patient coming in a few minutes. But we could talk again."

"Yeah, maybe." He stood up. "Listen, thanks for the coffee. I've, uh, got to do some thinking."

He crossed to the door and left.

STEVE STEPPED out onto the sidewalk and stood with his hands in his pockets, looking toward the parking garage where he'd left his car. After taking a few hesitant steps in that direction, he turned and went the other way up Light Street.

In a couple of her letters Sharon had mentioned a place called Clayton Florist where she liked to stop in and buy flowers. And she'd talked warmly about Sam Segal, the old guy who ran the place. He'd sent a huge arrangement of tulips and daffodils—Sharon's favorite flowers—to the funeral. The shop wasn't too far from here. Maybe Segal had some useful information.

At the courthouse on the corner of Light and Fayette, Steve turned west. It was strange to be tramping around downtown Baltimore, he thought, seeing which old buildings were still standing and which had been replaced.

His boots pounded the grimy sidewalk, but somewhere around the old bus terminal he stopped being aware of the scenery. He was thinking about Abby Franklin.

Now he remembered that first glimpse of her at the cemetery. He'd wondered if she was a friend of Sharon's. Then, back at the house when he'd found out she was his sister's shrink, he'd made some rash accusations. Well, maybe he'd jumped to the wrong conclusions.

The observation stopped him in midstride. A couple of days ago he'd been sure there was only room in his thoughts for Sharon. Now Dr. Franklin had moved in and taken up residence.

He turned the corner and headed up Howard Street. For a moment he was shocked at how run-down the old retail area looked. But the city scene faded into the background again as he started thinking about Abby's green eyes with their fringe of sooty lashes and the warmth of her tapered fingers pressing his.

Claiborne, keep this on a professional level, he advised himself. *You want a woman who's going to be hot and sweet and not give you any problems. Someone uncomplicated.*

A frown dug a furrow between Steve's eyebrows. Abby was nothing like the Asian women he'd been associating with recently. They'd been brought up to be submissive. Dr. Franklin could be gentle and caring when she wanted to be. But he'd be willing to bet she'd also taken assertiveness training. He knew he'd given her a hard time. And she hadn't buckled. She'd given as good as she'd gotten. Somehow, instead of turning him off, her spunk was turning him on.

With a determined effort he dismissed her from his mind as he reached Clayton Street, which was little more than a two-block-long alley near Lexington Market. The florist shop was in an ancient row house next to a parking lot.

When he stepped through the door, the sweet scent of flowers enveloped him, and for a moment he was back in his walled garden half a world away. As soon as he finished his business in Baltimore, he was going to go home, kick off his boots and sit on the veranda with a tall gin and tonic.

"Can I help you?" A balding, stoop-shouldered man was looking up from the rosebud corsage he was wiring together.

"Sam Segal?"

"You've got him."

"I'm Steve Claiborne, Sharon's brother."

The wrinkled face took on a look of sadness. "She was so sweet. Used to come in here and let me ramble on about old times. Did the family like the flowers I sent?"

"Yes. They were beautiful."

"It was the least I could do."

"I'm trying to figure out what happened. Why she—" He swallowed and started again. "Did Sharon tell you about anything that was worrying her?"

The old man looked thoughtful. "She didn't talk to me about her problems. But I could tell she was upset about something the last time she was in."

Steve's expression was eager. "What?"

"I'm not sure. Maybe it had something to do with her volunteer job."

"Where was she working?"

"Maybe she told me . . . but you know how it is. When you get old, things go in one ear and out the other."

They talked for a few more minutes. Steve didn't get any more information, but Segal insisted on giving him a bouquet of pink carnations. What the hell was he going to do with them?

FIFTEEN MINUTES after Steve had left, Abby was still sitting on the couch trying to understand what had transpired between the two of them. Something physical, she acknowledged. And something emotional.

Her thoughts turned to the men she'd dated. They'd all been safe, steady types. That had made her feel comfortable, except that lately she'd come to realize she was missing out on something.

On the other hand, getting into a conversation with Steve was like climbing into a roller coaster car. You went where the ride took you—up the long, heart-stopping inclines and then flying headlong down the hills with the wind whipping through your hair.

The outer door opened again, and Abby's head jerked up. She could see her new patient, George Napier, striding purposefully into the waiting room.

Rising, she smoothed her hair with a pat of her hand and went out to greet him. His wife had called up very distressed two days before asking if Dr. Franklin could possibly fit him in late in the afternoon that week.

"I ask my new patients to fill out a questionnaire," Abby began.

Napier ignored her and walked right into her office without being invited. Taking a chair, he started talking excitedly about the shoe business.

"I'm going to cash in my money market certificates and withdraw my retirement fund so that I can open a chain of shoe stores. I've got this dynamite new concept. It's gonna be great. Each store is gonna be in a converted luxury van so that I can bring the product right to the customer."

Classic manic symptoms, Abby thought. Almost a textbook case. "Mr. Napier—" She tried to interrupt, but he plowed on.

"Everybody needs shoes, and people are so busy that they don't even have—Do you know how many people are walking around in shoes that hurt their feet?"

Before the therapist could answer, he began to describe his promotional campaign that would have him featured on every national talk show and his picture on the cover of *Business Week*. Abby had the odd sensation that he was mouthing a memorized speech. Maybe he'd told so many people his ideas that they'd taken on the sound of a TV script.

When Abby quietly suggested that he reconsider withdrawing funds for the time being, he began to rant.

"Listen, I came here to get my wife off my back. If I'd known you were a woman, I wouldn't have bothered." As he spoke, he ripped a copy of *Psychology Today* in half and tossed it onto the floor.

"I'd like to help you, but if you don't think we're suited to each other, I could put you in touch with a male therapist."

He was a big, strong man with a receding hairline and teeth that would have benefited from an orthodontist's attention. When he stood up and shoved his face menacingly toward Abby's, she had to steel herself not to flinch.

"If I hear that you've stolen my idea, sister, I'm going to make you wish you'd never been born." Turning abruptly, he stamped out of the office, slamming the door behind him.

Abby took a few moments to catch her breath. With someone that out of control, the best thing was hospitalization. Sighing, she called the number his wife had given to discuss her recommendations.

The line clicked, and it sounded as if the call was being transferred to a new exchange.

"Mrs. Napier?" Abby questioned.

"Who is this?" a guarded voice shot back.

"Dr. Franklin."

The woman's voice warmed up several degrees. "Oh, yes. Dr. Franklin. I hope George kept the appointment this afternoon."

"Yes, he did. I'm afraid he's showing symptoms of being in an acute manic state."

"What does that mean?"

"He's excitable. Full of grandiose ideas and very angry if you refuse to go along with his schemes."

"I know that. What am I going to do?"

"I'd recommend hospitalization."

The woman cleared her throat. "Uh, our health insurance recently affiliated with the Sterling Clinic. Do they have psychiatric care?"

Abby hesitated, torn between professional ethics and her own bias. Right now she didn't feel particularly good about the Sterling Clinic. But she had a lot of respect for Jonathan Wyndham, and she'd had other patients who'd done quite well at the facility in the past. "Yes, they do, but I think you'd be better having a male doctor handle it. Your husband might respond better." She went on to say that Mr. Napier would probably be put on medication, but it might take several weeks for any therapeutic effect to be observed.

Mrs. Napier thanked her for the advice. But somehow Abby had the feeling that the woman wasn't going to follow it. In fact, there was something decidedly odd about the whole episode—although she wasn't sure why she thought so.

ADAM GOODWIN LIKED to think of himself as a chameleon. He was just as comfortable at a yachting party in Annapolis as a dimly lit bar in East Baltimore. He knew how to pick the right outfit for the right occasion. He was a good listener. He had a nice stock of amusing stories to tell. Usually he could find a touchstone—a shared point of view or a common experience—with just about anyone. Just the way he'd done that evening when he'd knocked on the door to borrow Sharon Claiborne's phone. He'd introduced himself as her new neighbor and they'd gotten to talking real chummy like. But he'd waited a couple of months before he'd asked her for a date.

It was all part of the strategy of selling himself, which was what you did when you peddled insurance. Or anything else. Get to be a good buddy. Gain their confidence. Then let them know what you could do for them. Sometimes the process was as subtle as a hint of expensive perfume drifting on the wind. Other times you could just reach out and nail them like a rolled-up newspaper coming down on a fly. Knowing which approach to take was part of the game. And knowing which angles to work. Every now and then when you were in the middle of one job, you could cop a little extra for yourself on the side. Like with Ezra Hornby. Once he'd pointed out the advantages for the Lazarus Mission of the deal he had in mind, it hadn't taken much effort to get the old guy going.

This evening Adam was loose and relaxed and open to a variety of possibilities. Score some coke. Get hooked up with a foxy lady. Have some fun. What good was money if you didn't use it to have a good time?

"Adam," the bartender at the Crazy Eight greeted him like an old friend.

"How ya doin'? Give me a Miller Lite, will ya?" Foaming glass in hand, he ambled toward the back of the long, narrow room where several of the regulars were shooting the breeze. Two or three greeted him by name. Several others nodded or waved in a friendly fashion.

"Hey, Adam, how ya been?"

"Can't complain." He pulled out a chair and sat down, crossing his long legs comfortably at the ankles.

"There was a guy around lookin' for ya."

"Yeah?" Adam took a swig of beer and wiped his mouth with the back of his hand.

"Tall fellow. Streaked hair. Tough. Had a scar on his forehead."

The insurance salesman kept his expression bland.

"He was asking questions about that chick you brought down here a couple of times," another voice piped in. "Sharon. The antsy one." The man laughed. "Man, was she out of her element."

Adam set his glass down very carefully. "Did you get a name?"

"Naw."

No name. But the description fit Steve Claiborne. Sharon's brother. Not the nice polite corporate executive—the other one, with the reputation for swinging first and asking questions later.

So Steve Claiborne was looking for him. What if he came bursting through the door right now? Adam looked nervously toward the front of the bar. Then he turned and checked the back exit. He'd left that way before. Once when Sharon hadn't been quite steady on her feet, and he hadn't wanted the hassle of maneuvering her through the crowd.

Adam took several swallows of beer and considered the situation logically. Steve was probably just on a fishing expedition. He couldn't know anything. Could he? Like, for example, what had really happened to his sister? Nah. Who the devil would tell him *that*?

THE MAN GLANCED over his shoulder. No one else was in the musty basement of 43 Light Street. Not after he'd arranged to give Lou Rossini a hot tip on a filly named Baby's Breath. With a set of special keys he opened the service door and stepped inside. Then he switched on a flashlight and played the powerful beam over the ancient equipment.

Some of the new stuff was almost tamper-proof. Nowadays there were more safety features than in the redesigned space shuttle. But not this baby.

Quickly he began to rewire circuits so that he could work them from a remote control. After it was all over, he'd put the stuff back the way he'd found it. Nobody was going to be able to figure out what the hell had happened.

ABBY WAS MAKING some notes in her patient records when the phone rang.

"Hello?"

"What are you doing working so late?" It was Jo.

"So what are you doing calling me at the office if you don't expect to find me here?" Abby joked. After the episode with George Napier, it was good to hear a friendly voice.

"I tried your home number first," Jo explained.

"Oh."

"I was down at the health department this afternoon, looking up some stuff for one of my clients and decided to do a quick check on Sterling."

"That was fast."

"Well, you know, why not? And I did find out something kind of interesting."

"Don't tell me Sterling was cited for a health department violation?"

"Nothing like that. Did you know the clinic takes a fairly high percentage of welfare cases? A lot of them from East Baltimore," Jo asked. "Even though they're in an upscale area, they have a higher percentage of indigents than any other hospital in the city."

"That's very public-spirited of them."

"I thought so, too. Until I did some more poking around. It's amazing the kind of connections you can come up with when you query a large data base."

"And?"

"There's a very high mortality rate among the Sterling welfare cases. A lot higher than with their private patients."

Abby's felt the fine hair on the back of her neck stir. More deaths at Sterling. This wasn't what she'd expected to hear. Now she tried to draw some logical conclusions from the new information. "Sounds as if that segment of their population might not be getting as good care. Or it could be that they're in such poor shape when they finally get to the hospital that it's impossible to save them."

"Could be. Or maybe Sterling picks up extra government funding to cover the expenses. They could be siphoning it off for some other purpose."

"Jo O'Malley, you have a devious mind. You don't really think that a reputable hospital system would be playing games with government money, do you?"

"You must not be reading the *Baltimore Sun*. A lot of so-called reputable corporations are padding government contracts."

"Did you come up with anything else?"

"Well, most of the welfare patients who died were seen first for an out-patient problem. I'm not sure what that proves."

Abby stroked her chin, but she couldn't draw any further inferences, either. "Well, thanks for checking. I owe you one," she told Jo.

"The next time I get a nut case who needs a shrink instead of a private eye, I'll send him over."

"Thanks a bunch."

Abby was smiling as she hung up, but the light expression faded quickly. She was the kind of person who liked to categorize things and put them in their proper place. But there was something going on at Sterling that she didn't understand and couldn't figure out.

Almost as soon as she'd put down the receiver, the phone rang again. This time when she answered, she was met with silence on the other end of the line—except for the sound of someone breathing.

"Hello?" she tried again. "Who is it? Jo?"

There was a pause of several seconds. Then the line went dead. Probably someone who realized they'd dialed a wrong number and were embarrassed to admit it, Abby told herself. But she was only half convinced. Shrugging, she replaced the receiver, finished up her paperwork and locked the office door.

The lights were off in the other offices, and the halls were quiet, giving the building a deserted feeling. The echo of Abby's heels on the marble floor rang through the empty space like bursts from a cap gun.

The exit sign at the end of the corridor was out, which cast the area in even more shadow. Under normal circumstances dim, empty hallways didn't bother Abby, but tonight she felt tiny goose bumps prickle her arms.

All at once she was seized with the irrational feeling that she was being watched by malevolent eyes. Cautiously she glanced over her shoulder. No one was there.

Then she peered down the hall in the other direction. The barest suggestion of movement drew her attention to the door at the north stairway. Was it open slightly? She couldn't be sure, and she wasn't about to go investigate.

Maybe her uneasy feelings came from the unsettling experience with George Napier, she told herself. He'd been pretty agitated when he'd stomped out of the office. Was he lurking at the end of the hall ready to jump out at her and beat her to death with the heel of a shoe?

The image was ridiculous, making her laugh nervously. Nevertheless, she jabbed the elevator call button with a lot more force than necessary. Nothing happened. After an endless minute, she punched the button again. As the machinery whirred to life, a feeling of relief washed over her.

Just then, the door at the end of the hall swung all the way open and a large man bolted out. In the dim light she couldn't make out any details. All she knew was that he was heading straight toward her.

As he bore down on her, she heard the elevator doors wheeze open. Somewhere in the back of her mind it registered that the lights must be off.

The man was running now. Abby took a quick step back. Instead of coming down on the floor, her foot encountered empty air. The car wasn't there.

"No. Wait," the man called.

It was too late. Abby had already lost her balance. Her fingers scraped against the edge of the doorway, but she couldn't save herself. In the next second she tumbled into the yawning elevator shaft.

Chapter Five

Reflexively Abby grabbed again for a handhold. But it was no use. A scream tore from her throat as she tumbled through the dark opening.

Then there was the sickening sensation of falling helplessly.

But it was only a few seconds before she slammed into a cold metal surface. As she hit, the shock of impact reverberated in her head like a Chinese gong.

"Abby!" a voice echoed from somewhere above.

Dazed and confused, she stared upward, struggling to focus—and to make sense of what had happened.

Steve. The doors. The elevator. What—

Vaguely she wondered why she hadn't fallen farther. Her head throbbed. Her thoughts were like gnats circling in her skull.

"Can you hear me? Abby?" Steve was leaning into the opening through which she'd tumbled.

In the next moment he landed as light as a cat beside her. His hand was gentle on her shoulder. "Are you hurt?"

"My head," she whispered. Then another thought pushed the previous one aside. "What are you doing here?"

He looked chagrined. "I decided you were right. I came back to talk. Then I saw the guy peering out at you from the stairs and wondered what the hell he was doing."

"Guy?"

"I'll tell you about it later."

When he bent down and lifted her shoulders, she sucked in a sharp breath.

"We'll take it slow. Is it bad?"

"Dizzy."

He sat her up. Her head slumped against his shoulder and her lids fluttered closed. It felt as if his fingers were stroking her hair. When they encountered the bump on the back of her head, she winced. "You're going to have a goose egg all right. You're damn lucky the car was right below the doorway, not at the bottom of the elevator shaft."

She shuddered. His words had just made her realize how close she'd come to disaster. With the realization, she felt herself unraveling like a frayed cord. Yet somehow she hung on to the shreds of her self-control. Her pride wouldn't let her go to pieces in front of Steve.

After a few moments he muttered, "We'd better get out of here. Can you crawl out if I boost you up?"

"I think so." But when he helped her to her feet, her knees buckled and she grabbed at his shirt front to steady herself.

Steve's arms came up to catch her, and the two of them stood like lovers in a close embrace. As he gave Abby time to regain her equilibrium, Steve's fingers stroked soothingly across her back. Not so long ago she'd thought of this man as an enemy. Now she felt protected.

"I'm a rag doll."

"You're entitled." He waited several heartbeats. "Ready?"

"I hope so."

Kneeling, he encircled her hips with his arms, and she felt his breath against her abdomen. Then he was lifting her toward the square of light above them. She felt her skirt riding up, felt his fingers against her panty hose. But this was no time for modesty. Her own fingers clutched for purchase on the metal track at the edge of the doorway.

The man was strong. He gave one more powerful thrust upward, and she got her shoulders onto the floor. Then she was rolling out into the hallway.

"Are you all right?" he called out.

"Yes."

"I'm coming up."

"Hey, wait. Don't forget my purse."

Steve's chuckle drifted up out of the darkness. "Trust a woman to remember her purse, even when she's down for the count."

A few moments later he climbed out of the gaping elevator doorway with her pocketbook slung over his shoulder. She noticed he wasn't even breathing hard. Perhaps this sort of thing was all in a day's work.

After helping her up, Steve gave her an assessing look.

"I can walk."

They started slowly down the hall toward her office. She didn't protest when he put his arm around her for support.

Fumbling with her bag, he retrieved a key ring. Probably it was bad manners to jimmy the lock with your arm around the occupant of the office.

"The brass one on the end," Abby informed him, her voice shaky. Reaction was setting in, and she was starting to tremble. It was a relief to sink onto the couch in the office.

After closing the outer door, Steve turned back to Abby. "Do you have a first-aid kit?"

"In the bathroom." She pointed toward the door on her right.

A few minutes later he came back with his hands full. Apparently he'd also found the refrigerator. He put an ice pack on the back of her head and then took her hands and gently washed them with a towel.

Abby looked down, surprised to discover they were scraped and bleeding. Now that she had time for an inspection, she saw that her suit was stained with grease. Her free hand touched one of the streaks.

"Don't worry about it, Abigail."

"Nobody calls me that and lives."

"I do. It suits. Abigail van Perfect."

"Is that what you really think of me?"

"No. But I don't think you want to pay for a fifty-minute session to find out."

"You mean you think I should pay for the information?"

"Why not?"

The man was baiting her. Maybe to take her mind off the sting of the antiseptic he was applying to her palm.

Closing her eyes, she leaned back and let him continue. After finishing with her hands, he looked up. "Anyplace else hurt?"

"I don't think anything is broken. But I'll probably have some bruises tomorrow."

After checking out her legs and shoulders, he began cleaning up her face. When the cloth laved her cheek, she looked up from under lowered lashes. It was a strange sensation, having someone minister to her like this—

particularly someone like Steve Claiborne. She'd discovered he could tease when he wanted to. Now there was a sensitivity—even a warmth—in his expression, something she hadn't seen before. The combination was surprising.

When he realized she was studying him, he cleared his throat. "You're looking better."

She was about to say "Thanks" when he added, "Chalky white isn't your color."

"Next time I fall down an elevator shaft, I'll make sure I've freshened my makeup."

He tried to bite back a grin and didn't quite succeed. "You must be feeling better, too."

She nodded, expecting him to smile. Instead there was a watchful expression on his face.

"What's wrong?"

"Shh." Getting up, he walked quickly but quietly to the outer door and flung it open. No one was in the hall.

"Stay there. I'll be right back."

Steve was gone for about a minute, and Abby felt her heart rate accelerate as the seconds ticked by. When he appeared in the doorway again, she looked up questioningly.

"I guess my back-alley instincts are working overtime. I thought I heard someone outside."

"It could have been the building. It's old and creaky."

"I suppose you're right."

As he stepped into the office, she saw that he was holding a slightly crushed bouquet of pink carnations.

"You found a delivery boy lurking in the hall?"

"And I wrestled him for the flowers." Steve laughed and explained where they'd really come from. "I guess I dropped them in the excitement," he added. "They were on the floor in the stairwell."

"There's a vase in the closet."

Steve found the vase, filled it and set the flowers on the desk. Then he turned back to Abby. "Now that we've beautified your office, let's give you a quick once over."

"I thought you did."

"You have quite a bump on the head. I want to make sure you don't have a concussion." Sitting down beside her on the sofa, he crooked his finger under her chin, tipped her head up and peered into her eyes.

Abby swallowed. "How are they?"

"A very unusual shade of green. And your pupils are the same size—the way they're supposed to be."

"Oh. I mean good." Being this close to him now was surprisingly disturbing. Or perhaps it was simply because her guard was down.

"Blink for me."

She followed instructions.

"Fine. Did you lose consciousness when you hit?"

"I don't think so."

"And you're not feeling sleepy now?"

"No." A little disoriented, maybe. But not from the bump on her head. She was still staring into his eyes. "Uh, how did you get to be an expert on concussion?"

"In my line of work you get to be an expert in a lot of areas."

"Um." She made an effort to snap out of her trance. "We'd better report the elevator problem before someone else falls in."

"Right." His hand dropped away from her chin as if he'd suddenly remembered that he was still holding on to her. He shook his head, a slightly bemused expression on his chiseled features.

Abby gave him the number. When he called, he found that another tenant had already reported the malfunction to Lou Rossini, and the service people were on their way.

"Satisfied?" Steve asked.

"Yes."

"Are you up to talking?"

"I guess."

He dropped into the easy chair facing her. Then he saw her wince as she changed positions. Right now she probably felt like a sack of potatoes that had fallen off the back of a truck. A stab of protectiveness edged with guilt knifed into him. From the psychological wound flowed the need to take care of her, make the hurts disappear. He'd felt that way with Sharon, too.

"I think we ought to get you home."

"Maybe you're right."

As Abby stood up, she realized she was still shaky on her feet. She didn't object when Steve slung his arm around her waist. By mutual agreement they took the south stairway—the one that didn't lead past the elevator.

"You're in no condition to drive," he told her.

"I'm only a couple of blocks away. I walked over."

"My car's right across the street. I'll take you back."

As they stepped outside, she saw that it was already dark. A little shiver zinged up her spine, and suddenly she realized that every shadow on the street was going to conceal an imaginary menace. "I'm not going to object."

"Good." Steve paused and looked up and down the street before ushering Abby out the door. Then, making only a slight allowance for her injuries, he hurried her across the alley to the parking garage where he'd left his Corsica.

ABBY DIDN'T KNOW how close she'd come to the truth. From the alley across Light Street, a hulking figure slunk back into the gloom.

There must have been some kind of screwup. He'd been waiting around to see an ambulance pull up at the front door. But the only truck had been from the elevator repair service. At least they wouldn't find anything wrong. He'd made sure he'd removed the temporary override controls before he'd come down here.

He cursed. Now Abby Franklin was walking out of the building under her own power. Not even a broken leg. And Sir Galahad was still with her. Everything would have worked out fine if he hadn't come along.

Despite the cool evening breeze off the water, the man's palms were sweaty, and he wiped them on his twill slacks. Now what the hell was he going to do?

A FEW MINUTES later Steve and Abby pulled into the parking area under her building. Abby was starting toward the exit when she heard a high-pitched voice squeal her first name.

Beside her, Steve whirled to face the source of the interruption and stepped in front of Abby as if he were shielding her from danger. Startled, she didn't immediately realize who was calling her. Then she spotted Melissa Wexler.

"Dr. Franklin," she heard the nine-year-old's mother correct her daughter. At the same time Steve stepped back and shifted into a more relaxed posture.

"It's all right, Mom. We're friends," the little girl insisted as she skipped toward Abby and Steve. She eyed the pair and took in the psychologist's disheveled appearance. "What happened to you?"

"She had a bad fall," Steve explained. "And I'm bringing her home."

"Are you okay?" Mrs. Wexler and Melissa both asked.

"Just a little shaken up."

Melissa looked slightly guilty. "I haven't called you because I just finished putting this rocket together. Now I'm back to working on your puzzle. I've got part of it. But it's hard," she said in a rush of words.

For a moment Abby didn't remember what her young friend was talking about. Then she smiled. "I'm sure if you keep trying, you'll solve it."

Steve had been watching the friendly exchange between the little girl and the young woman. But when the elevator arrived, he switched his full attention to Abby and noted the way her face suddenly drained of color.

As the mother and daughter bustled inside, he took hold of Abby's arm.

"It's okay," he murmured.

"I know." Abby took a deep breath and stepped across the threshold, but her throat clogged as the car began to ascend. What if it fell? No, that was ridiculous. Still, she was glad Steve held on to her elbow as they rode upward.

Melissa turned to Steve. "Abby dumped her last boyfriend. Are you her new one?"

"Melissa!" Mrs. Wexler gave her daughter a disapproving look.

Steve glanced sideways at Abby, noting that her face had regained some of its color. In fact, it was a bit flushed. "We're just friends," he explained.

Abby let out a sigh of relief when the car reached the eighth floor. As the door closed behind them, she glanced at Steve. "Do you think I have the makings of a full-blown phobia?"

"If you're talking about the elevator, of course not."

"What else would I be talking about?"

"Dumping boyfriends."

"Steve!"

"Just kidding." His expression turned serious again. "You had a bad experience with an elevator. You're entitled to be nervous. Which way is your apartment?"

Abby pointed to the right.

"Little Miss Wexler is ten going on fifteen," Steve said, changing the subject again as they started down the hall.

"No, nine going on thirty-five." Abby corrected. After she opened her door, she expected her escort to say good-night. She was surprised when he followed her into her apartment. "Steve, I'll be fine."

"After that conk on the head, you shouldn't be alone."

If her brain had been in better shape, she would have told him she was going to call a friend.

"You're going to feel either a hell of a lot better or a hell of a lot worse in the morning. Which way is the bedroom?"

The assumption that she was simply going to follow his plans like an obedient child made her bristle, yet she didn't have the energy to challenge his assertiveness. Without waiting for her reply, he started down the hall, checking the rooms. Abby followed.

When they reached her bedroom, he walked briskly across the carpet and turned down the spread.

"You need any help getting undressed?"

Some of the fog dissipated. "Of course not."

"I'll be in the living room. Call me if you want anything."

Abby left her ruined suit in a heap on the bathroom floor, pulled off her panty hose and climbed into bed in her slip. She half expected to find herself lying awake for hours. Instead she was asleep almost as soon as her head hit the pillow.

Steve had been lying when he'd told Abby he was going into the living room. Instead, he stood outside her door, listening to the little rustling sounds of her getting ready for bed. He suspected she hadn't bothered to put on a nightgown and wondered what he was going to encounter when he opened the door.

He waited until her breathing was soft and even. Then he stepped back into the room. A shaft of light from the hall fell across the sleeping woman on the bed. She was curled on her side, the covers up around her shoulders.

Relaxed in sleep, she was no longer the competent psychologist. In her place was a damn sexy woman whose full bottom lip pouted slightly and whose tousled hair spilled across the pillow.

The image brought a familiar stab of sexual awareness—and another unaccustomed wave of protectiveness. He recognized them both as dangerous impulses.

Abby Franklin didn't mean anything to him, and he planned on keeping it that way.

Silently he backed out into the hall and closed the door. He'd told her he'd stay to make sure she was all right. And he'd do that. But there was other business to attend to right now.

The room up the hall was her office. Slipping inside, he closed the door and turned on the light. For a moment he felt a pang of guilt at invading her privacy. Then he shrugged and sat down at the desk. His life—maybe hers—depended on finding out as much about her as he could. She might not have realized the implications of her fall. But she hadn't seen the burly-looking guy peering out of the stairwell. Two to one he had arranged a nasty accident for Dr. Franklin tonight, which confirmed Steve's suspicion that someone was desperate to make sure the real facts about Sharon's death stayed buried.

Somebody thought Dr. Franklin knew something. Or just possibly she was hired help who'd served her purpose. For a moment his teeth clenched. He didn't want that to be true. But if it was, he was going to find out.

For the next hour and a half he methodically went through Abby Franklin's records. Not just from her practice, but from her personal life. Bank statements. Checkbooks. Calendar. Correspondence. Income tax information. She was a very systematic and organized person. He even thumbed through a stack of old concert and theater programs. As he worked, he carefully put everything back just as he had found it.

By the time he finished he was feeling even guiltier. But the emotion was tinged with relief. He knew a great deal about the business of the woman he'd rescued tonight, and the only vice he could uncover was a tendency toward compulsive shopping—as revealed by her three-page credit card statements.

In some ways he envied her. Abby was a respected professional. She had a warm relationship with her parents and she knew where she was going. He'd never been that sure of his life. His attitude had always been every man for himself. Now he couldn't help worrying that he and Sharon had dragged Abby into a shadowy world she wasn't prepared to cope with.

It was after midnight when he went back to check on her. Quietly he opened the door. In the light from the hall he could see that Abby was lying on her back with her arms above her head.

She looked innocent—and submissive. Again he couldn't help noting that sleep had softened and blurred the no-nonsense image she worked so hard to project, leaving a very appealing femininity. Seeing her like that made him even gladder that he hadn't found anything incriminating when he'd searched her records.

As he stood in the doorway, she shifted, and the covers drifted down to her waist, making the unconsciously sexy pose all the more tantalizing.

He was drawn forward by the irresistible, sleep-warmed scent of her body and the translucent glow of her skin in the dim light.

He couldn't stop a little fantasy from flicking through his mind. Her green eyes heavy-lidded with passion. Those slender white arms reaching out to clasp him around the neck and pull him down to the bed with her. The scene was only in his mind, but his body's reaction was all too real.

It would be prudent to back out of the room and leave her apartment, but he had a mission to accomplish. Sitting down on the edge of the bed, he gently reached out toward her shoulder.

"Abby."

Her eyes opened—momentarily disoriented and then wide with alarm. In the split second before she screamed he covered her mouth with his hand. "Don't. It's all right."

Her gaze questioned his.

"I told you I was going to wake you up to make sure you were all right." As he saw comprehension dawn on her features, he removed the hand.

"I'm going to ask you some dumb questions. What's your name?"

"Abby Franklin."

"Abigail."

"I thought we settled that."

"Your address?"

She supplied it, and he watched her lips as she recited the information.

There was a tension between them now that had nothing to do with concussions and everything to do with a man and a woman who have silently acknowledged they're attracted to each other and find themselves alone in the middle of the night.

Was Melissa right? "Are you dating anyone seriously?" That wasn't what he'd thought he was going to ask. But the question in his mind had simply slipped out.

She arched an eyebrow. "That's kind of personal."

"I'm feeling kind of personal, Dr. Franklin."

"I'm not Dr. Franklin all the time."

"I know."

Suddenly it was impossible not to lean forward and brush his lips against hers.

He was simply satisfying his curiosity, he told himself. If she turned her cheek, he'd pull away. But she was pliant and breathy and perhaps as curious as he.

This wasn't smart, Abby thought, even as her lips parted under his. It wasn't rational. It wasn't safe. But she couldn't hold back a small sound of pleasure as her mouth opened under his. Perhaps it was from being thrown so badly off balance tonight. Or maybe it was a response to this new, unexpected side of Steve Claiborne. But any logical thought was quickly swept away on a wave of sensation.

She quivered with anticipation as his tongue stroked her lips, investigated the corners, swept seductively across the soft fullness. Then he was reaching possessively above her head to lock his fingers with hers. Their hands clasped, loosened and clasped again in a rhythm that accented the building tension.

She didn't know which one of them deepened the kiss. She only knew that the heady taste and texture of his tongue dipping into her mouth brought every nerve in her body to throbbing life. He muttered something rough and sensual.

She could feel his heart pounding wildly against her breasts. She could feel her own blood racing hotly through her veins. But it was all happening much too fast.

Chapter Six

Stop. She had to end this insanity now.

He felt the change in her—from warm and pliant to resisting. All at once he realized that he was trespassing. Lifting his head, he stared down at her, his own confusion mingling with hers.

He'd only come in to make sure she was all right. Maybe he was the one who needed to have his head examined. Slowly his fingers unlocked from hers. She lay with her arms still above her head, gazing up at him. Passion mingled with astonishment in her eyes. He reached down to stroke a thumb across her still-dewy lips.

"I think your responses are, uh, normal."

"Normal for you, maybe," she swallowed. "But I think I've given you the wrong idea."

"I should be sorry for taking advantage of the situation."

"But you're not."

He grinned and pushed himself off the bed. "I'll see you in the morning. Go back to sleep.""

"I'll try." As he reached the door, she called his name. "Steve."

"What?"

"Thanks for being a gentleman."

"I'm not." Before he could prove the point he ordered his feet to take him down the hall to the living room—and the couch that wasn't quite long enough for his six-foot-plus frame.

Alone in the dark once more, Abby adjusted the pillow and pulled the covers up to her chin. Steve Claiborne had thrown her for a loop right from the start. He was still doing it.

Perhaps the only satisfaction was in knowing that she'd affected him as much as he'd affected her. She couldn't understand her own behavior. Unfortunately she couldn't leave the analysis at that. She'd been taught to dissect motivations and emotions, and she wasn't able to silence the questions that Dr. Franklin kept asking.

When did you find you'd become attracted to this man?

Do you see a future in the relationship?

Do you feel anything more substantial than superficial sexual attraction?

What are you going to do about it?

She was too well trained not to ask the questions. But she was too drained to put much energy into her answers. This was something entirely different from her previous relationships with men. It was vibrant and exciting.

But the excitement didn't cancel out the danger. There was a lot she didn't know about Steve Claiborne. More importantly, no matter how sexy he was, the man had a lot of emotional baggage. Running away to India hadn't solved his problems. And neither would having a quick affair with Abby Franklin.

Several hours later she awoke to a unique experience, the smell of freshly brewed coffee and cinnamon drifting down the hall to the bedroom. Abby stretched. The back of her head was still tender, but beside that she didn't feel too bad. As she sat up, she remembered the little episode in the middle of the night, and her cheeks heated. Looking across to the mirror over her dresser, she inspected her wrinkled slip. In the morning light it was almost as revealing as a sheer nightgown.

And the man who'd seen her wearing it was out there in the kitchen eating breakfast. Since she doubted Steve was going to have amnesia, probably the best way to minimize the damage was to make a point of putting some distance between them. Instead of going out to meet him in a robe, she took a quick shower and dressed in a pair of cotton slacks and a camp shirt.

Still, she felt as if all of her nerve endings were on red alert as she walked down the hall toward the kitchen. Stopping just outside the door, she eyed Steve. He was sitting at the white Formica table by a window that looked out over the harbor, drinking a mug of coffee, reading the sports section of the *Baltimore Sun* and obviously enjoying the sun-warmed ambience of the breakfast nook. For a moment she was struck by how at home he looked.

From his deliberately relaxed pose, she sensed he was just as determined as she to dispel any lingering tension from the night before. Instead of focusing on the two of them, he swept his arm toward the marina and shopping pavilions across the harbor.

"I can't get over the way the area has changed. Back when I was growing up, this used to be one of the roughest neighborhoods in the city. Now you can buy peanut butter fudge and designer leather, but you can't find a simple T-shirt without a cute message."

Abby glanced at the clean knit shirt her guest was wearing. It said Maryland Is for Crabs. He must have bought it that morning, and he also seemed to have found a razor in her bathroom.

"I like the Inner Harbor this way. I also like your shirt," she added.

"You'll also like the breakfast I picked up." He gestured toward the basket of enormous, sticky cinnamon rolls on the table. "Have one."

Abby rarely indulged in sweets for breakfast. But the baked goods looked too mouth-watering to pass up.

She sat down, and he poured her a cup of coffee. "How are you feeling?"

"Better, thanks." She broke off a piece of sweet roll and began to eat.

"Good, because we need to talk." All business now, he folded the paper and stuck it on the empty chair beside him.

"About what?"

"About Sharon. Yesterday I wasn't sure how much I wanted to tell you. This morning I'm thinking there are some things you ought to know—for your own protection."

Abby set down her mug with a clank. "That sounds like a line out of *The Godfather*."

"I'm not trying to be melodramatic. Think about it. Do you honestly believe the Sterling Clinic isn't in the middle of some kind of cover-up?"

Abby shrugged. Then she remembered yesterday's conversations with Jo and her own inability to get Sharon's records. "A friend did some checking for me at the health department—"

"And?"

She summarized what Jo had found out about the welfare patients.

"Well, that's very interesting. So Sharon's not the only one who left the place in a body bag," Steve mused.

"But I don't see how her death is connected. Besides, people die in hospitals all the time."

"Not psychiatric patients." For a moment they were both silent, then Steve sighed. "All right, let's talk about how Sharon wound up in the hospital in the first place."

"Derrick says he had her committed because she was on drugs. And if—"

"Oh, sure," Steve interrupted. His chair scraped on the floor as he got up and paced to the window. "Except that I've never known anyone who was more antidrugs. Her best friend in high school had gotten into coke. She was driving three other girls to a party and ran into a tractor trailer. They were all killed. The only reason Sharon wasn't in the car was that she had a bad cold and didn't feel like going to the party."

"She never told me that."

"Maybe because it was something she'd already come to terms with. Or maybe it wasn't relevant. But, I'm telling you, if Sharon was on drugs, then somebody was giving them to her without her knowing what was happening."

Abby nodded slowly, not entirely convinced. Privately she was thinking about all the patients she'd treated who'd gotten sucked into addictions before they realized what was happening.

Steve had turned back to face her, and he must have read the ambivalence on her face. "You don't believe me."

"Who would do that—and why?"

Steve hooked his thumbs over the edges of his pockets. Last night he'd told himself he could trust Abby. Now that the moment of truth had come, he admitted that it was still hard to trust anyone. Yet he needed to talk to someone about his suspicions. "Maybe her ex-husband. Or her new boyfriend Adam Goodwin."

"She wouldn't have let Miles get that close to her again."

"Probably, but I've been checking around. She was pretty close to Adam, from what I've been able to find out."

"Why would he slip her drugs?"

"For money. He seems to go through a lot of it. And her trust fund might have come in handy. Or maybe he likes women who are dependent on him."

Abby was impressed with the amount of detective work Steve had done since he'd been back in town. And, in truth, there was one aspect of Sharon's life that had still worried her when the young woman had decided to discontinue therapy. Sharon's need for affection made her a bad judge of men. What was more, she often tried to push things too fast and then was left wondering why so many relationships went sour.

"You're going to pursue the Adam Goodwin angle?"

"Yes."

She had the feeling he was going to leave and get right back to his digging. Then he sat down at the table again. The intensity of his gaze was disconcerting.

"There's something else we've got to talk about. Somebody thinks you know something, and they're nervous about it."

"Someone thinks *I* know something?" Despite her instant denial a shiver ran up Abby's spine. She locked her fingers under the seat of her chair to steady herself.

"How else do you account for your little joyride in the elevator shaft?"

"I fell through the door because I saw you running toward me and didn't realize who you were."

"Yes. But remember, I told you there was a man lurking in the stairwell watching you."

Abby thought back over the minutes before the accident. "I saw the door move. That's why I was so jumpy in the first place."

"I'm willing to bet that if I hadn't come along, the guy was planning to rush down the hall toward you when the elevator doors opened. The lucky part is that the car stopped on the floor below your office. Otherwise you might have broken your neck."

Abby shuddered. Someone had been watching her.

Steve hesitated for a moment and then came around to her side of the table. When he put steadying hands on her shoulders, she leaned back into the strength of his arms.

"Abby, I went over to 43 Light Street this morning and checked things out." He laughed. "In fact, I almost got my toe shot off by Lou Rossini."

Abby's own laugh helped loosen the uncomfortable knot in her chest. "When you get him going, he can be like a lioness guarding her cubs."

"Yeah. He's real concerned about you. I guess he feels guilty about not being in the building when the accident happened."

"I'll have to make sure he understands it wasn't his fault."

"After I took his cap gun away from him and explained I was trying to find out what happened to you, we got to be best buddies." His fingers kneaded Abby's shoulders, and she leaned her head against the hard wall of his stomach. Neither one of them spoke for several heartbeats, and Abby closed her eyes.

"I had a look at the elevator control box."

The gritty quality of his voice made her eyes snap open.

"Somebody was pretty careful to put everything back the way it was supposed to be," he continued. "But I could tell from the way the dust had been disturbed that they had been fiddling with the circuits. My guess is that the guy watching you rigged a remote control. He was planning to send the car to the bottom of the shaft and then open the door after you pushed the button. That's why he had to know what you were doing."

Abby gulped. "What happened?"

"Probably when I came along he got flustered and screwed up."

Abby felt uncomfortably short of breath. "But that doesn't prove it was something connected with Sharon," she insisted. Somehow it was important to hang on to that idea.

"Oh?"

"A few of my patients get...out of control. There was a man yesterday who was in a paranoid manic state. My last patient, in fact. The one I was going to see right after you left. Maybe he was still hanging around and..." Her voice trailed off.

"I didn't realize psychology was such a dangerous profession."

"It usually isn't."

"What does your paranoid manic look like?"

Abby described George Napier.

Steve shrugged. "He was big. It could have been him, but I'm not sure. I didn't see his face. Anyway, the guy ran up the stairwell, and I decided I'd better see what he thought was so interesting out in the hall. That's when I spotted you."

"What were you doing on the stairs?"

"I'd been standing in the lobby for ten minutes ringing for the elevator." His fingers tightened on her shoulders. "Listen, let's stop dissecting this. The point is, I want you to be careful. Like, for example, I wouldn't walk home from work in the dark. In fact, I wouldn't even go to work. Why don't you just take a couple days off and go to the beach?"

Yesterday she'd cringed at dark shadows. Now, in the bright morning sunlight, she didn't want to believe his ominous assessment. When she sat up straight, his hands dropped away from her shoulders.

"Steve, I appreciate your concern. But I have patients who depend on me. And there isn't any proof that this is all some conspiracy."

"You think *I'm* being paranoid, Dr. Franklin?" He came around the table and glared down at her.

"I think you're looking for someone to blame for your sister's death."

His features twisted. "Thanks for the psychological insight."

Abby realized she'd gone too far, but he didn't give her a chance to clarify the remark.

"You can bet that when I find who railroaded her into the Sterling Clinic, they're going to be damn sorry," he promised. Without asking for any further comments, he turned and strode toward the front door.

"Steve, wait."

"Why? You don't want to listen to anything I've got to say."

"Tell me where you're staying."

He gave her a narrow look. "What difference does it make?"

"If I find out anything else, I'll let you know."

"Sure. Great. I'm at the Hampton Hotel. The number's in the phone book." Without further discussion, he turned and left the apartment.

THE COMPUTER NETWORK was tied into facilities around the world—London, Rio de Janeiro, Hong Kong, Sydney, Riyadh—anywhere there was money to spend on big-ticket, one-of-a-kind items. The buyers were people whose wealth was beyond imagining. Yet they protected their anonymity as vigorously as the world's intelligence services guarded the identities of their agents in the field. Great fortunes weren't something to be flaunted across the front pages of tabloids. They were resources to be respected, quietly increased and used to consolidate one's personal power. In a way the accumulation of money was like immortality. It secured the future. And it could create a life of such pampered indulgence that even death was unimaginable.

Frances Backmann was at the nexus of the computer network. Time of day meant nothing in the air-conditioned subbasement data processing center where she worked. When you provided a service to clients around the world, you worked a flexible schedule.

She sat in a six-hundred-dollar, ergonomically designed chair in front of a control panel that drove four integrated high-resolution color screens. One of them recorded a seven-hundred-and-fifty-thousand-dollar offer, which she processed and redirected to the dozen other agents participating today.

Even as her fingers keyed in the information, her mind was busy. Seven hundred and fifty thousand dollars. What a joke. They'd never get it for that. The amount was almost insulting. Last week they'd had a much older piece that had gone for twice as much.

Messages flashed across the bottom of her screen. She put some on hold and responded to the ones she knew were most urgent. She had no illusions about the people she was dealing with. But controlling the auction suffused her with a heady sense of power. For a girl from Camden who'd put herself through the University of Maryland, she'd come a long way.

Another bid came through. A million one. She smiled to herself. Even at one percent her commission on this one was going to be very nice.

Behind her she sensed the presence of a tall figure. Her boss. He was also her lover—which made things very convenient.

"I'd like to move this one out tonight. Tell them we're going to have one more round. They'll have to make their best offer." Frances nodded even as her fingers began to flick across the keys. "And then we'll celebrate. Champagne and escargots and then a nice long soak in the spa."

The silky voice made her tingle with anticipation. He wasn't just offering a banquet and lovemaking. There'd be a present, too. The jade necklace or the Russian sable she'd hinted about. But with this man it was always business before pleasure. First she had to accomplish what he wanted before she got her reward.

STEVE CLAIBORNE STOPPED in front of the door to his downtown hotel room. The almost invisible strand of hair he'd placed across the door and frame was still there. It looked as if no one had been in the room since he'd left yesterday afternoon. Still, once he was inside, he checked the other little booby traps he'd left. No one had searched his luggage or the bureau drawers.

Satisfied, he stripped off his jeans and shirt and headed for the shower. Abby Franklin's couch hadn't been designed as a bed for a man his size. He needed a couple hours of sleep before he went out and started shaking the bushes again.

He tried not to think about Abby. But as he lathered his muscular body with a pygmy-size bar of deodorant soap, he gave up the struggle. Despite the abruptness with which he'd left her apartment, he acknowledged that she'd gotten under his skin in a remarkably short time. He hadn't met many women like her. She was a surprise package of brains and beauty. And he wasn't all that sure he liked the combination. For one thing, she was too damn perceptive. Sometimes when she looked at him with those forest-green eyes, he felt she was probing all the secrets he'd carefully hidden from the world. Other times it was as if those eyes were a magnifying glass focusing the rays of the sun on his skin. And if he didn't jump out of the way, he'd get burned. Bad.

He closed his eyes and tipped his face up into the hot spray, trying to wash away newly born feelings he didn't know how to cope with. Somehow being with her last night had given him a glimpse of what he'd missed in life. Warmth. Closeness. A special kind of communication between a man and a woman. Not just sex, but something more powerful.

No. Stop thinking like that, he ordered himself, squeezing his eyes more tightly shut. It was dangerous to get too involved with anyone. They'd just end up stomping all over you. He'd learned a long time ago to keep his own counsel and hide his vulnerabilities behind a tough-guy exterior.

He hadn't gone in for meaningful relationships. Women moved in and out of his life, but he hadn't wasted much time talking to them. Hell, most of them didn't even speak English beyond the bare essentials.

Sharon was one of the few people who'd seen another side of his personality, and it hadn't really been an open exchange. When she'd needed a shoulder to cry on, he'd been there—until last week when he'd let her down.

His features contorted, and he lowered his head so that the needle spray pounded on the back of his neck. If only the hot water could wash away his guilt. And if only Dr. Abby Franklin wasn't so damn insightful about what he was feeling.

After turning off the water, Steve stepped out of the shower and began to towel his hair dry. When the phone rang, he stopped abruptly. Not many people knew where he was staying. Was Abby calling? He felt a stab of anticipation at the thought.

Droplets of water from his naked legs and torso dripped on the rug as he strode across the bedroom. "Hello."

"Steve Claiborne?" It wasn't Abby. The woman's voice was low and throaty.

"Who wants to know?"

"Sharon told me it was hard to get a straight answer out of you."

"Who is this?"

"Her friend Michelle."

"How did you get my number?"

There was a soft laugh on the other end of the line. "I have my ways. But that's not important. I understand you're looking for Adam Goodwin."

"Yes."

"He's agreed to meet us at the Blue Star in half an hour. Do you know where it is?"

"No."

"Fells Point. Turn right a couple of blocks past the marine terminal."

"Why has he agreed to meet *us*?"

"I guess you'll have to show up to find out." The line went dead.

Well, so much for taking a little nap, Steve thought as he finished drying off and began to get fresh clothing out of the dresser. All at once he felt supercharged. When you stirred the pot, eventually something bubbled to the surface. And this might be it.

EVER SINCE STEVE CLAIBORNE had paid that little visit to the antique shop, Miles Skinner had been debating what to do. With shoulders the size of Idaho and a face as dangerous as Dirty Harry looming over him, it had been hard to think. Now that he'd had a few days to reflect, he'd decided it was better to have someone like Steve Claiborne in your corner than across the ring. He had some information Sharon's brother would be interested in, some stuff he'd heard on the street about Adam Goodwin. Maybe he could trade it for Claiborne's goodwill. The guy didn't have to know his ex-brother-in-law had already worked the other side of the street—by letting the opposition know where he was staying.

After digging out the card with the Hampton Hotel number, he phoned the desk. "Steve Claiborne's room please."

The phone rang ten times and then switched back to the desk. "I'm sorry. Mr. Claiborne is out. Would you like to leave a message?"

"No." Miles hung up, feeling a mixture of disappointment and relief.

STEVE ARRIVED at the Blue Star five minutes early and parked across the street where he could take a look at the place. On Saturday afternoon the bar wasn't terribly busy. But the progressive rock music was loud, he noted as he approached the open door.

Once inside the dimly lit main room, he stood looking over the customers. A blonde with spiky hair and a black net blouse through which he could see dime-size circles of skin tipped her head to one side and smiled invitingly. Steve ambled over. "You're Michelle?"

"Sure am."

He pulled out a bentwood chair and sat down. "Where's Adam?"

She shrugged. "Must be held up in traffic. But that's okay. We can get to know each other." There was something about her manner that put him on his guard—as if her agenda wasn't exactly what she'd advertised.

When a waitress glided over and asked what they'd like to drink, Michelle ordered a fuzzy navel. Steve asked for a bottle of Japanese beer. Under the table the blonde slipped off one sandal and walked her toes along his ankle and calf.

"You say you were a friend of Sharon's?" He pushed his chair back so that he wasn't in quite such easy reach.

"Uh-huh." She gave him a little pout. "She told me a lot about you. So I feel like we're already friends."

The drinks came. Studying him from under lowered lashes, Michelle took a sip of her orange juice and peach schnapps. Steve slowly poured his beer into the glass.

He watched as the girl dug through her pocketbook and produced a pack of cigarettes. After putting them on the table, she continued to shuffle through the black leather bag. Then she made a disappointed face. "No matches. There are some on the bar." One hand still in her purse, she pointed to the other side of the room. "Could you bring me some?"

"Sure." When Steve reached the bar, he almost kept going right out the front door. Something told him that Michelle was stalling, and Adam Goodwin wasn't going to show up anytime soon. At the last minute he changed his mind and came back to the table. This was his first real break and he couldn't just walk away.

"So what about Adam?"

"He's always late."

She seemed to relax visibly when he took a few more swallows of beer. Maybe she'd sensed his ambivalence about staying.

"I didn't think Adam was very good for Sharon," Michelle confided, lighting her cigarette and dragging smoke into her lungs.

"Oh?"

"I think one of the things he liked about her most was her money. You know, her trust fund."

The room had suddenly begun to feel very warm, and Steve took another fast gulp of cold beer. It didn't help. He could feel his heart starting to jump erratically inside his chest; the rock music was pounding to the same beat inside his skull. Trust fund. Yeah, he'd been wondering about something like that himself.

But now it was getting damn hard to think. When he looked up at Michelle, he couldn't focus on her face. At that moment reality slammed into his brain like a melon splattering on the sidewalk. Of all the stupid jerks... he'd let eagerness overcome caution and fallen for one of the oldest tricks in the book. While he'd been politely getting Michelle that pack of matches, she'd been slipping something very potent into his drink.

All at once voices, music and colors began to swirl around him like dancing needle pricks against his skin. His head was an expanding helium balloon—full of thoughts as substantial as clouds.

A hole had opened up in the baseboard beside the table, and a troop of white mice came marching out. He started to laugh. The mice turned into coral snakes, and the laugh turned into a silent scream.

His fingers scraped the edge of the table as he struggled to hold on to some shred of coherence. He had to get out of there. Now. When he tried to stand up, he lurched back into his seat.

"Easy, honey." Michelle was at his side, her voice solicitous, her fingers digging into his forearm. He wanted to push her away, but his muscles had turned to maple syrup. "My friend's not feeling good. Somebody help me get him out of here."

No! Not that! His mind screamed. The words burst like soap bubbles before they could form in his mouth.

A large man materialized on Steve's other side. Together he and Michelle hoisted him to his feet.

No!

Half dragging, half carrying him, they steered him out the door and toward a car waiting at the curb. The open back door looked like a shark's mouth. He felt himself being sucked inside with the force of water gurgling down a drain.

"Thought you were pretty smart, didn't you, sucker?"

He recognized the man waiting in the back seat and shook his head in confusion.

"Easy does it."

Something sharp bit into his arm. Then blackness swallowed him up.

Chapter Seven

There was a sharp rap at the door, and Abby jumped. She'd wanted to dismiss Steve's warning, but his words had stuck in her head like a Post-it note in the middle of an empty bulletin board. Tiptoeing to the front door, she peered through the peephole. The distorted image was that of Laura Roswell.

Abby flung the door open, and Laura embraced her. "I was over at the office, and Lou told me about the elevator. I haven't seen him so upset since the sewage leak in the basement last year. He kept telling me he'd never go to the races again."

Abby managed a weak laugh. "At least maybe I've reformed him."

"Thank God you're in one piece," her friend continued. "Are you all right?"

"Just a little bruised."

The two friends looked at each other. There was a sparkle of mischief in the lawyer's blue eyes. "So, do you want to sue the management company?"

"Only if we can get a million dollars."

Laura laughed. "They'd probably raise all our rents by two thousand dollars a month to cover it."

"Well, if you put it that way. Maybe it's not such a good idea."

"But there ought to be some liability insurance. What if you'd really been hurt?"

"I'll take it under consideration, Counselor."

Abby led the way into the living room and stopped abruptly. But Laura had already taken in the untidy sofa cushions and blanket draped over the arm.

"Who's been sleeping on your couch?"

"Steve Claiborne, Sharon's brother. But it's not as exciting as it sounds."

"Oh?"

Abby folded the blanket and straightened the pillows. "Steve's the one who rescued me, and he came back to make sure I was okay."

"And nothing at all personal happened?"

Abby's cheeks heated. "Not much."

"What's he like?"

"Sexy. Tough. Dangerous."

"Honey, that sounds like a bad combination."

"Well, I doubt if I'm going to be seeing him again. I think staying out of the Claibornes' way is the safest course. Besides," she rationalized, "Steve didn't like my analysis of his motivation."

"Men. They're willing to tell you every little thing you're doing wrong. But when you dare to criticize, you're a bitch."

Abby gave her friend a direct look. "You're not talking about men in general, are you?"

Laura sank into one of the sofa chairs. "Why do I have a friend who's a psychologist?"

"Are you up to a counseling session?"

Laura nodded slightly and took a deep breath. "Bill keeps telling me he's busy building up his practice, and he doesn't seem very interested in what I'm doing. I feel like we're losing touch.''

"And you care about the relationship?"

"We were so much in love, and I thought that we could make a two-career marriage work. Now I'm starting to feel like we're two strangers living together."

Abby fixed them each a cup of tea and let her friend pour out her anxieties. It was more rewarding to counsel Laura than to come to any conclusions concerning her own mixed feelings about Steve.

"You look as if you're feeling better," Abby observed an hour later.

"I do. Thanks. I think I'm going to try talking to Bill and see if we can get some of this out in the open. Maybe he'd like to go away for a romantic little weekend where we can just concentrate on each other."

"That might help."

"The question is, does Bill care enough to try?"

"Relationships are a risk." That observation turned Abby's thoughts around to her own single status. She'd always told herself the right man just hadn't come along. But would she recognize him if he did?

A vision of Steve the way he'd looked bending over her bed last night popped into her mind. He would make an exciting lover. But to jeopardize her emotional stability with him would be crazy. Or was she just so conservative that she'd stopped taking risks?

"But I've talked your ear off," Laura was saying. "Is there anything I can do for you?"

For a moment Abby toyed with the idea of sharing her own doubts. However that was the last thing Laura needed. "Well," she said, "the Greeks have taken over Festival Hall this weekend. Let's walk over and check out the gyro sandwiches."

Laura's eyes twinkled. "You know I can't go to one of those festivals without pigging out on fried dough."

"Every nationality has its version of fried dough. But you can't beat Greek baklava. Let me get dressed and we'll check the place out."

A half hour later they started down the hall. As Abby waited for the elevator, she felt her hand tighten around the strap of her pocketbook. She been on edge going up yesterday. Now she realized she'd never step into another elevator with her old casual trust.

"Is there any way to find out who was named in Sharon Claiborne's will? Or on her insurance policy?" she asked Laura to distract herself.

"Once it's probated, the will's a matter of public record. I'd have to do some checking on the insurance." The lawyer gave her friend an assessing look. "But I thought you were going to stay out of the Claibornes' business."

Abby pursed her lips. "Yes, I was, wasn't I? Somehow I just can't let it go."

"Well, maybe a little therapeutic eating will clear your mind."

Abby nodded. She hadn't been to one of the city's ethnic festivals since last year. It was always relaxing to listen to the music, admire the exotic costumes and stop at the craft booths. But then why did she feel like an overwound watch spring? she asked herself.

HIS HEAD. Two-inch spikes pierced his brain.

His body. Stripped naked and strapped down on a padded table.

Nightmare.

"He's awake."

Reality.

Steve opened his eyes and tried to find the speaker. The image wouldn't come into focus. That as much as anything made panic rise in his throat like the taste of green persimmons. A fine sheen of perspiration bloomed on his skin.

Strong fingers pressed against his shoulder. "Relax," a woman soothed. "The visual disturbances are from the drug you OD'd on."

OD'd? His swollen brain strained with effort. Was his hearing affected, too?

"No...I..." he choked out and then stopped. It was almost impossible to make his cracked lips form the words.

He tried to sort through the vague memories tumbling through his consciousness. The Blue Star. Michelle. Then—confusion.

"Let...me...up."

"I'm sorry." Another speaker. A man. This time the voice came from somewhere behind his head. "But you're a danger to yourself and to others."

"It would help if you could tell us about your delusions," the woman encouraged. "What is it you think happened to your sister?"

Confusion mixed with anger. Steve strained against the straps that held him down. They didn't give. They only cut into his wrists and ankles. But the pain helped clear his head. "Go to hell. I'm not telling you anything."

"I'm afraid you're mistaken, Mr. Claiborne. You're going to tell us a great deal."

The woman's sharp nails trailed across a scar on his hip, and his skin crawled as if scorpions were scurrying across him. Heart pounding, he struggled to see the faces hovering above him. It was like looking through a grease-smeared lens.

A cold cotton ball dabbed his arm, and he tried to jerk away. The straps held firm. Then there was the sting of another needle.

ABBY HAD NOT ONLY ENJOYED baklava for dessert, she'd also succumbed to one of Baltimore's more unique traditions—fresh lemon sucked through a peppermint stick.

After putting away the handcrafted silver earrings she hadn't been able to resist, she called her answering service. She found that Mrs. Shrewsberry needed to cancel an appointment. And Cecile Claiborne wanted to talk to her.

Cecile Claiborne? After the scene at the funeral reception, she hadn't expected to hear from the woman again. Curious, she dialed the Claiborne residence.

"Dr. Franklin. Thank you for calling back." The voice was several degrees warmer than Abby remembered.

"Is there something I can do for you?"

"First I wanted to apologize for my boorish behavior at the funeral. I was upset, and I really wasn't myself."

Abby could imagine just how hard it was for someone like Cecile to make amends. "I understand," she murmured. "A death in the family is a very trying time for anyone."

"I worried so much about Sharon. She had the Claiborne tendency toward—" there was a pause "—instability."

"Oh?"

"Yes. It's the same with Stephen. You don't know from one moment to the next how he's going to react."

Abby could identify with that. But she wasn't sure where the conversation was leading.

"He was here this morning threatening me. Then he started ranting and raving about you," Cecile enlightened the psychologist. "Frankly, I was frightened, and I thought you ought to really be on your guard. The safest thing for you would be to avoid any contact with him."

"He can be rather overwhelming," Abby admitted. Had Steve left her apartment and gone straight to Cecile's? she wondered.

"Derrick didn't tell me much about his family before we were married," Cecile went on. "It was only afterwards that I discovered that grandfather Edward had committed suicide. They don't talk about it much. But apparently he snapped—just like that. Kind of like what happened to Sharon."

Just snapped? Like Sharon? Her patient had left that detail out of the family history. Had she known about her grandfather? Was it even true? And what did that mean with regard to Steve's behavior? She'd attributed his mood swings to the stress of his sister's death. But he'd been alienated from the family years ago. Was there an underlying component to his erratic behavior that she didn't know about? Or to Sharon's behavior, for that matter?

"Thank you for calling," Abby managed.

"If he threatens you, let me know and I'll get Derrick to do something."

"I appreciate your concern."

Abby got off the phone as quickly as possible and stared out the window at the boats bobbing along the wharf. Despite everything there was something about Steve that she liked very much. Were her emotions overriding her professional judgment?

Abby got up and wandered into the kitchen with some vague idea of making dinner, but she found she wasn't really hungry. Instead of opening the refrigerator, she opened the telephone book and looked up the number of the Hampton Hotel. Before she let her speculations run wild, she'd get Steve's side of the story.

"Steve Claiborne, please," she said when the desk clerk answered.

"I'm sorry. Mr. Claiborne checked out this afternoon."

"He did?"

"Well, he didn't come in himself. He had a friend settle his bill and collect his things."

"A friend?"

"His girlfriend, I believe."

How many women did he have in town? she wondered. "Did he leave a forwarding address?"

"We only have his home address—in India."

Abby's fingers twisted the phone cord as she tried to take in this new information. "His girlfriend. What did she look like?"

"Young. Pretty. Spiky blond hair. Excuse me, I've got another call. Do you want to hang on?"

"No. Thank you very much." Abby hung up slowly. When Steve had left her apartment, she was sure he was going to continue his private investigation. Now he'd suddenly checked out of his hotel. Was he hiding? Or had he left town? Both alternatives were oddly disturbing.

As she stood beside the phone, it rang again and she snatched the receiver from the hook. "Hello?"

"That was quick." The speaker was Jo O'Malley.

Abby sighed. "I don't know what I was expecting."

"Well, let me ask you a question. Have you ever used the computer terminals at the Sterling Clinic?"

"A few times."

"Then keep tomorrow morning open."

"What's up?"

"Boy, are you in luck. Sterling is upgrading their system software this weekend."

"And?" Abby prompted.

"One of the operators told me the new security procedures won't be installed until tomorrow night. If you want to have a look at their computerized patient files, all you have to do is go in and log on as 'prime user' tomorrow morning."

"That easy?"

"The information's very reliable."

"Thanks. I think I'll take you up on the suggestion."

"I assume you're going to check on Sharon Claiborne."

"Right."

"Just out of curiosity, why don't you see if you can pull the records on some of those welfare patients?"

"Good idea." She copied down the names as Jo read them to her.

"Well, that should keep you busy," her friend remarked.

"Um . . . say . . . uh—"

"Something else I can do for you?" Jo asked.

"How easy is it to check an old death certificate?"

"In Maryland?"

"Yes."

"You have to know the person's name and the county where the death was reported. The certificate is a matter of public record."

"I think the name is Edward Claiborne. I guess he would have died sometime in the early part of the century. And I hope he lived in Baltimore."

"I'll see if I can find out anything. But it'll have to wait until Monday."

THE RICHLY PANELED WALLS and thick carpet of the room did nothing to sooth the belligerence of the two individuals who glared at each other across the desk. They both had a lot to lose in the present situation and a lot to gain by working together effectively. But the partnership was showing the strains of both success and the specter of exposure.

"There's too much riding on this gig for you to mess it up with a stupid stunt," the one in charge rasped.

The one on the defensive bit back a sharp retort. "I thought we were each taking care of our own business."

There was a sigh. "Yes, but you don't go off half-cocked and do something that could gum up the whole works."

"Getting rid of Dr. Franklin seemed like a good idea. She's sticking her nose in where it doesn't belong, and that's dangerous."

"We're trying not to litter the Baltimore-Washington corridor with bodies of prominent people."

There was a harsh laugh. "Just the bodies of nonentities."

"Stop worrying about Abby Franklin. We've got her completely neutralized. She's not going to find a damn thing, and then she'll go back to taking care of her own patients."

"But—"

"Listen, we're controlling things from a different angle."

"You mean Steve?"

"Yeah. Once we find out if he really knows anything, he's expendable."

"You'll find out if he told Dr. Franklin anything significant?"

"Of course."

"You're sure he'll talk?"

"With sodium pentothal, he'll tell us his grades on his junior high report card if we want to know them."

"If he implicates Franklin, then you'll get rid of her, too?"

"Yes. And I'll think of something more efficacious than that dumb elevator trick."

SUNDAY WAS PROBABLY a good day to nose around the Sterling Clinic, Abby decided as she pulled into the staff parking lot. It was half-empty.

And there was hardly anyone in the administrative wing. Yet every time she passed a door, she kept expecting someone who knew her to stroll out. When she tried to imagine explaining what she was doing there, her palms began to sweat.

Stepping into an alcove, she wiped her hands against her skirt and tried to concentrate on the hospital layout. She knew there was a computer terminal at each nursing station. But using one of those was asking for trouble. It was safer to find a workstation in one of the labs.

The door to the biotech lab was unlocked. Abby slipped inside and reached to lock the door behind her. No, that would be too conspicuous.

Sitting down at the terminal, she let out the breath she'd been holding. So far so good. After the hassle in the records office, it gave Abby a perverse pleasure to log on as a "prime user."

When she asked to see medical records, she was told to type in the last name of the patient.

Claiborne.
Two records found.

1027242 Claiborne, Sharon.
1027885 Claiborne, Stephen.

Abby stared at the screen unable to take in the information. Steve Claiborne was a patient at the Sterling Clinic? Had he gotten sick yesterday and been rushed to the hospital? Quickly she moved the cursor to the second listing and pressed Enter. An admission form flashed onto the screen.

As Abby began to read, the color drained from her face. Steve had been admitted yesterday—just a couple of hours after he'd left her apartment. How was that possible? Particularly if he'd stopped at Cecile's. According to the admitting physician, he'd suffered an acute psychotic breakdown and was under restraint in the violent ward.

Acute psychotic breakdown? The man had been upset, but she certainly hadn't seen any evidence of that kind of personality disorder.

Her hand was shaking so badly that she had trouble entering the next command. First she requested a printed copy of Steve's record. Then she did the same with Sharon's. As the printer began to hum, she glanced over her shoulder, feeling like a burglar who had rung the bell opening a cash register drawer.

When the printer finished spitting out the request, she stared at the listings. She didn't understand what was going on here. Could Steve have been reckless enough to have checked himself in as a patient to investigate the hospital from the inside? A stunt like that would be pretty dangerous unless he had the cooperation of a staff physician. Surely he couldn't have set something like that up on a few hours' notice.

The name in the upper right-hand corner of the form was Dr. Lewis Gerheiser. It wasn't familiar. Which was odd, because Abby thought she knew everyone on the psychiatric staff. On the other hand, she hadn't been here in several months. Maybe Gerheiser was new.

There was no use speculating about the man. Perhaps the best course of action was to get out of the clinic with this stuff before she was discovered and charged with illegal entry to a computer system.

As she opened her purse to stuff the records inside, she saw the list of charity patients she'd gotten from Jo. Printing out that information would be pushing her luck. But she was willing to bet she wasn't going to get a second chance with the computer.

Still, it was hard to make herself sit back down at the workstation and type in the list of names when the coils of tension in her stomach threatened to cut her in half. As she finished, she could feel cold perspiration running down the back of her neck.

The machine printed out the first page and then began to beep. Oh, God, what was wrong? Abby jumped up and inspected the feed mechanism. The paper was jammed.

She was so absorbed with trying to align the holes on the edges of the paper with the sprockets that she didn't hear footsteps behind her.

"Can I help you?"

Abby whirled around, her eyes wide.

"What are you doing here?" The speaker was Katie Martin, a research physician who had recently gotten a grant to do family histories of patients with genetic diseases. She and Abby had met at a staff party and liked each other. But their paths hadn't crossed recently.

Abby willed her voice to steadiness. "Just getting some records I need for a report." She'd never told a lie like that before and was surprised at how smoothly it had come out. But maybe once you took the first step into criminal activity, the rest was easy.

Abby's heart leaped into her throat as Katie leaned over the machine and adjusted the paper. "This printer is like a fussy old lady. Everything has to be just so." She touched the On Line button, and the printer head began to move again. "If it gives you any more trouble, you might want to use the one at the nurses' stations."

"Umm..."

Katie started for the door and then turned. "We could go down to the cafeteria for a cup of coffee when you're finished. I'd like to catch up on what you've been doing."

"I, uh, have a date this afternoon. That's why I was trying to get this stuff done and get out of here."

The other woman grinned. "I wouldn't want to make you late. But let's get together sometime."

"I'd like that."

As she watched Katie's back disappear through the doorway, Abby felt like a secret agent who'd just survived a dangerous encounter behind enemy lines. Then another thought made her heart start hammering against her ribs. What if the physician casually mentioned to the wrong person that she'd just run into Abby Franklin? They'd be down here in a flash to take her into custody.

When the printer stopped, Abby tore off the sheets and stuffed them into her purse. Then she logged off and fled the office. But she didn't know that the log-off procedure had changed—or that the installation work on the new computer system was causing delays. When she left, the terminal was still on line. As her departing footsteps echoed down the hall, the printer cranked out the last file she'd requested, and the records sat there in the paper tray like a neon sign advertising someone's unauthorized access.

Chapter Eight

Steve was floating in a warm, comfortable cloud of pink carnations. The petals caressed his naked skin. The spicy scent filled his nostrils. It was wonderful—and suffocating. He had to get out of there. Somehow he couldn't drag himself away.

"Steve."

It was an effort to open his eyes, but the sight that greeted him was worth it. Abby Franklin was running toward him through the flowers, her arms outstretched. She was barefoot but wore a white lacy sari. Through it he could see the tantalizing curves of her body.

"Abby. You came to get me out of here!"

"I can't get you out."

The disappointment was so acute that it brought tears to his eyes.

"I came to be with you. Do you want me here?"

"God, yes."

She knelt beside him, and he pulled her into his arms. The sari was gone. Somehow she was as naked as he. They rolled together in the flowers, laughing and kissing and crushing the carnation blossoms so that a haze of cinnamonlike fragrance wafted around them. The taste of her, the feel of her soft breasts in his hands, were intoxicating.

He clung to her. She was the only thing that seemed real.

"Abby, I want to make love to you."

"Oh, yes, Steve. Oh, yes."

She was under him, smiling up, her face eager. Then she was gone and he was utterly alone.

ABBY FORCED herself to walk across the parking lot at a normal pace. But she kept expecting to feel a hand clamp down on her shoulder and a gruff voice ask her where she thought she was going with confidential patient information.

As soon as she reached her car, she scrambled inside, started the engine and jerked into reverse. But when she reached the end of the drive, she looked back at the clinic building. Steve was in there, and not as a medical patient. He was upstairs in the psychiatric wing. What were they doing to him there?

All at once she felt uncomfortably short of breath, and her knuckles whitened on the steering wheel. She almost turned the car around and sped back to the parking lot. But what good would that do? She couldn't simply march in, say there had been a mistake and demand a patient's release. She had to have some facts. And the first thing she'd better do was read those reports so that she'd know what she was supposed to be dealing with.

Her foot hovered uncertainly on the brake. It was difficult not to pull up at the curb and take a look at the printouts. But there was no point in giving them a hurried glance. She needed time to study the material.

PANIC WELLED UP in Steve's chest. He tried to push himself to a sitting position, but his arms were too limp.

There was no sense of time passing. But now a voice was piercing his brain like sharp, pointed tweezers plucking out information. He wanted it to go away so that he could sleep. Maybe when he woke up, Abby would come back. But the voice wouldn't let him be.

"When was the last time you saw your sister?"

"At the funeral." Steve's lips moved, but he wasn't in control of the physical response or of the words oozing out of his brain like molasses from a broken pitcher.

A pedantic voice interrupted the questioner. "How many times do I have to tell you, the answer's going to be literal. You have to ask the question in the right way, or you won't get what you want."

"When did you last see Sharon alive?"

"Two years ago."

"Have you been in contact with her since?"

"I called on her birthday."

"Did she send you a letter?"

Steve's face contorted. "Yes."

"What did she want?"

"My help."

The questions went on. He was powerless to hold back his answers.

HALF AN HOUR LATER Abby laid Steve's and Sharon's medical reports on her kitchen table, acutely conscious that she and Steve had eaten breakfast there yesterday morning. Hours before that they'd been lying on her bed exchanging hungry kisses.

She didn't want to think about that. Instead, she focused on the way he'd acted at breakfast. He'd been considerate, concerned and angry by turns. His emotions had never been far from the surface. But she would have called him upset—not psychotic.

Quickly she read through the report on Steve that Dr. Lewis Gerheiser had written. Then she studied the data on Sharon, which had also been submitted by Gerheiser, and her eyes widened.

The report on Steve was an exact duplication of the first page of Sharon's record.

"Patient brought in by family who complained of irrational, belligerent behavior and incoherent speech.... During initial interview, patient tried to assault a member of the medical staff and was placed in restraints.... Patient refused to answer questions and was isolated in the disturbed ward . . ."

There were subsequent notes on the patient's progress twelve and then eighteen hours after admission. The entries remained identical.

It was as if someone had simply copied the material from one computer file to the other. The only editing was a change in the pronouns—from *she* to *he* and *her* to *him*.

Abby cupped her chin in the palms of her hands. Naturally she knew that certain mental conditions ran in families, but she'd never heard of identical medical reports. Each patient was a unique personality, with at least some individual variation in symptoms and behavior.

But that was beside the point. Steve Claiborne might be angry and impulsive, but she'd come to know the man, and she'd stake her reputation on his basic mental stability.

So what was going on here?

The only explanation she could think of was so monstrous that it was hard for her not to dismiss it out of hand. But it made a kind of horrible sense, if you admitted the possibility that someone was desperate to stop

Steve Claiborne from asking questions about his sister's death. What better way than to claim he was crazy and haul him into a psychiatric hospital? If you were in a hurry for medical jargon to justify the kidnapping in case someone asked embarrassing questions, you could copy the information from his sister's file. Then, when you had more time, you could alter some of the detail, in case someone wanted to compare the two files.

God, no, her mind screamed. But as she sat staring at the reports, she began to shiver.

EZRA HORNBY STARED at numbers on the computer screen on his desk in the shabby office at the back of the Lazarus Rescue Mission. Wearily he rubbed his tired eyes. He'd prayed long and hard for guidance. But holding things together was getting harder every day.

Take the mission food budget, for example. He'd been going over the numbers for the past three hours, trying to figure out how to serve five hundred well-balanced meals a day with funds for four hundred. He could do it if the government hadn't quit giving out surplus cheese. You could fill guys up on pasta and potatoes, but you had to provide some protein and fresh fruits and vegetables.

Pushing back his chair, he stood up and stretched. Then he allowed himself the pleasure of turning to face the wall of framed pictures behind his desk. Today the smiling faces of politicians and celebrities didn't give him the usual lift. All those famous people had told him what a wonderful job he was doing. Few of them had put their money where their mouth was.

Not one of them knew what it was like to hit below rock bottom. But he did. Thirty years ago demon alcohol would have destroyed him if he hadn't found salvation. After that, he'd committed his life to helping others find the light.

There was a pony of bourbon in his desk drawer. Sometimes he got it out to remind himself what temptation looked like. Now he opened the drawer, took out the bottle and held it to the light. The amber liquid seemed to reach for him, generating a heat of its own that he could feel through the glass. Even after all these years it was a reminder of the fires of hell. His Adam's apple bobbed. With the willpower he'd forged in the furnace of faith, he held it aloft for prayerful seconds. Then he tenderly laid it back in its velvet-lined resting place and closed the drawer.

Deliberately he turned his attention back to the practical problems of the Lazarus Mission. It was a crying shame the way things were going in this country. Federal funding had all but dried up. And charitable contributions hadn't made up the difference. The rich were keeping their money for themselves, and the poor were ending up on the streets.

Sometimes he felt like the little Dutch boy with his finger in the dike. But if he gave up, the sea was going to sweep in and drown the hundreds of lost souls who depended on him.

He'd tried, but he just couldn't do it alone. This month he'd been counting on the money Sharon Claiborne had left him. Then he'd found out he wasn't going to get it until the insurance people were satisfied that everything was hotsy-totsy.

He sighed. He'd been trying to avoid emergency measures, but the time had come to exchange some more special merchandise for ready cash. First he retrieved a coded computer file. After consulting the list, he dialed a number that wasn't written down in his phone directory.

"Can I help you?" the cultured voice on the other end of the line inquired.

"This is the Angel of Mercy. I'd like to make arrangements for another delivery."

"I'm sorry. We're not taking any new merchandise at the moment."

"But—"

"Call back next week."

The phone line went dead, and Ezra was left staring in disbelief at the receiver.

REPUTABLE MENTAL HOSPITALS didn't hold people captive for ulterior motives. Yet logic didn't stop the goose bumps that spread over Abby's skin.

She folded her arms across her shoulders and rubbed. But she couldn't rub away the chill that seemed to have sunk into her bones. She'd been trained to think of the mental health profession in positive terms. But that wasn't always the case. In the Soviet Union, former regimes had punished dissidents by declaring them insane, slapping them in mental institutions and subjecting them to dangerous drug treatment.

When you thought about it, totalitarian states didn't have a patent on that kind of behavior. Anyone with a big enough secret to hide could silence the opposition with similar techniques. The question was, had Sharon and then Steve stumbled onto something so big that they had to be eliminated?

Steve had been convinced his sister's death was part of some plot. He'd even insisted that the elevator incident was no accident. She'd tried to counter his emotional arguments with cool logic. Now she reached up to touch the bump that still marred the back of her head. Much as she wanted to believe otherwise, she was afraid he might be right.

Still, there was no real proof of the conspiracy her mind was manufacturing. How could she find out what was really going on? she asked herself. The sensible thing would be to start with Steve's family. The report said they were the ones who'd committed him. But after her previous experience with Derrick, she was pretty sure she wasn't going to get any answers from the Claibornes. Then the back of her neck turned to ice. Cecile had called a few hours ago and talked about Steve's instability. What a perfect way to prepare someone for the idea that he was in the hospital. It sounded like the family had arranged this.

What if she confronted the clinic? That was no good, either. They'd already prevented her from seeing Sharon's records. If she asked about Steve, she'd simply tip her hand that she was suspicious.

Abby began to pace restlessly around her apartment. She felt the same need to do something that had gripped her when Sharon had called. No. This was different. She hadn't known where Sharon was. But she knew that Steve was in the Sterling Clinic.

Abby picked up the two reports and studied them again. Steve's had been entered yesterday and Sharon's . . . Her eyes found the date, but it took several moments for her to understand what she was seeing. The date on Sharon's was May 15. Abby thought back. That was the morning Sharon had called her. But Derrick had said his sister had been in the hospital for several weeks. Abby felt little prickles dance down her spine. Derrick couldn't have gotten that wrong. He must have been lying, or someone was lying to him. Either case meant that Sharon hadn't called from the hospital at all. What in God's name was going on? And what about Steve?

She was willing to bet her license to practice that the hospital staff wouldn't let her through the locked door of the disturbed ward without a court order. By the time she got one, he could be— She stopped herself from finishing the terrible thought.

She didn't realize she'd made a decision until she found herself calling Jo.

"I take it you're phoning because things worked out with the computer at Sterling."

"Yes. Thanks for the tip."

"What did you get?"

"More than I bargained for."

"Oh?"

Abby quickly told her friend about Steve being committed and the strangely identical records on the Claiborne siblings.

"You're right. It sounds like something isn't exactly kosher at Sterling."

"Jo, I've got to get in there."

"Are you thinking of breaking and entering?"

"I figured you could come up with something creative."

Jo laughed. "Let me do some calling around. I'll get back to you as soon as I can. By the way, maybe you'd better tell me what sizes you wear."

Two hours later Jo walked into Abby's apartment, carrying a small suitcase. Inside were white nurses' uniforms, stockings and shoes.

As Jo laid out the props, she explained her strategy. "Just like other hospitals in town, Sterling has been hit hard by the nursing shortage, so they've been using a registry to fill temporary vacancies."

Abby eyed the uniforms. "And we just joined Med-temps Unlimited? Is this really going to work?"

"The exciting thing about this business is that you never know until you get right in the middle of a job."

Abby gulped. "Oh, great."

"I checked with Medtemps. They have requests to fill vacancies in several departments. Including psychiatric."

"But—"

"You've got the knowledge of the hospital and medical jargon to pull it off. I've got the credentials to make us look official." From a manila envelope she produced two laminated ID cards in the names of Gladys Wells and Shirley Brisbane. The picture of Gladys looked like Jo. The picture of Shirley was brunette with only a vague resemblance to Abby.

"This is going to pass inspection?"

"No one looks exactly like their ID. Trust me. This'll get you in."

His thoughts were like scattered scraps torn from old photographs. With great effort he could pull them together into mended pictures. But the images didn't always make sense.

Someone came, lifted his shoulders and held a cup of water to his dry lips. Eagerly he slurped up the cool liquid and collapsed back against the sheet.

He was in a bed now. He'd been on something harder. A table. Someone had been asking him questions. He couldn't remember any of the answers. Voices drifted around him like static-filled radio transmissions. He wanted Abby. The touch of her hand. The comfort of her lips.

"Give me a hand, will you?"

"What do you need?"

"I've gotta shave his chest. He's scheduled for surgery in the morning. Then we'll have one less problem to deal with."

He felt something wet slap against his skin, then the familiar stroke of a razor.

JO HAD FOUND OUT that the night shift came on at midnight. Abby used the intervening time to tell the detective what she knew about the hospital's procedures and layout. As they started to discuss strategy, she was seized with a strange feeling of unreality. Was sane, sensible Abby Franklin really planning something this crazy?

"It might look funny if two new nurses arrive at the same time in the psychiatric unit," Jo pointed out.

"Maybe we should separate," Abby suggested. "One of us could pretend to be assigned up there. The other could be coming from the lab to do blood work."

"You're getting the hang of it," Jo approved. "Does that report you have give Steve's room number?"

"Three fifteen."

They were both keyed up and anxious to leave. As they sat in the living room, they went through a pot of coffee, two bags of corn chips and a jar of salsa.

Finally it was time to get ready. After changing her clothes, Abby looked at her reflection in the bathroom mirror. A bright-eyed, nervous-looking nurse stared back. Jo, dressed in an identical outfit, came up behind her.

"What do you think?"

"I think we're nuts," Abby responded.

"You can call it quits right now."

The bats that had invaded Abby's stomach beat their wings sickeningly, and the salsa and corn chips she'd been gobbling threatened to rise in a tide up her throat. She knew her whole professional career might be on the line for pulling such a crazy stunt. Yet the thought of what Steve must be going through bolstered her resolve.

"Let's do it," she said with more courage than she really felt.

HE DIDN'T REMEMBER where he was or how long he'd been here. The only thing he knew was that he had to get the hell away. Before something—What? Something terrible. That was all he remembered.

He lay with his eyes closed, feigning sleep and trying to gather his strength.

They were in the room again, watching. He could feel their piercing eyes, hear their stagnant breath.

"If we just gave him another shot, we wouldn't have to keep checking on him all night."

"Yeah, but they want to avoid any more contamination if they can. Anyway, he's not going to be our responsibility much longer."

The door closed. Cautiously he opened one eye. He could barely pull the scene into focus. After long moments, he satisfied himself that the room was empty. It took every ounce of strength he had to push himself to a sitting position. When his bare feet touched the floor, his knees threatened to buckle. He was just inching toward the door when it opened again.

"Help! He's out of bed."

Steve rushed at the nurse whose eyes were big with alarm. He took her down with a heavy thrust of his shoulder. But the lunge sent him off balance, and he didn't have enough stability to recover. He sprawled on top of her, and her cry for help brought heavy feet pounding down the hall. Even as he struggled a needle bit into his arm.

"Told you we should have given him . . ." The words faded out as the black tar pit of oblivion sucked him in again.

IN A WAY, it was disturbing to find out how easily a couple of impostors could walk into the basement of the Sterling Clinic. Although Abby held her breath as she presented her ID card, she and Jo were checked through almost at once by a bored security guard who was more interested in the late night talk show he was watching on TV than his job.

Once they'd rounded the corner, Abby and Jo exchanged glances. "See," the detective whispered. "Piece of cake."

They had decided that Abby would go upstairs first. Jo would slip into the lab, take a blood test tray and meet her.

"The lab's up on the next floor?" Jo confirmed.

"Right."

"Then I'll see you in a few minutes."

Abby prayed that she looked calm and professional as she stepped off the elevator onto the third floor. But so much perspiration was trickling down from her armpits that she wondered if her uniform was going to start leaking.

The nursing station was in a separate area on the right. As Abby stepped through the door, the night supervisor looked up. The nameplate on her desk identified her as Mrs. Shaw.

"Who are you?"

Abby swallowed and pitched her voice a bit lower than usual. "Shirley Brisbane—from Medtemps."

"I thought they weren't sending anyone until tomorrow."

"I came back from vacation early," the counterfeit nurse improvised.

"Thank God for small favors," Mrs. Shaw harrumphed. Then she took a long pull on a can of Diet Coke. "This place has been a zoo tonight. A couple of patients got into a fistfight at dinner and had to be separated. Then one of the loonies in the disturbed ward assaulted a nurse."

Abby must have looked alarmed because the woman continued. "It's okay. He's sedated again. I don't know what they were thinking about, letting his medication wear off. But the orders came straight from downstairs."

"What would you like me to do?" Abby inquired.

"You ever worked this unit before?"

Abby shook her head. She'd decided it was safer to pretend she didn't have any familiarity with the setup.

"Well, it's like most psychiatric units—with the dangerous cases segregated. They're beyond the locked door on the left side of the hall. That corridor is off-limits to everybody except authorized staff. Got that?"

"Yes." Abby and Jo had talked about the locked ward. Since she'd visited patients there, she even knew the key was in the center desk drawer. Now she itched to leap across the room and grab it. But she could hardly do that under Mrs. Shaw's nose.

"Okay. I'd like you to start off with a bed check. But just on the right side of the hall."

"Fine."

For Abby, stepping out of the nurses' station was like crawling out of a dark mine shaft into the sunlight. She dragged a deep breath into her lungs before starting across the dayroom to the patients' wing. What was keeping Jo? she wondered as she opened doors and made sure everyone was in bed. Most were sleeping deeply, as if sedation were routine procedure.

Fewer rooms than she expected were occupied. Either the Sterling Clinic was cutting back on psychiatric services, or there was a temporary lull in admissions.

Come on, Jo, she silently urged. Had her friend gotten caught? Were they coming for her next? She tried to swallow, but her mucus membranes had turned to cotton.

Abby was all the way down to the end of the hall when Jo finally rounded the corner carrying a lab kit. "What took you so long?" she demanded, no longer able to keep her voice steady.

The private detective had a devilish gleam in her eye. "I told Mrs. Shaw I'd be glad to cover for her if she wanted to go to the ladies' room and have a smoke." Jo pulled a large key out of her pocket.

"I'm scared spitless. But you're getting a kick out of this, aren't you?" Abby inquired wonderingly.

"It's the challenge of the thing. Besides, I'm not quite as cool as I look; I've just had more practice."

"What if she misses the key?"

Jo pressed her lips together for a moment. "Probably she's not going to. In fact, if she has a couple of more sips from that Diet Coke of hers, she's going to be kind of sleepy."

"You didn't—"

Jo shrugged. "It seemed like the prudent thing to do under the circumstances."

This wasn't the time to argue morality with her friend, Abby decided as she started across the hall. She whispered a silent prayer as she slipped the key into the lock.

It fitted, and they stepped into a short corridor painted institutional green.

The unit was much smaller than the main psychiatric ward. As Abby recalled, only a handful of disturbed patients were housed in the half-dozen rooms that lined the corridor. Room 315 was the first door on the right. As soon as they stepped inside, Abby knew something was terribly wrong. The room smelled fetid, and the man-size form on the bed was draped from head to toe with a white sheet.

"Oh, my God! Steve!" Abby gasped.

There was no response from the bed, just the finality of death.

Chapter Nine

Abby made it across the room in three giant steps and snatched the sheet off the unmoving form. The first thing she saw was a dead man's face. The second thing was a recent incision that split the chest from sternum to belly button.

Jo clamped bloodless fingers around her friend's arm. "Steve?" she whispered.

"No." The syllable was the only one Abby could manage for several seconds. She stared at the corpse. His face was leathery and waxy yellow. His hair was shaggy and unkempt. He looked as if he'd just stumbled in from skid row, except that he wasn't going anywhere under his own power.

Jo reached out and tried to lift his right arm. His fingernails were ragged and dirty. When the arm didn't move easily, she whispered. "He's been dead for several hours. What the hell is he doing here?"

Abby shook her head, fighting the salsa-tinged queasiness that was creeping up her throat. When she'd tried to imagine what was going on at the Sterling Clinic, she hadn't dreamed of finding a dead body stashed in the locked psychiatric ward. Who was he, indeed? She offered silent thanks that it wasn't the man she was looking for. But the printout had said the new patient was in room 315. If that was just a copy from Sharon's record, where was Steve? She couldn't cope with the possibility that he wasn't alive.

Jo touched her arm. "I think we'd better find your Steve Claiborne ASAP," she whispered.

The private detective searched one side of the corridor. Abby took the other. When the first two rooms she looked in were empty, she felt her panic rise. She was just backing out of the second when Jo called out from across the hall. "This him?"

Terrified of what she might see, Abby hurried over to investigate. From the doorway she recognized the man laid out on the bed. "Yes, it's Steve."

As she took three more fearful steps to the bedside, she saw the shallow rise and fall of his chest. He was alive! Abby's own chest clenched with fierce joy. The intensity of her reaction took her by surprise, but she didn't have time to analyze her emotions. Instead, she made a swift assessment of the patient's condition. His skin was cold and clammy. His pulse was slow. And a line of recent needle marks dotted the skin of his arms. When Abby pulled down the sheet that partially covered his body, she saw blond stubble and recent razor nicks. Tenderly she smoothed her fingers against his cheek. He didn't open his eyes or turn his head. The lack of response made her eyes sting, and she blinked to clear them.

"Ever seen a mental patient in this kind of shape?" Jo questioned. "I mean, someone who's supposed to be in a prestigious clinic?"

"I've never seen *anyone* in this kind of shape—except in a hospital emergency room. A drug overdose might do this. But he's not an addict. I saw his arms a couple of days ago, and he didn't have those needle marks. Even if they thought he'd OD'd, they sure wouldn't leave him alone—and without any monitoring equipment. It's as if they don't give a damn what happens to him, just so he's not giving them any trouble.''

Jo eyed the sleeping man's chest. ''I hate to say this, but it looks as if they've prepped him for the same operation that killed his friend across the hall.''

''Yes,'' Abby whispered. She'd broken into the clinic expecting to find Steve drugged—probably to keep him quiet. And she'd worried that his life might be in danger. Now she didn't know how to interpret what she was seeing. But there was one thing she did know with gut-wrenching certainty. ''We've got to get him out of here.''

''Right. But how?'' For once Jo was at a loss. ''We can't just walk him out the door—not in that condition. I don't suppose you could give him a shot to wake him up, could you?''

''It would be a terrible risk when I don't know what they've given him.'' Even as she spoke Abby's mind scrambled desperately for a solution to the problem. Then she remembered Steve's crack about patients leaving in body bags. ''Somebody's got to remove that body across the hall pretty soon,'' she mused.

''And?''

''So we pretend they gave us the job. Only we put Steve in the body bag instead of the dead guy.''

Jo looked at her friend in admiration. ''You may get your private eye license yet.''

''I rather doubt anything we've done tonight comes under the heading of licensed activities,'' Abby shot back.

''Don't get technical on me.''

Jo stayed with Steve while Abby went after the supplies they needed. As she passed the nurses' station, she silently admitted she was grateful her friend had been farsighted enough to neutralize Mrs. Shaw. The woman's head was on her desk, and she was snoring softly.

Several minutes later Abby was back with a rolling cart and a body disposal kit. Since Steve was naked, they wrapped him in a blanket before poking some air holes into the bag and folding him inside.

Someone had to be checking on Steve during the night. If they got him out of here without getting caught, it was going to be a miracle.

"What if he wakes up?" Jo asked as they struggled to shift the drugged man onto the cart. Even with two of them it wasn't easy. He was big and heavy.

"We're dead meat," Abby managed through gritted teeth.

"Are you always so reassuring?"

The psychologist didn't bother to answer. She was still thinking about their chances of pulling off this desperate operation.

Jo began to push the cart. With Steve's weight on top, a wheel squeaked, and they both froze.

"Slow and easy," the detective muttered to herself.

"Wait a minute." Abby grabbed the lab kit from where Jo had set it on the floor and stuck it on the lower shelf.

"What's that for?"

"I want to find out what they gave him." She didn't add the qualifier that was on her mind. *If we get out of here.*

If she'd let herself analyze what they were doing, Abby might have collapsed in a heap on the tile floor. Instead, she began thinking in terms of milestones. They didn't have to do it all at once. Just one step at a time. Get into the regular part of the psychiatric ward. Lock the door. Cross the dayroom. Push the cart down the hall to the elevator. Each goal they reached put them closer to freedom.

It was fifty steps down the hall and another fifty across the dayroom. When they drew abreast of the nurses' station, Jo put the key back in the drawer. "I hope these creeps spend a long time trying to figure out what happened to their surgical patient," the detective gloated as she held open the door. Abby started to push the cart into the hall and stopped dead in her tracks. Coming toward her from the elevator was a large, slightly bucktoothed man with a receding hairline. Her own scalp prickled, and the bump on the back of her head began to throb.

The last time she'd seen the man he'd been dressed in a suit and had called himself George Napier. Now he was wearing a green hospital orderly's uniform.

"You handle this," Abby managed as she pulled a curtain of dark hair in front of her face and turned partially toward the wall. The advantage she had was that he didn't expect to run into her here, either, she told herself. Yet black spots began to dance in front of her eyes. If she had to stand still for very long, she was going to keel over.

Almost anyone else would have been at a loss. Jo hardly missed a beat. When the orderly came abreast of them, she gestured toward the cart. "We're taking him down."

"Sorry I wasn't here to help," the man answered pleasantly. He passed them and continued down the hall. Abby half leaned on the cart as she gave it a push. "We've got to get out of here," she whispered.

Jo trotted ahead and pushed the elevator button. Luckily the car was still on their floor. When the doors closed behind them, Abby sagged against the wall and closed her eyes.

"Who was he?" Jo asked.

"A patient of mine, I thought. The last patient I saw on Friday before the elevator accident."

"Sheez."

"If he finds out Steve is gone . . ."

"Don't worry. We'll be out of here before they suspect a thing."

Abby's numb brain clung to Jo's reassuring words even as her fingers clung to the cold metal handle of the cart. As soon as the elevator door opened, they set to work as a silent, efficient team. Abby pushed the cart to the hospital's back entrance, her pulse racing like a timing mechanism gone crazy. She kept expecting sirens to go off and a loudspeaker to announce that two women posing as nurses had stolen a patient.

Their luck held. There was no one near the back door. Abby handed Jo her keys, and the detective retrieved the car. There was nothing decorous about the way they heaved Steve off the cart and into the back seat.

Then Jo was barreling down the long drive, and Abby was leaning over the back seat and clawing the heavy plastic off Steve's face with her fingernails.

THE MAN WHO SOMETIMES called himself George Napier liked the night shift. The name he'd been born with was George Nesbitt. On his hospital employment forms he was George Nash. Nobody came around to check up on you at night, and you didn't have to have your work done until just before you went off duty. As he ambled down the hall, he pulled a candy bar out of the breast pocket of his green uniform and took a bite.

The back entrance to the locked ward was through a supply closet at the end of the hall. Only selected employees knew about it or had a key. George was humming as he closed the door behind him. He hoped no one was going to be angry about the nurses having to get rid of that cadaver. But he had been in the middle of a hot poker game downstairs with the custodians and hadn't wanted to give up his seat.

He took a contemplative bite of chocolate and peanuts. Come to think of it, who'd given those nurses the order to remove that body? There weren't many people around the hospital clued into the real situation—especially on the night shift. Was somebody bypassing him? Then he thought about the man in room 320 whom he was supposed to be checking every half hour. He'd spiked the guy up enough to put a water buffalo to sleep for the night.

George stuck his head in Claiborne's room. It took several seconds to register that the bed was empty.

"Holy gee!" Somehow the guy had gotten up again. But he couldn't have gone far. Sweat broke out on George's upper lip as he began to open doors. Every room was empty except 315. The body was still there.

His mouth fell open. Those nurses. The body bag. The awful truth slammed into his chest so hard that he sagged against the wall. Those blooming women had snatched the kidnap victim right out from under his nose.

TWO MILES FROM THE HOSPITAL Jo pulled into a dimly lit parking area behind an office building and cut the engine. Opening the doors so they could work, they stripped the body bag off Steve. He didn't stir or wake up. Abby pressed her fingers against the pulse in his neck. It was still slow—but stronger. Trying to make him more comfortable, she rolled him onto his side and drew his legs up. After tucking the blanket more securely around him, she wadded up the body bag and tossed it into a dumpster.

"Okay, so we've kidnapped an unconscious, naked mental patient. Now what?" Jo asked when her friend returned to the car. "Doesn't he need some medical attention?"

Abby pressed her knuckles against her lips. She was caught in a terrible dilemma. As far as the authorities knew, legitimate doctors had been treating Steve at the Sterling Clinic. If she took him to any other hospital with this fantastic story—or any other—she risked having him fall back into the clutches of the bastards who'd done this to him. On the other hand, what were the medical consequences of trying to deal with this herself? She smoothed her palm against his chest and was reassured by the steady beat of his heart. "They wanted him alive for an operation. So the drugs they gave him weren't lethal. When they wear off, he should recover. I just have to take him to a safe place and wait."

"Not by yourself, you're not."

"Jo, I've already pulled you too deeply in this."

"So what's the big deal about a little more?"

"We have to be logical," Abby insisted. "The most important thing is to get Steve out of town—take him somewhere they won't be looking for him. But first I'm going to draw a blood sample. Do you have a lab you can trust to give you confidential results?"

"Sure." But Jo wasn't going to drop the previous subject so easily. "You have a particular hideout in mind?"

Abby had been racking her brain. Now an answer came to her. "A friend of my parents has a place down in St. Michaels, and I have permission to use it. Wayne's still in Florida and won't be using the house till later in the summer. It's on about six acres right by the water, so no-body will bother us."

"Abby, are you sure you can handle Steve by yourself? I mean, what if he's violent when he wakes up?"

"I'm trained to deal with situations like that," she insisted in her best therapist's voice.

Jo still looked doubtful.

"I'll call you when we get to the shore. If I'm having any trouble, I'll let you know." As if the matter were settled, Abby climbed into the back seat, picked up the lab kit and extracted cotton and antiseptic. Although she wasn't licensed to perform medical procedures, she had a great deal of lab experience. Now it was easier to concentrate on drawing a vial of Steve's blood than think about what she was getting into.

"If you won't take me along, I'll keep nosing around while you're gone," Jo said. "Now I'm damn curious about what's really going down at Sterling."

Abby withdrew the needle from the sleeping man's arm and turned to her friend. "Jo, for God's sake, be careful. Whoever did this to Steve plays rough."

"Don't worry. I'm not stupid."

Abby inserted a stopper in the tube of blood and handed it to the detective. "Keep this in the refrigerator overnight and take it straight to the lab in the morning. And I want to ask another favor."

"Anything."

"Would you call my secretarial service, and tell them to notify my patients that I've been called out of town on an emergency? Tell them I'll reschedule appointments when I get back." She racked her brain, trying to remember what else needed attention. "I almost forgot the class I'm teaching at Goucher. Could you call and tell them the same thing?"

"No problem." Jo looked down at Steve's face. His left eyelid had begun to twitch. "Abby, I feel rotten leaving you with this guy." She held up her hand when the psychologist started to protest. "Just promise to call me the minute you get to St. Michaels."

"I will."

The two women embraced. Abby clung to her friend. "Thanks," she murmured.

"Take care of yourself."

"I will. But I'd better get going."

They changed places, and Abby drove Jo back to her car. Then she was on her own.

GEORGE NASH BALLED his hand into a fist and socked it against the wall so hard that a chunk of plaster came loose. Suddenly his skin felt as cold as that stiff across the hall. Unless he could think his way out of this mess, he might as well start measuring himself for a pair of concrete shoes.

Hold it. He snapped his fingers. Across town was a place where he could pick up a guy about Claiborne's size and coloring. He could drug him up, bring him back to the hospital and pop him into the empty bed across the room. Yeah, and maybe he could mash up his face so that no one would realize who it was. Except he knew that the lab had already done the blood typing. So switching dog meat wouldn't work.

When his hands started to shake, he thrust them into his pockets. He had to get Claiborne back. What if he called the police and issued an all-points bulletin? Maybe that would work. Unless the boss found out.

His fists tightened again. Damn those bimbos to hell. This was all their fault. The little redhead had even said something to him. The cheeky twit. He'd like to wrap his fingers around her throat right now.

The trouble was, he had to find her first. And Claiborne. Think, he commanded himself. Think. The women. If he could only get a line on the women. He was positive he'd never seen the redhead before. But the brunette. He hadn't been paying much attention to her. But now he realized that she'd been trying to hide her face. Why? Had she recognized him? Yeah, that was it. Now that he thought about it, he knew he'd seen her before. He just couldn't remember from where.

But he had to.

ABBY HADN'T HAD much time to dwell on the consequences of her actions. Now, as she headed east out of the city, her mind started to churn, and the thoughts that bobbed to the surface were like unappetizing lumps in a bowl of rancid stew.

Back in the office building parking lot she'd cavalierly dismissed Jo's comment about kidnapping a mental patient. But what if the clinic already knew Steve was gone and had informed the police? They might be looking for her right now.

The thought brought her foot down harder on the accelerator. When she realized what she was doing, she eased up on the pedal. The clinic was doing something illegal; they wouldn't dare call in the authorities. Would they? Still, the last thing she needed right now was to get pulled over for speeding.

Unfortunately the police weren't the only unsettling possibility. The psychiatric ward supervisor, Mrs. Shaw, had said one of the ''loonies in the disturbed ward'' had assaulted a nurse. It was a sure bet she wasn't talking about the guy who'd been split up the middle like a

Thanksgiving turkey. The only other patient over there was Steve. Had the massive doses of drugs they'd pumped into him made him violent? Or was he just desperate to get away?

Abby stole a quick glance over her shoulder, and her heart squeezed painfully. Steve hadn't moved. He looked so helpless.

She'd gotten him out of there. He was safe now. She wasn't going to let anything else happen to him. Except for one more terrible possibility that she didn't even want to think about. But it kept knifing its way back into her thoughts with the relentlessness of a surgeon's scalpel. The clinic had needed Steve alive. But not for long. They weren't concerned about his ability to function later. What if the drugs they'd given him had damaged his brain?

Oh, Lord, not that, Abby prayed. *Dear Lord, not that.*

It was a two-and-a-half-hour drive to Wayne's summer place on Maryland's Eastern Shore, a narrow strip of land separated from the rest of the state by Chesapeake Bay.

By the time Abby reached the bay bridge, her stomach was in knots. Luckily she had the exact change to pay the toll, so she didn't have to risk one of the toll takers wondering about the unconscious man in the back seat.

Driving across the six-mile-long span that joined the two shores of the bay had never been one of Abby's favorite activities. Now she gripped the wheel and focused her eyes on the road straight ahead as the bridge climbed high above the choppy water below. It was a windy night. As Abby reached the crest of the span, she tried to ignore the cross-currents buffeting the car. But it was hard to hold the vehicle in the slow lane.

A tractor trailer approached on the left and sounded its piercing horn. In reaction, she swerved toward the right, almost scraping the concrete barrier. As the truck sped by on her left, it whipped the car even more furiously in its wake. Abby fought to keep the car on an even keel.

Steve must have been startled by the horn. Or perhaps he was responding to the vibrations. For the first time since Abby and Jo spirited him out of the hospital, he groaned. Then he muttered something unintelligible and kicked against the front seat.

Abby jumped. They were finally on the downgrade. But they wouldn't be off the bridge for several miles.

"What!" The voice from the back seat was rough and urgent. "Stop! No. Don't do that again."

Abby risked a quick glance over her shoulder. Steve had pushed himself to a half-sitting position. A muscular arm reached toward her. Then he was grabbing the seat belt shoulder strap where it hung from the doorframe.

Suddenly she was jerked back against the seat. The strap dug painfully into her chest and throat.

"Steve. No," she gasped. "Let go. You're choking—" the plea ended in a cough.

Another truck passed, and the car shook from side to side. Steve was too weak to hold on and was thrown back against the seat once more.

He grunted.

Abby coughed and rubbed her throat. "Are you all right?"

Steve didn't respond or stir again. How was he? Had he hurt himself? As the minutes ticked by, her chest grew tighter and tighter. But glancing over her shoulder was dangerous, and there wasn't anything she could do until they were on solid ground again.

She focused all her energy on getting off the bridge, but the moment it was legal to pull off the highway, Abby nosed the car onto the shoulder and jerked up the emergency brake. Scrambling out, she opened the back door and leaned inside.

"Steve?"

He didn't answer. Nor did he stir when she smoothed her fingers against his shoulder.

"You're safe now," she murmured, wondering if he could hear her. "I'm taking you to a place where you can get better."

Still no reaction. But his breathing seemed more normal, and his color was better.

Abby leaned over and pressed her lips against the blond stubble on his cheek. "I know it was horrible. Just hang on for a little while longer."

Somehow he seemed to respond to the gesture and the gentle words. She watched with relief as he settled back against the cushions into what looked like more normal sleep.

Abby was tucking the blanket back around his shoulders when a red-and-blue flashing light filled the rear window. A police car had pulled onto the gravel behind her. For a moment her heart stopped and then started up again in double time. Had the hospital issued a bulletin, after all? Was she about to be arrested?

Quickly she closed the doors. Then, willing her knees not to give way, she turned to face the khaki-clad state trooper marching toward her. In the darkness his features looked grim, and Abby forgot to breathe.

"Having some trouble, ma'am?"

"I was just stopping to check on my husband. It's so embarrassing." She pressed her fingers against her mouth for a moment, trying to project a feeling of chagrin. "You know how it is. He...uh...he had one of his anxiety attacks in the middle of the bridge."

The officer peered into the window. But since the doors were closed, there wasn't much he could see in the darkness besides the indistinct form of a reclining man.

Don't wake up now, Abby ordered silently.

"You don't have to feel bad about it," the trooper was saying. "Lots of folks hate to cross that sucker." He jerked his thumb in the direction of the bridge. "One time I had a guy who got a quarter of the way across before he stopped right in the middle of the road and refused to move his vehicle. We had to drive it across for him."

Abby nodded in agreement. "I don't like it much, either. But Bill always makes me drive."

"Anything I can do?"

"No. This has happened before. I just need to get him home and into bed."

"Well, your being a nurse and all, I guess you know what to do."

Nurse? Then she remembered the uniform she was still wearing. "Yes. That's right."

"You all take care."

Abby slid behind the wheel and pulled back on the road. Her knuckles were white on the wheel as the cruiser followed behind her.

The trooper stayed with her for several miles. Didn't he believe her story? Or was he tailing her just in case she needed some help? When the patrol car turned off into a darkened shopping center, Abby breathed a sigh of relief. She didn't want him to see her take the turnoff toward St. Michaels, in case someone asked questions about her later.

She shook her head in amazement. Another crisis averted by the nimble Dr. Franklin. Probably in her whole life she'd never told as many lies as she'd manufactured in the past twenty-four hours. It was disturbing that they were tripping off her tongue so easily.

Forty-five minutes later she began looking for Wayne Templeton's driveway. He was a good friend of Abby's parents. As a girl, she'd visited his summer place on the Miles River many times. When she'd grown up, he'd given her permission to use the house whenever she wanted in the off-season. She'd come down for weekend vacations several times during the past few winters, but she wondered what her host would think about this particular visit.

When she spotted the brick gateposts of Bachelor's Cape, she turned into the long driveway that wound through a stand of loblolly pines. It was four in the morning, and the Cape Cod-style house was a black silhouette against the night sky.

Abby had forgotten how dark and still it was in the country. She could hear waves lapping against the shore about twenty-five yards beyond the house. But she couldn't see the river.

Exhausted, she clasped the steering wheel and rested her head for a moment. Her arms ached with the tension of the past few hours. She'd made it here. Now she had to find the energy to get Steve out of the car.

The first thing Abby did was retrieve the key from the ledge above the window next to the front door. Inside, there was a living-dining-kitchen combination and two small bedrooms downstairs. The master suite was on the top floor, but there wasn't any question of trying to get Steve up the stairs.

After turning on a few lights, she made sure there were sheets and a blanket on the double bed in one of the bedrooms, then she went back to the car. She and Jo together had had a tough time getting Steve onto the cart. There was no hope of carrying him to the house by herself. But she didn't know what she was going to encounter when he woke up. The best she could hope for was getting him in a half-awake state where he could walk but wouldn't give her much trouble. Still, she wasn't feeling particularly sanguine when she pulled the door handle.

When the door opened, Steve's legs sprang out and he groaned. She hoped it was just from shifting his cramped position. Sliding onto the seat, she gently shook his shoulder.

"Steve."

He jerked upright, and the blanket fell away from his upper body as he flailed his arms. His fingers found her hair and held. Even in his weakened state he was a strong man.

"You bitch. You're not going to—"

"Steve. It's Abby. Please. You're hurting me."

"Abby?" His eyes focused on her face. "Abby." The painful grip in her hair loosened.

"Steve, you're safe."

"They got you, too?" He grabbed her hand and started to pull. "We have to get away."

It was too much to hope that he'd be rational so soon after what they'd done to him. Yet the desperation in his voice made her eyes glisten. He must be reliving a nightmare too horrible to contemplate.

She put a restraining hand on his shoulder. "We're safe," she repeated gently but firmly. "You've got to believe me."

"No. Can't stay here. Got to run. Before they..." The words trailed off abruptly.

There was no way to cut through the disorientation. For a moment she cursed the sadists who'd done this to Steve.

Right now she couldn't do anything about his confusion, but perhaps she could use it. "That's right. We'll find a place to hide."

He lifted his head and focused on her, some of the fogginess leaving his eyes. It was as if he knew for the first time who was speaking to him. "The pink carnations."

"What about the carnations?"

"You did come to help me." His voice was hoarse.

She didn't understand what he was talking about, but that wasn't important. "Yes, I'm right here," she soothed. She gripped his hand, and he squeezed her fingers almost painfully. "We need to get into the house," she murmured as she pulled the blanket up around his shoulders.

It was awkward getting out of the back seat. When Steve stood up on shaky legs, the covering dangled around his thighs and gaped apart in front. But indecent exposure was the least of her worries. The important thing was getting him up the porch steps and through the front door.

Even the few feet from the car to the house seemed to sap his strength so that he leaned more heavily against her. As they started to climb the steps, he teetered precariously on the treads and they both almost tumbled into the bushes. Abby righted them, but Steve's weight was like an anchor dragging her down.

"Just a little more. We're almost there," she puffed as she opened the screen door.

By some miracle Abby steered Steve to the bedroom. It was a relief to shift his weight to the bed. "You can sleep here. They won't find you," she soothed.

"Have to stay awake. Get away before they—" But he was already collapsing against the pillows. As matter-of-factly as possible, she stripped off the blanket. It was a symbol of the hospital and the horrors Steve had experienced there. If she'd had the strength, she would have torn it into shreds. Instead, she hurled it toward the door and turned her attention back to Steve.

He was naked now—just the way he'd been when they'd found him strapped into bed, but the urgency of getting him out of the hospital had taken precedence over everything else. Now they were alone, sharing the intimacy of the small bedroom, and God knows how long they were going to be here together.

She sucked in a steadying breath, silently admitting that it was impossible not to be affected by his masculinity. He might be unconscious, but his body was magnificent. His chest was broad, his hips narrow, his stomach absolutely flat, and... Abby struggled to bring the assessment back to a professional level. His well-developed muscles spoke of excellent physical conditioning. That as much as anything else might help him get through this trauma.

"Steve, you're going to make it," she whispered. "We'll get through this together. I promise."

He didn't respond.

Sitting down beside him, she took his hand and clutched it against her chest as if the gesture could transfer some of her determination to him.

Chapter Ten

The 4:00 a.m. strategy session was held in the director's conference room. Four men and one woman sat in padded leather chairs around the long table.

The woman was willing to wait and see how events unfolded. If this whole thing blew up in their faces, she could have her bags packed and be in Hong Kong before anyone knew she was on the Sterling payroll. Meanwhile, she'd play whatever role was necessary.

One of the men was furious. A cautious type, he didn't take unnecessary risks. So he'd studied this proposition from every angle before he'd concluded the safeguards were adequate. Now it looked as if some hireling had screwed the whole thing up.

Another of the men didn't have time for emotions—either fear or anger. He was too intent on damage control. The third wished to hell he'd never gotten sucked into this. And the fourth man was sweating like a pig who was next in line at the slaughterhouse.

"All right, George," the interrogator began in a voice that was all the more frightening because it was so calm. "Take it from the beginning again, and don't leave out any details. The team finished questioning Claiborne at eight."

"Yes."

"And his escape attempt was at 11:00 p.m."

"Yes."

"Why did you leave him alone after that?"

"He was heavily sedated. He wouldn't have gotten up under his own power if someone had shouted fire in his ear."

"But you were supposed to stay with him."

"I—"

"If you'd stayed in the room the way you were supposed to, nobody else would have been able to get him out of there." The cool logic was like a schoolmaster lecturing a wayward boy just before he brought a birch rod down across his knuckles.

George winced. Under the table his hands were clasped together in a death grip. He'd been changing into his street clothes and getting ready to split when two security guards had closed in on him. Too bad he'd stopped to change.

Another voice broke into the discussion. It was the woman. "Raking George over the coals isn't getting us anywhere. We've got to concentrate on finding Claiborne before he can tell anyone what happened to him."

The man on the hot seat looked toward her, unable to suppress the first glimmer of hope he'd felt since they'd brought him up here.

When she spoke, her voice was reassuring. "I know you're feeling bad about this. But any detail you can give us might help. For example, what did the nurses look like?"

Maybe there was a chance to get out of this in one piece, he told himself. Now he spoke up with more animation than he'd shown all evening. "The smart mouth one had Orphan Annie red hair. The other one...the other one . . . I've been trying to think, see. I know her. I just—'' His eyes suddenly widened as if he'd won the lottery. ''It was that Franklin woman. The one you sent me to check out.''

''Abby Franklin!''

''Yeah, her.''

''I was right all along. We should have gotten rid of her,'' one of the others bit out.

''Well, things aren't as bad as they seemed a few minutes ago,'' the woman interjected. ''We know who has Claiborne. We just have to scoop the two of them up.''

SHE COULDN'T SIT here all night, Abby told herself. After tugging the blanket and bedspread from under Steve's legs, she covered him and stood staring at his sleeping profile. It wasn't safe to leave him alone, and she was too exhausted to try to sit up in the straight-backed chair across the room and keep guard. Besides, he probably wasn't going to wake up again for several hours. She'd be in better shape to deal with him if she got some rest.

She had just kicked off her shoes when she remembered she'd promised to call Jo. The phone was on the wall in the kitchen. Her friend answered before the first ring had finished.

''Abby?''

''Yes.''

''Is everything all right?''

''As good as can be expected.'' There was no point in talking about the bridge or the policeman.

''How's Steve?''

''In bed sleeping. And I'm exhausted. I can hardly stand up.''

''I'll bet. Before you conk out, give me your number there.''

"It's safer if you don't know it."

"You're right." Jo agreed.

"I'll call you tomorrow." Abby was already starting to unbutton the nurse's uniform. Back in the bedroom she tossed the outfit onto the chair and climbed under the covers in her slip.

She'd been running on adrenaline for hours. Now fatigue washed over her like a warm ocean wave, knocking her down and pulling her under. Without much struggle she surrendered to sleep.

IT WAS AMAZING how fast you could tear through five thousand dollars, Adam Goodwin thought as he staggered up the steps to the front door of his Federal Hill town house. All it took was a little help from your friends. When the word got around you were treating the crowd, everybody was your buddy.

He stood panting at the top of the six-stair flight. It was also amazing how badly coke and booze mixed. His head felt like a smashed muskmelon. And the morning sun peaking over the top of the church across the street was like a hot poker stabbing into his eyes.

Squinting through slitted lids, he tried to get the key into the lock and finally succeeded. As he stepped across the threshold, his foot slid across a manila envelope.

With a curse he grabbed for the wall. Only a miracle kept him from landing on his ass on the floor.

When he caught his breath again, he looked down at the envelope. What kind of moron would slip a booby trap like that through the mail slot on Sunday night? They ought to be sued. With a snort of disgust he picked up the envelope, crossed to the kitchen and dumped it into the trash.

The room smelled as if something had died there in his absence. Then he realized he'd left the shells from half a dozen crabs in a heap on the kitchen table. Pulling over the trash can, he swept the whole mess inside and shoved the lid back down. Then he went to the bathroom and threw up.

It helped a little. But his head was still pounding like a synthesizer going full blast. The best thing to do was have a shot of whiskey, crawl in bed and sleep all day. But on the way to the liquor cabinet he saw that the red light on the telephone answering machine was blinking.

Swearing again, he hit the button.

"This is Fred Edgewater from Concord Insurance. It's 10:00 a.m. Friday. Please get in touch with us as soon as possible. We need to speak to you concerning the claim for death benefits made on the Sharon Claiborne policy."

Good, they were finally paying off, Adam thought. Too bad he hadn't been home to get his messages all weekend.

The machine clicked again. "This is Fred Edgewater again. It's Friday at four. We need to get in touch with you right away. Please call me at home. The number is 555-6021."

The third message was from Ezra Hornby. "Concord Insurance called and asked if I knew where you were. What's up?"

"Don't worry. You'll get your money," Adam muttered. Then Fred Edgewater's voice filled the room again. "Mr. Goodwin. It's Sunday at 2:00 p.m. I have some urgent documents for your signature. I'm sending them by messenger service this afternoon. Please call as soon as you look them over."

Urgent documents? Messenger service. From neutral his mind lurched into third gear and his gaze swung toward the trash can. Head averted, he opened the lid, fished down through the rotting crab mess and extracted the stained envelope. The return address in the left-hand corner was Concord Insurance.

After slitting the end with a kitchen knife, he tossed the envelope into the sink, took the contents into the living room and sank into his leather recliner. In his present condition it wasn't easy to focus on the print. But the words "claim denied" leaped out at him like the bat signal over Gotham City. His hand started to shake, and he had to set the papers down on the coffee table. A sick feeling gathered in his chest as his eyes scanned the text.

Suicide was one of the exclusions. Damn. He hadn't been worried about that when he'd drawn up the policy. And he'd known damn well the death wasn't suicide. The trouble was, he couldn't tell that to the claims officer.

Why couldn't the clinic have stuck to the original plan and made it an accidental drug overdose? Now he wasn't going to get his cut. And Ezra Hornby was out fifty thousand dollars. Which meant the old toad was going to be hopping mad.

But what could Hornby do? Certainly not go to the police. That thought was the only comfort Adam took with him as he staggered up the stairs and collapsed across his bed.

ABBY SNUGGLED further under the covers. She was hovering at the edge of consciousness, but she didn't want to wake up. Warm breath feathered her cheek, sending subtle little tingles along her nerve endings. An unaccustomed weight pressed across her breasts. Her eyes fluttered open and encountered a hairy, muscular arm.

Cautiously her gaze followed the tanned skin to the juncture of a broad shoulder and then up to the tousled blond head of the sleeping man inches from hers.

Steve. His presence beside her was reassuring—and disturbing. Somehow during the early morning hours they'd drawn together like lovers reluctant to relinquish contact. No, not lovers, she reminded herself. It was just the basic human need for warmth and comfort. Hers just as much as his, she admitted silently.

She studied Steve's face, unwilling to pass up the opportunity the morning had handed her. There were dark circles under his eyes, but otherwise his color was good. His features were relaxed, his lips slightly parted. Her eyes swept over the texture of his skin. His cheeks and jaw were covered with blond stubble. There were fine lines at the corners of his eyes and the barest suggestion of grooves from nose to mouth. Yet in sleep he looked younger and more approachable than she'd ever seen him. Then her gaze flicked to the scar at his temple. It was a vivid reminder that the man who slept so peacefully beside her was tough—and dangerous. The worst part was that she didn't have a clue about what to expect when he woke up.

Gingerly Abby tried to wiggle out of Steve's grasp without disturbing him. But as soon as she moved, the arm across her chest hardened to solid oak.

Instinctively she tried to pull away. Before she could blink he was on top of her, his hands circling her wrists and pinning them to her sides. A hard thigh trapped the bottom half of her body against the mattress. His eyes burned down into hers.

"What the hell's going on?" he spat out.

Fear sliced through her, but she struggled to keep her voice calm and reassuring. "Steve. Everything's all right. I promise."

"I said, what's going on?"

"You were kidnapped and drugged."

"You can make up a better story than that."

His voice was harsh, but she caught the shadow of doubt behind the menace in his eyes.

"What's the last thing you remember?"

"I..." The doubt spread across his face like water pouring out of a burst main. "I...oh, my God."

The strong hands that held her captive suddenly loosened. Without a word he rolled onto his back and lay staring at the ceiling.

"Steve..." Abby leaned over him, reversing their positions. "What's the last thing you remember?" she repeated.

"Michelle. The Blue Star Café. Michelle put something in my drink," he answered dully.

"And after that?"

"Not a damn thing."

Her fingers stroked his face. "It's all right."

"Yeah. Sure." He grimaced. The grimace turned into a groan and he pressed the heels of his hands against his eyes.

"Steve?"

"It feels as if somebody just stuck a knife into my head and twisted the blade."

Abby waited, her heart going out to him as she watched the pain etch the lines more deeply into his face. If only she could do something. But even an aspirin would be a bad idea at this point. Finally the spasm seemed to ease, and they both breathed a sigh of relief.

"What day is this?" he asked.

"Monday."

His eyes flicked to the window. The sun was still low in the east. "Monday morning. The Blue Star Café was Saturday morning. I've lost…almost forty-eight hours." He started to push himself to a sitting position and winced.

"Your head again?"

"No." He was staring at the row of needle marks running up his arm.

Abby's gaze followed his.

For a long moment he was immobile.

"Steve, everything's going to be all right," she murmured. *And pray God it's true,* she added silently.

"Don't kid me, sweetheart. Somebody's been screwing with my mind, haven't they?"

"Somebody drugged you."

"More than one dose."

"We're going to figure out what happened. But right now you need to rest. And I need to get dressed."

For the first time he took in her attire. "Parading around in your slip again. Dr. Franklin, this is getting to be a habit." The ghost of a smile flickered around his lips.

She smiled back. "Humor's always a good sign."

When she began to slide off the bed, his hand circled her wrist again. Once more Steve's expression had become tense. "Was I, by any chance, being 'treated' at the Sterling Clinic?"

"Yes."

"Where are we now?"

"A safe place. A summer house on the Eastern Shore. It belongs to a friend of my family."

"You mean we're hiding from the authorities?"

"That's right."

Steve leaned back and closed his eyes. Almost at once they snapped open again. "You got me out of there, didn't you?"

Abby nodded, not trusting herself to speak as she thought about the frightening events of the night before. "How?"

"It's a long story" was all she could manage at the moment.

"What if they'd caught you?"

"They didn't."

The hand that held her wrist captive loosened its hold. But instead of withdrawing, his fingers turned and pressed against her palm. "Thank you." The words were low, barely above a whisper.

She had the feeling he didn't use that phrase often.

In the next second he confirmed her suspicion that he wasn't comfortable with the tender scene. "I'd better get up," he muttered. He started to pull back the covers and then stopped abruptly. "God Almighty. I'm as naked as a jaybird. What did you do with my clothes?"

Color flooded her cheeks. "I didn't do anything with your clothes. I'm afraid you were only wearing a blanket and a sheet in the hospital."

His blue eyes deepened as they took in her tousled hair, moved on to her flushed face and slowly traveled down to linger on the lace appliqué cupping her breasts.

His perusal warmed her skin, and her hands fluttered at her sides. "I couldn't leave you alone, not the way you were last night."

"The question is, did I leave *you* alone?"

"You were asleep."

"Damn! Missed my chance."

When she saw the corners of his lips twitch, her own quirked up. "I'm glad you're feeling better." But despite her smile Abby's voice was thick with emotion. It took a pretty remarkable man to laugh at himself after what he'd just been through.

He kicked a naked leg from under the covers. "Do you suppose you could find me something to wear?"

"I hope so."

"I think that would be safer for both of us," his wry observation echoed behind her as she turned and left the room.

Several hours later the noonday sun reflected off the river as a pair of sea gulls skipped along the waves. Dressed in jogging clothes borrowed from their absent host, Abby and Steve sat on the wide back porch of Wayne Templeton's beach house.

The sweatpants and shirt hung loosely on Abby's slender frame. The pants rode up Steve's calves, and the shirt barely met the waistband. The two of them could have been getting ready for an audition at the Comedy Store, except for the grim nature of the conversation.

Earlier Steve had tried to lift his own spirits with a bit of humor. Now his mood had swung down, and he sat with his hands wrapped tightly around a mug of cream of tomato soup. Once he'd gotten out of bed that morning, he'd realized how unsteady he was on his feet—and also that he was starving. Abby suspected he hadn't eaten anything since the cinnamon buns at her breakfast table on Saturday.

Since she didn't want to leave Steve alone, she had to work with the limitations of Wayne's larder. If it didn't come out of a can, a box or a fast-food freezer pack, Wayne didn't have it.

As Steve sipped his soup, Abby gave him an unobtrusively assessing look. Even though he'd been weak, he'd insisted on showering and shaving without her hovering around. When he'd joined her in the kitchen, she'd half expected him to ask about his shaved chest. But he hadn't mentioned it. Hadn't he noticed? Or didn't he want to talk about it?

While they'd eaten breakfast, she'd filled him in about the rescue. His expression had turned grim when she told him about her and Jo meeting up with George Napier.

The idea of asking him if he wanted to try hypnosis to recover his memory had crossed her mind. But she was afraid to suggest the technique when she didn't know what kind of medication he'd been given. Flashbacks were a definite possibility at this stage of the game, and they could be dangerous, both to him and to her.

He thunked his mug down on the table in front of the wicker sofa. "How long am I going to be a basket case?"

"You're not a basket case. You simply can't remember a short period of time. That can happen to people who drink too much—or have gotten high."

"I didn't do either one—as far as I know."

"Not deliberately."

"What the hell am I supposed to do about it?"

"The memories could come back over the next few weeks."

"Sweetheart, we don't have a couple of weeks. We've got to figure out what's happening at the Sterling Clinic. Now." Steve closed his eyes for a moment, then he turned and gave Abby a direct look. "I'm sorry. I'm giving you a pretty hard time, aren't I?"

"It's all right."

"No, it's not." He sighed. "Once, when I was a kid, I fell out of a tree. Hitting the ground knocked the wind out of my lungs. Do you know what that feels like?"

His words had brought back a sharp, painful memory. "Yes. A boy pulled me off the monkey bars at recess once. It was horrible when I hit the blacktop. I remember the sense of total panic, as if I'd never be able to draw in a breath again.''

''Yeah. That's it. The fear that you'll never be able to breathe again. That's what it's like for me now. Only it's not physical. It's mental.''

''Oh, Steve, I know. It's got to be terrible for you. I'd be frightened and discouraged.''

His expression was guarded, as if he wished he hadn't given her so much insight into his emotions.

''This didn't happen because you're weak,'' she offered softly.

''I'm used to making my own decisions and taking responsibility for my actions. Do you have any idea what it's like to have that taken away from you? When there's not a damn thing you can do?'' he said between clenched teeth.

''Yes.''

His eyes lifted questioningly to hers.

''When Sharon called and I couldn't help her. That was the way I felt.''

''Probably you're wishing you'd never gotten mixed up with the Claibornes,'' Steve muttered.

She held her gaze steady with his. ''No, that's not the way I feel.''

Silence stretched between them again.

''I've just thought of something we could try,'' Abby offered.

Steve turned to her eagerly. ''What?''

''I was in the ward where they were holding you. If I tell you what I remember about the place, maybe that will trigger some memory of *yours*.''

His face registered equal parts enthusiasm and apprehension. ''All right. Let's give it a try.''

Abby began to describe the third-floor ward. "There was a locked door. And all the rooms opened off a short hall." As she talked, she charted Steve's physiological reactions. His respiration accelerated, and beads of sweat broke out on his upper lip.

"A room with green walls," he interrupted her. "I remember that. I was strapped to a table like a Christmas goose. There was a man standing on one side and a woman on the other."

"Do you remember their faces?"

He squeezed his eyes shut. "It was all fuzzy, as if my vision were distorted."

An idea hit her. "Was he a big bucktoothed man with a receding hairline?"

Steve's head jerked up. "Yes! How did you know?"

"I saw him just as we were leaving. It was the same guy that came to my office Friday afternoon calling himself George Napier."

"Then I was right."

"I'm sorry I didn't want to believe you."

"I understand. When you're an honest, upright citizen, it's hard to think in terms of people running around kidnapping and murdering. You know, when I first came back for Sharon's funeral I was thinking that someone had murdered her for her money—like maybe Miles Skinner. Now we both know something a whole lot bigger than that is going on."

Abby nodded slowly.

"But when it came to the crunch, you believed enough of what I was saying to come looking for me—and break me out of there."

Their eyes locked. Somehow during the past twenty-four hours their relationship had changed dramatically. Steve had started sharing some of his most private thoughts with her. But he still didn't like the feeling of being dependent.

Well, depending on each other was the only way they were going to figure out what was going on at the Sterling Clinic—and stay alive.

Chapter Eleven

Steve stood up and began to pace back and forth along the length of the porch. Abby watched him, aware that by now, midafternoon, his anxiety level had escalated.

"What's wrong?" she asked.

"Suppose I just don't give a damn anymore? Suppose I just want to get the hell out of Baltimore and back to my nice safe business flying weapons into Afghanistan?"

The words made Abby's chest tighten painfully. She knew Steve was tired and disheartened. But she couldn't let him give up. Perhaps it was time for some shock tactics. "You know," she began quietly, "in the room across the hall from you was a dead man—with a fresh surgical incision down the middle of his chest."

He stopped pacing and stared at her.

"Steve, when you took a shower, didn't you notice that your chest was shaved?"

"I was lucky to be standing up in the shower."

So he'd just blurted what he'd been too hardheaded to admit this morning, she realized. But he wasn't even thinking about that. He was pulling off his sweatshirt and looking at the stubble that replaced the spattering of blond hair across his chest.

"What in the...?" But even as he spoke, the blood drained from his face and he swore. "They were talking about an operation in the morning."

"What kind?"

"And then we'll have one less problem to deal with."

"What?"

"That's what someone said just before they started shaving my chest."

Abby watched him struggle to control his features and understood how badly the snatch of memory had shaken him. The knowledge that someone had turned the tables on him so completely was almost as destructive to his sense of self-worth as the realization that there had been nothing he could do to save himself. His tortured expression made her heart turn over. Scrambling out of her chair, she crossed the room and wrapped her arms around him. At first he just stood very still, but he didn't draw away.

Her cheek was pressed against his chest so that the recent stubble scratched her face. But she didn't want to break the contact; she wanted to feel the steady beat of his heart. Her hands stroked against the taut skin of his back. By slow degrees she felt his muscles relax.

His arms came up to circle her waist. She felt the hair on the top of her head stir and imagined his lips nuzzling through it. She'd come over to give him comfort. All at once she knew she was drawing as much emotional energy from the contact as she was giving.

"Abby, look at me."

The gravelly quality of his voice made her feel as if she were standing on shifting sand. Slowly she tipped her head up. His blue eyes were like twin search beacons giving her no place to hide.

"It didn't hit me until now how far you went out on a limb for me."

"I couldn't leave you there."

"You're the damnedest mixture of stubbornness and bravery I've ever met."

"No, I . . ." She wasn't sure what she had been about to say. The thought was swept away as he lowered his head and captured her lips with his. There was nothing tentative or tame about the kiss. It was more primal than civilized, more savage than refined. He'd been hours from death, and the woman in his arms had stolen into the enemy camp and won his freedom. Holding her now was exhilarating and suffused with an intensity he'd never experienced.

His lips were urgent and demanding on hers. They were also firm and hot and very, very sexy. She opened to him without hesitation. There was only the need to taste, to know, to satisfy.

She trembled in his embrace and reached up to anchor her arms around his neck. His fingers shook as they combed through the dark richness of her hair.

The kiss was a celebration of life, an acknowledgment of mutual hunger, a sharing of more than pleasure.

When she arched against him, his hands slid down her back to her hips. An involuntary little moan escaped from her mouth. He drew it in as eagerly as he pressed her against his arousal.

One hand anchored her to him. The other found the hem of her sweatshirt and slipped underneath to revel in the warm skin of her back. God, she wasn't wearing a bra! He shifted her slightly so that he could cup one breast. The nipple was taut and strained against his fingers.

Somehow the knowledge that he was at the brink of pulling her into the bed where they'd spent the night brought back a measure of sanity.

He lifted his head. Her eyes fluttered open. Slowly, reluctantly, he drew back, but not so far that he couldn't rest his hands on her shoulders and then stroke his fingers down her arms.

They stood staring at each other, neither knowing quite how to cope with the emotions that had flared between them with the heat and intensity of a summer lightning storm.

"Abby, it would be really easy to get carried away—and blame it on the situation," he finally muttered.

Was that what he thought? The casual assessment hurt, and she lowered her eyes. Or perhaps he didn't know how to deal with his sudden defenselessness. She wasn't sure how to cope with her own raw emotions. The difference was, she wanted to reach toward him, not turn aside. But there was no way to force that kind of intimacy. It had to be offered up as a symbol of trust. Without that there could be nothing real between them. Only white-hot passion. It would be glorious while it lasted. But it wouldn't be enough for her.

"You're right. I guess we'd better get back to figuring out what's going on at Sterling," she murmured.

His look of relief was like a dagger stabbing into her heart.

"I . . . I'll be back in a little bit." She turned and fled the room, wondering how long it would be before she could face him calmly again.

THE PERSISTENT POUNDING WAS like a jackhammer in his skull. Half asleep, Adam Goodwin pulled a pillow over his head and willed the noise to stop.

The knock came again. It was the door. Probably some salesman pushing vacuum cleaners or cemetery lots. Why didn't the jerk just go away?

The noise continued. Apparently the only way to make it stop was to throw whoever was out there down the front steps.

Cursing, Adam rubbed his bloodshot eyes and made his way along the hall. He opened the door and saw Ezra Hornby on the front stoop. Before he could shut the door again, the squat little man had muscled his way into the foyer.

"I thought it was understood. You're not supposed to come here," Adam muttered.

Hornby ignored the admonition and delivered one of his own. "I see you've been carousing again. You look like you've been to hell and back. Don't you know that alcohol is the devil's tool?"

"If I need to take a guilt trip, old man, I'll call up my folks. What do you want?"

"Money. We had a deal. If you can't get me the whole thing, I need twenty thousand by the end of the week."

"Are you out of your mind?" Adam's head had started pounding again. It was hard to think.

"You said I'd have the check by now," Ezra insisted.

"They aren't—" Adam started to blurt out the bad news from the claims department and then thought better of it "—ready to settle yet."

Hornby's eyes took on a shrewd look. "Some guy from Concord Life was calling me up and asking all sorts of nosy questions."

"I'm sure they'll get it all worked out," Adam assured him.

"I can't wait for that. I've got mouths to feed and souls to save. And I'm not going to let you stand in the way of

God's work. I'll be back, and you'd better be ready to pay up.''

Hornby delivered a five-minute sermon before he finally turned and left. As Adam watched him limp down the block toward the bus stop, his mind scrambled for a way out of this mess. It had seemed like a surefire money-making idea when he'd thought up the scheme of changing the beneficiary on Sharon's insurance policy. After she'd found out he was an insurance agent, she'd asked him to take her husband off her policy and switch the death benefits to Steve. But he'd held on to the form. A month ago he'd altered the paper and changed the beneficiary to the Lazarus Mission, but he'd kept the old date so that no one would be suspicious. Now he didn't know what the hell he was going to do. Hornby as an ally was fine. As an enemy he was trouble.

Adam had begun to sweat. There had to be a way out of this mess. Maybe he could get the money from that bastard Jonathan Wyndham. Now that was an idea. But he'd have to figure out how to make the approach.

THE TENSION BETWEEN THEM made things a lot more difficult. By four o'clock Steve was exhausted, and they weren't making any more progress in reconstructing his stay at the Sterling Clinic. After persuading him to take a nap, Abby called her answering service.

There were several messages. The first was from Melissa Wexler, the little girl to whom she'd given the puzzle box. She'd get back to her when she returned to town, Abby decided.

The next two messages made the hair on the back of her neck prickle. They were both from Dr. Donald Kellogg, the surgeon she'd run into at the Sterling Clinic. He said he had to talk to her and left a number. She wondered what he wanted, but she wasn't going to risk calling him without consulting Steve.

Next she phoned Jo.

"Everything still going all right?" her friend asked.

"Basically."

"Abby, there's a warrant out for your arrest."

She'd half expected to hear something like that. Now she couldn't help gulping. "For what, exactly?"

"Breaking and entering. No mention of kidnapping. And no mention of me."

"I see." Abby struggled to keep her voice calm. "What about Steve?"

"Nothing about him, either. I guess they figure if they find you, they'll find him." Her friend cleared her throat. "You haven't used your credit cards, have you? They can trace you through the transactions."

"I haven't used them."

"Good. Do you have enough cash, or do you want me to send some?"

"I've got enough."

"I located Edward Claiborne's death certificate."

"Good work."

"He died of a heart attack," Jo related.

"So Cecile was lying to me. Or maybe her husband was lying to her."

"Now, I've also got the information on the blood sample you took from Steve."

"You've been busy."

The detective reeled off a list of drugs that had been in Steve's system. Two were powerful sedatives. One was an illegally manufactured hallucinogenic, the other was an agent used by the army to interrogate prisoners.

As she absorbed the information, Abby sank into the chair by the phone. All that stuff dumped into the man's system without regard for the consequences. No wonder his emotions were swinging like a pendulum. It was lucky he was able to talk coherently.

"Abby?"

"Sorry. I was just trying to take it all in."

"Pretty bad, huh?"

"Bad enough."

"What else can I do for you?"

There was a sudden noise from Steve's room, as if a heavy body had collided with a piece of furniture.

"Thanks for everything. I'll call you tomorrow," Abby told Jo quickly, and hung up.

She looked up to see the man they'd been discussing standing unsteadily in the doorway. His face was flushed and his pupils dilated. The rise and fall of his chest was rapid and shallow.

"Steve?"

He didn't answer.

"Steve?"

He focused on her as if seeing her for the first time. "What are you doing here? What's going on?"

Abby's stomach knotted. He'd woken up disoriented again. Maybe taking a nap hadn't been such a good idea. "You're safe. At a friend's house."

He tipped his head to one side, and it was several seconds before he spoke. "You told me that this morning, didn't you?" he asked slowly.

"Yes."

His hands balled into fists at his sides, and he swore. "We've been here all day, haven't we? Or am I just making that up?"

"Yes, we've been here. But it's all right if you're feeling confused. I was just talking to Jo, the friend who helped get you out of there," she went on quickly. "I took a blood sample before we headed down here, and she got back a report from the lab. So I know exactly what they gave you at Sterling.'' The moment she'd uttered the words, she wished she could call them back. Probably he wasn't ready to hear the worst.

He strode across the room, his expression fierce, and took her by the shoulders. ''Tell me!''

In a matter-of-fact voice she gave him the list.

His arms dropped to his sides. ''Hallucinogens,'' he muttered. ''No wonder these weird images keep drifting through my head.''

''What?''

''I don't know. Sometimes I'm floating in a sea of pink carnations and you're kissing me.''

''You dreamed about me?'' Her voice was soft.

He swallowed. ''Yeah. Sometimes.''

She suspected he wanted to change the subject. ''At least we know the sodium pentothal is the reason you're having so much trouble remembering details. It has an amnesiac effect.''

''But that's not why they gave it to me. They were asking me questions, weren't they? And the stuff makes you talk,'' he grated. ''What do you think I told them?''

''Everything you knew, I expect. The lucky part is that you didn't know much. We still don't.''

He started to laugh, not hysterically but with a measure of control.

She looked up at him, her own relief washing over her face.

''You're right. We don't know much,'' he agreed. ''Which is the only saving grace in this whole sicko situation.''

ADAM HAD TRIED to reason with the insurance company. After listening quietly to his arguments, Fred Edgewater had told him the Sharon Claiborne case wasn't being handled by the local office anymore. If he wanted more information, he'd have to get in touch with New York.

He sat by the phone contemplating the kind of conversation he was probably going to have with some anonymous administrator in New York who would want to know why the change of beneficiary form had been turned in late. When you didn't know a guy personally, you had about as much chance getting him to see things your way as you did spitting into the wind and hoping it wouldn't blow back in your face.

So he'd picked up the phone and called in a few favors. At least it was reassuring to find out that he could raise five thousand dollars by tomorrow morning. Maybe that would be enough to keep the self-righteous Ezra Hornby's mouth shut. But when he'd called the mission, he'd been told that the old man was unavailable.

He had an urge to talk about his troubles, but there was no one he could really spill his guts to. The funny part, when he thought about it, was that Sharon Claiborne had come the closest of anyone to meeting his needs. She'd been so warm and funny and passionate. But she'd had a way of sucking up affection that made him nervous, and she'd expected so damn much from the relationship—and from *him*. He'd decided somewhere along the line that a guy like him couldn't live up to her standards.

She'd been volunteering down at the Lazarus Mission, which was how he'd gotten to know Hornby. It hadn't been hard to win the old guy over. A five-hundred-dollar contribution was all it had taken.

But he'd always figured there was something about Hornby that was "off." Or maybe it was the old "it takes one to know one."

When Sharon had come to him with worried stories about guys disappearing from the mission, he hadn't really been all that surprised. He'd checked things out and discovered a sort of underground railway that went right from the Lazarus Mission to the Sterling Clinic. Only the guys that got on had bought a one-way ticket.

Once he'd let the people at Sterling know he was in a position to do them a big favor, it hadn't been any more trouble to score a little extra himself. He'd thought it was all nailed down. Now the deal was about to blow up in his face like a trick cigar.

He half wanted to get out of the house, but he couldn't face an evening of smiling faces and chitchat. On the other hand, he wasn't able to face going down in flames without some fortification.

He took a bottle of bourbon, an ice bucket and a tumbler up to the bedroom, turned on the television set and tuned in the Cable News Network. There was nothing like global misery to put your own problems in perspective, he told himself.

Perhaps if the television hadn't been on, he might have heard the lock being picked on the back door. Or if he hadn't downed two tumblers of bourbon, he might have been alarmed when the floorboards in the hall creaked. As it was, he stared uncomprehendingly at the menacing figure that suddenly filled the bedroom door.

"Whaddya want?" His speech was slurred.

"Oh, I think you'll be able to guess."

"LET'S TAKE A BREAK for the rest of the evening," Abby suggested as she and Steve did the dinner dishes together.

He sighed. "Maybe you're right. I feel as if I've been banging my head against a wall all day."

"You've made better progress than most people. But sometimes memories come back when you're not trying so hard."

Steve didn't answer as he dried the last plate and put it back in the cabinet.

"Why don't you see what's on TV?"

"Okay."

When she joined him in the living room, Steve was watching a newscast from Baltimore. "At least there's nothing about us," he told her. After the sports and weather, there were only game shows, so he turned the set off again and picked up one of Wayne's fishing magazines. But Abby could see that he wasn't really concentrating on largemouth bass. Quietly she got up and went back to the kitchen. When she returned several minutes later, she was carrying a tray with two mugs and a plate of cookies.

"What's that?"

"Hot chocolate."

"Hot chocolate. I haven't had that in years."

After passing him a mug, Abby sat down on the other end of the couch. Steve took a sip and licked the line of brown foam off his lip. Then he reached for a cookie.

He looked more relaxed than Abby had ever seen him. "Tell me about India," she prompted as she drew her knees up and got comfortable. "Do people really ride on elephants?"

He laughed. "Only for show."

"You like it there?"

"Mostly. But this is a good time to be away. It's the hot season right now. And then comes the monsoon."

"Did you learn to speak the language?"

"There are about fourteen major languages, and they're broken up into hundreds of dialects. I can order a beer or ask a woman to bed in half a dozen." Suddenly he realized what he'd just said and took a couple of quick swallows of his chocolate.

Abby looked down into her own cup, pretending that the last remark hadn't made her pulse jump. "So tell me about your house," she requested.

"My house. Yeah. It's in Jamshedpur near the Bay of Bengal. I live outside of town on a ten-acre plot." He went on to tell her about his day-to-day life.

Abby listened in fascination. "I'd like to see your garden."

"You'd love it."

They stared at each other for a wordless moment. What would it be like to visit him there? Abby wondered. "You get stuck in your own little corner of the world and don't realize how different things can be," she finally observed.

"Anything else you want to know?"

"How did you get that scar on your forehead?" The question just tumbled out.

"In a bar fight."

"Now you've really got me curious."

"A friend of mine and I were playing fan-tan in Hong Kong. It's a Chinese betting game where you try to guess how many coins or counters are left under a bowl after a certain number have been taken away."

"It sounds fairly tame."

"In Hong Kong it draws the same crowd as craps. And in this case, the other guys at the table thought they had a couple of easy marks. They were playing with the local equivalent of loaded dice.''

"And you weren't going to just get up and walk away?''

He sat forward. "Not and leave my fifteen hundred dollars behind.''

"But you got cut up.''

"Sweetheart, you ought to have seen the other guys. The lucky part is that we got away with our money before the cops showed up.''

They talked for a half hour longer, both enjoying the quiet closeness.

"You were right. It was nice to get my mind off the Sterling Clinic,'' Steve finally said.

Abby could see that he was getting tired. "We've both had a long day. Maybe we should get some sleep,'' she suggested.

Steve ran his finger around the rim of his empty cup. "Last night, we, uh . . .''

"I don't think you need me tonight.''

There was a long, pregnant pause as they stared at each other.

"Where are you going to sleep?''

"On the couch. In case you wake up or something.''

"I think the hot chocolate is going to have me down for the count. Thanks for thinking of it.''

"Yes. Good night.''

They both got up and stood awkwardly for a moment in front of the sofa. Then Steve turned away toward the bedroom.

Around ten Abby changed into an oversize T-shirt she'd found in Wayne's bureau. She'd owe him a new wardrobe, she thought wryly, when this was all over.

After taking a paperback mystery from the bookshelves, she settled herself on the couch. But the book lay unread on her chest. Instead, she kept glancing at the closed bedroom door.

Steve had seemed fine when he'd gone to bed. But he had a long way to go before he was fully recovered. How did he feel now that he was alone in the dark? She wanted to go in and see if he was all right. But she understood his need to be by himself.

Finally she turned off the light, pulled the blanket up around her shoulders and courted sleep. But it was as elusive as a dream lover.

Was she doing the right thing trying to handle this alone? she asked herself. She felt like a rookie demolitions expert trying to defuse an unexploded bomb. The trouble was, she didn't know exactly when or where the booby traps might lurk. But there was no one she could trust.

She had to comfort herself with the assessment that Steve seemed to be getting better. This evening she'd been charmed by his exciting life in foreign lands. Places and events were safe topics. But emotions still made him uncomfortable.

Yet even when they weren't talking about how they were feeling, the emotional involvement kept deepening for both of them. It was right there, humming below the surface of every conversation. The realization was as frightening as it was exciting.

Even under the best of circumstances there were so many reasons why Steve Claiborne wasn't the right man for her, she told herself. And these were the worst of circumstances. Yet she couldn't turn off her feelings. She desperately wanted to help him through this trauma.

More than that, she longed to strip away the layers of scar tissue he'd been accumulating since his childhood.

The need wasn't just that of a therapist to reach a troubled patient but of a woman to reach a man who could be important in her life.

She'd been so deep in thought that she hadn't been paying much attention to her surroundings. Now she realized that the wind had begun to pick up. As she listened, a gust howled around the eaves and rattled the old windows.

When a branch scraped against one of the panes, Abby jumped. It would be easier to sleep, she told herself, if nature cooperated.

Sometime after midnight she finally drifted into a troubled slumber. Hours—or was it minutes later—a noise woke her. At first she thought it was the wind assaulting the eaves, then she heard a frantic shout above the din.

She was heading toward the bedroom when Steve burst through the door. In the light from the kitchen she could see that he was wearing only a pair of briefs. But more than that, his eyes were wide, his skin was drenched with perspiration and his muscles were coiled with the tension of a tiger about to spring.

"Steve!"

"If you touch me again with that needle, I'll kill you."

Needle. She focused on the word. He must be flashing back to the hospital. Abby ran toward him. "I'm not . . . it's Abby."

Her words didn't seem to register. He was caught up in some horrible scene from his lost forty-eight hours. She tried to grab his arm. He wrenched away and sprinted for the door. As he threw it open, a gust of cold air almost tore it out of his hand.

"Steve! Wait!"

He was already disappearing into the darkness, and she wasn't sure if he could hear her above the wind. Barefoot, she followed him through the open doorway.

In the moonlight she could see his form rapidly disappearing. He was in a hurry. But he was heading in the direction of the river.

Her heart pounded in terror as she dashed after him. Wind whipped her hair against her face. Gravel dug into her bare feet, but she hardly felt the bite.

"Steve, stop!" she screamed, feeling the night snatch her words away.

His long-legged stride didn't slacken. He was on the dock now, rushing toward the dark water. She reached the wooden boards just as he plunged off the other end into the blackness.

Chapter Twelve

Abby's breath was coming in jagged spurts as she ran along the fifty-foot dock. When she reached the end, she stood panting and scanning the river. An arm broke the surface of the choppy water and seemed to clutch upward at the sky.

Steve. Fear pounded in her chest. *Save him.* Without any hesitation she jumped in.

Abby hit the water feetfirst and felt icy cold sluice over her like the runoff from a glacier. Her muscles contracted in reaction, and she felt herself sinking. There was nothing she could do but plummet downward like stone.

Her feet hit the rocky bottom, and the jag of pain shocked her body into action. She pushed upward through endless waves of drifting sea grass. Finally, when her lungs were about to burst, she broke the surface. There was just time to gulp some air before a wave slapped her in the face.

She hadn't stopped to think. She'd just acted. But she'd never been much of a swimmer. Now she flailed desperately in the rough water as she tried to get her bearings. She wasn't going to save Steve. She wasn't even going to save herself.

"Abby!"

In her confusion she wondered if someone had called her name. But she was sinking again, and mindless panic seized her as she felt icy water close over her face once more.

Just as her head slipped below the surface, a strong arm grabbed her around the chest and pulled her up. "Abby."

She coughed water out of her throat and struggled to clutch at muscular shoulders.

"Relax. I've got you."

Somehow she obeyed the command. Steve. He had her.

He turned her over, slung an arm across her chest and began to tow her toward the bank. Waves still slapped around her nose and mouth, and she sputtered to breathe. But she knew Steve wasn't going to let her go. He was strong, and he gave every indication that he knew what he was doing.

Now that she wasn't lashing out with her arms and legs, she felt her whole body begin to shiver in the frigid water. When he reached the bulwark of rocks along the shore, he anchored her hand to a boulder.

"I'll get you out of here in a second," he said as he hoisted himself up. Then he turned and grabbed her hand.

As soon as they were both on the bank, her teeth began to chatter. The T-shirt she was wearing felt like a layer of ice against her skin. His arms came up to fold her close, but he couldn't warm her in the blustery night air.

"We'd better get back inside," he muttered, swinging her up into his arms.

She linked her fingers around his neck and pressed her face against his cold chest. Once he reached the house, he stepped across the threshold, set Abby down and turned to slam the door. It was warmer inside, but she had to struggle to control her chattering teeth.

"What in the name of God were you—" He stopped abruptly, staring at her.

Suddenly she felt self-conscious knowing that her wet T-shirt was clinging to her body like a second skin.

"You can't swim," he said slowly.

"A little. I can swim a little."

"But you jumped in—"

"To get you," she finished the sentence.

"I don't know which one of us is crazier," he muttered. "My God, woman, you could have been killed."

"Steve, I couldn't let you drown."

In just a few short days she'd come to know this man's expressions more intimately than any other human being's. That he was deeply moved showed in the unaccustomed softness of his face, the way his lips were barely parted.

The realization that she'd laid her life on the line for him without a moment's thought for her own safety was almost too much for Steve to cope with. That and the fierce, almost defiant, look in her eyes brought him across the few feet that separated them.

He wasn't sure what he meant to do. He wasn't sure of anything except the sudden urgency of his need to touch her, hold her, cover her mouth with his.

She raised her face to him, and the warmth of her breath was a balm against his river-chilled skin. His mouth melded hungrily with her. Her body melted against his. The cold water had brought her nipples to hard peaks that teased the stubble on his chest.

The contrast between the wet chill of her skin and the warmth flooding within made her gasp. She felt as if she were heating from the inside out so that any water still glistening on the surface would evaporate as steam. Except that it was the demanding pressure of his lips against hers, the sudden tension of his muscles, the desperate straining of their bodies against each other that generated the fire.

A shudder that had nothing to do with their freezing swim racked Abby's slender frame. An answering tremor seized Steve.

"My God, Abby."

"I know."

"I dreamed about making love to you like this. Even when I was half out of my head I knew how much I wanted you."

"Oh, Steve."

He captured her mouth again in a fierce, hungry kiss. When he stepped away from her, she cried out in protest.

"Sweetheart, we have to dry you off."

She hadn't realized her skin and hair were still soaking until he spoke. So were his. "You too. You'll catch your death of cold."

"I doubt it."

He led her to the bathroom and stripped the sodden shirt over her head. Then his briefs joined the small pile of wet clothes. She looked up to find his gaze caressing her body.

"Beautiful." His voice rippled with emotion.

Quickly he pulled one of the large, fluffy towels off the rack. First, folding her close, he began to rub her body. The heavy fabric teased her back and shoulders, bringing the blood tingling to the surface of her skin. When he shifted his attention to her front, she sucked in a deep gust of air as the terry cloth gently abraded her nipples.

She braced her hands against his shoulders, and her head dropped to his chest. Her cheek and then her lips played with the blond stubble.

"You're asking for it," he said in a husky tone.

Towel-clad fingers stroked the insides of her thighs, sending a wave of heat through her body. Then the towel fell to the floor, and he was teasing her satin flesh with his fingers, sliding them higher and higher toward the place that ached for his touch.

Groaning deep in his throat, he pulled her into his arms. Need, desire, an agony of wanting rocketed through him.

"I can't get close enough," he gasped.

"Neither can I."

Passion robbed her legs of strength. As she sagged against him, his strong arms pressed her into the fiber of his bone and muscle. Then he swept her up and carried her the few feet to the bedroom.

They tumbled together onto the bed.

"Abby, I can't wait any longer."

Within seconds, he was inside her. She gasped and his body went very still. His eyes searched for hers.

"That was pleasure, not pain."

He gazed down at her, as if he had just realized what this night might mean for the two of them. Then he closed his eyes.

Her fingers threaded through his hair. Her lips found his cheek. As if he no longer had control of his actions, his hips began to move.

After a moment, she matched him in perfect rhythm and then surprised him with her own counterpoint.

"Good. That's so good." The words were torn from his throat.

They moved together—man and woman—losing their separate identities as the intensity built.

Each stroke coiled the energy within them tighter and tighter.

Her fingers dug into his back. His hands reached to lift her hips and pull her closer. Broken little murmurs of pleasure tumbled from her lips.

He called out her name.

The final coil of the spring snapped, catapulting her into a soul-melting release. The moment seemed to shatter. Her hands still clutching Steve's back were the only anchor to reality.

She saw him throw back his head. She felt his body racked with the same spasms that were still echoing through hers.

Afterward they held each other for long moments. Finally he settled her at his side and reached to pull the covers up around them.

She nestled in his arms, wondering how to tell him what the experience had meant to her. "I'm glad that happened," she murmured.

He was silent for several heartbeats. "I'm not."

The words stung, and her head jerked up. "What do you mean?"

"The last thing you need right now is a disabled veteran of the Sterling Clinic wars."

"Let me be the judge of what I need. And you're not a disabled veteran."

"Not physically. It's the mental equipment that's not functioning too well. I almost got us both drowned," he rasped. "What in hell is wrong with me?"

"Nothing."

"Sure."

"Steve, it was a flashback. From the hallucinogens. You thought you were still in the hospital and you tried to get away. I don't know. Maybe it was the noise from the wind that started it."

He rolled onto his back and stared at the ceiling. "The cold water snapped me out of it. Maybe you'll have to throw a glass in my face the next time it happens," he said with a mirthless laugh.

"Let's hope it won't happen again."

"But you don't know if it will."

Under the covers she linked her fingers with his. "We'll face it together."

"Don't fool yourself about there being a future for the two of us. I'd be lying if I tried to say that making love with you wasn't fantastic. But that doesn't mean happily ever after. I'm a lousy risk. I've never been able to make relationships work. Not with women. Not with my parents."

"Steve, your parents weren't your fault. They didn't know how to—or didn't care about—giving their children the emotional support they needed. That's why you and Sharon drew together. You were trying to supply the love your parents didn't give you."

She thought the words would comfort him. Instead, he sat up and gave her a dark look. "You might as well know something else. I didn't like listening to those tapes I took from you. I mean, I didn't like hearing what Sharon really thought about me."

"I knew that was going to be true. That was one of the reasons I told you the information was confidential."

"And I don't like the fact that you know so damn much about me. Personal stuff I haven't told you."

Abby's voice was low. "I'm sorry. But whatever you got out of those tapes, you must know that Sharon loved you."

"Yes. But sometimes she demanded more emotionally from me than I could give her. And I'm pretty sure I can't give you what you're looking for, either. You want a home and kids and a husband who comes home every night, don't you?"

Abby swallowed. "I haven't thought about it in exactly those terms."

"Well, don't think about *me* in those terms."

"All right, I won't think about you in any particular terms. But I'm afraid that at the moment we're stuck with each other," she said in a level voice, unwilling to let him know just how much his words had hurt her.

"Abby, I'm sorry. Come here." He wrapped his arms around her and pressed her close, his fingers combing through her hair. She was offering him something he'd always been afraid to ask for, something he was still afraid to ask for because he knew all too well that a person could take back what they'd given.

"Once when I was a little kid I begged for a pair of cowboy boots for Christmas," he said, unable to keep his tone even. "I was so proud of those boots that I wore them to school every day for a week. Then my father got angry about something stupid and took them away as punishment. Right then I vowed I'd never ask the old man—or anyone else—for anything again." That was the closest he dared come to putting his feelings into words.

Her heart turned over at the thought of what that unbending man had done to his little boy. The boots were just a symbol in Steve's mind, but over the years the symbol had woven itself into the fabric of his life. "Just because something was true when you were a child, it doesn't have to be that way forever,'' she murmured. ''Sometimes if you don't let someone who cares about you know what you want, the answer is an automatic no.'' She felt the tautness in his body as he considered her statement.

''What if you don't know how to ask?''

''Start with something easy and uncomplicated. I know you're tense. Would a back rub feel good?''

''Yes.''

''Then turn over.''

His eyes sought hers. Then he silently shifted his position, and she began to knead his shoulders just as he'd kneaded hers that morning in the kitchen. But the physical therapy wasn't her only motive. She knew it would be easier for the two of them to talk if he wasn't facing her.

''Steve, my life has been a lot different from yours. In some ways I had an ideal childhood. But that also meant I was insulated from some harsh realities.''

''Maybe that's better.''

''It isn't always an advantage. Once I broke a spun glass ornament my mom had gotten from her grandmother. Mom didn't even spank me. But knowing I'd disappointed her was the only punishment I needed. When I was a kid, I put a lot of effort into being 'good.'''

''Most kids want to please their parents, I guess.''

She gave his shoulders a harder squeeze and began to work her hands down along his spine. ''I had the usual kind of teenage rebellion when I was in high school. So when this college guy named Brad Fairfax invited me to a party, I was really mad when Mom told me I couldn't go. A girlfriend said I could say I was spending the night at her house.''

She felt the muscles in his back bunch. ''I don't think I'm going to like the rest of this story.''

"But I want to tell it because it's the worst thing that ever happened to me. In a way, it set a pattern for *my* life. Brad picked me up at my friend's and took me to the party. At first I felt really daring. Then I realized there was a lot of drinking and drugs, and I wanted to leave, but Brad pulled me into one of the bedrooms. He was drunk, and the next thing I knew he was ripping off my clothes. I was so scared I started crying and screaming, but no one paid any attention, maybe because of the loud music. Or maybe nobody cared." Abby gulped, surprised at how strong the memory was. "I guess the only reason I got out of there with my virginity intact was that he passed out before he could get all my clothes off."

Steve turned over and took her in his arms. "That must have been horrible."

"I couldn't tell anyone how terrified I'd been, not even my girlfriend. But I made sure nothing like that ever happened to me again. I realize now that after that I stopped taking risks. My relationships with men have been pretty bland—because I thought I wanted things that way. But there was no real spark, no real excitement."

"You've had too damn much excitement since you met me."

"Steve, there may not be much time, and I want to explain—"

"There's going to be time! We're going to get out of this."

"Indulge me. It's suddenly become terribly important for you to understand how I feel about you. Meeting you made me realize there can be very good reasons not to play it safe."

"Abby, I . . . care . . . about you."

She knew he hadn't made the admission lightly. She wanted to tell him that she was falling in love with him. But she wasn't sure he was ready to hear it. "I care about you, too," she whispered.

Outside, the wind picked up again. It assaulted the house like a harbinger of the other threatening forces zeroing in on the man and woman in the downstairs bedroom. But for the moment the two of them were still warm and safe in each other's arms.

Steve kissed Abby once more, and she snuggled into his embrace. This time it was slow and sweet and sensual—lovemaking to drive away fear and apprehension.

GEORGE NASH WALKED back and forth across the length of the little room. It was almost like being one of the patients. They weren't treating him badly, but they hadn't let him out of the clinic since Abby Franklin had sprung the Claiborne guy.

What were they worried about? He was in this too deep to go to the police. Or maybe that was the best thing to do. If he blew the whistle on the whole operation, he might get some kind of immunity.

The door opened and he looked up expectantly. It was Frances Backmann, the lady who was in so solid with the boss.

"How are you doing?" she asked.

"Oh, just fine. And you?" He hoped he'd kept any note of sarcasm out of his reply.

"You know, the chief of staff is very angry about your breach of security."

George swallowed.

"But I like you, George. And I've been putting in a good word for you."

"Thanks." What was she leading up to?

"We've decided that the best thing for you is to get out of town for a while. How does a vacation in Brazil sound?"

It sounded too easy. "What's the catch?"

"We need you to set up something."

"Like what?"

"Our contact with the police has finally paid off. Abby Franklin was spotted on the Eastern Shore. As soon as we find out exactly where she is, somebody's going to have to go down there and bring her back."

"How do I fit into things?"

"I'll tell you as soon as we have the plans firmed up."

A FLOCK OF GEESE honking over Bachelor's Cape woke Abby. Opening her eyes, she stared at the sleeping man who'd turned his back to her sometime during the night.

She reached out to touch his shoulder but pulled her hand back. Making love with him had been wonderful, but she'd be kidding herself if she thought things between them were settled.

Abby pressed her fingertips against her closed eyes. Perhaps the midnight swim had something to do with the pain that had begun to drum in her head. Sighing, she slipped out of bed and pulled on the sweat clothes she'd worn the day before.

In the living room she found her purse. When she opened it to get out some aspirin, a sheaf of computer paper spilled out.

She stared at the forms, realizing they were the other medical reports from Sterling. She'd been concentrating so hard on Steve that she'd forgotten all about them.

She was thumbing through the printout when he came into the living room also dressed in yesterday's clothing.

Glancing up, she noted that he looked a bit unsure of himself.

He stared at her as if he were debating what to say. Then he focused on the papers. "What's that stuff?" he asked.

"Computer printouts from Sterling."

"How did you get them?"

"I was over there twice on Sunday," she began to explain. "When Jo and I got you out, that was my second trip. Before that I logged onto the computer system and stole a bunch of records. That's how I knew you were there."

"You have my record? Let's see what kind of bull they made up."

"Yours was an exact copy of Sharon's. Down to the report of your violent behavior at admission."

He swore and reached for the papers.

"It's not here. Yours and Sharon's printouts are back in my apartment," she told him. "But I guess I never took these other ones out of my pocketbook. They're from those indigent patients I told you about—the ones who died at Sterling in the past few months."

"So let's take a look at them," he suggested quickly.

She sensed that he was grateful for the constructive activity. It was easier than trying to jog his own memory—or delve any more into their personal relationship. Exchanging confidences in the middle of the night was one thing; continuing the conversation in the morning was a lot more difficult.

For the moment Abby was in complete agreement. Trying to cope with his memory loss put a tremendous strain on both of them. And they didn't have the leisure to sit around talking about how they felt.

Steve sat down at Wayne's white tile table and tore the computer printout apart while Abby made instant coffee and fixed them bowls of cold cereal. Luckily their host kept a supply of boxed milk on the shelf, so they didn't have to eat the bran flakes dry.

Abby joined Steve at the table, and they both silently began to spoon up cereal as they shuffled through the papers.

"What's this notation on line sixteen?" Steve asked after several minutes.

Abby set down her coffee mug, picked up one of the forms and studied the legend. "I'm not sure, but I think it's for tissue typing."

"Is that standard hospital procedure?"

"I don't think so." Abby scanned her set of forms. They all had the notations.

"What about the cause of death?" Steve asked. "I've got everything here from heart failure and aplastic anemia to cirrhosis of the liver. There doesn't seem to be any pattern."

Abby nodded. "I don't see one, either." Then another thought struck her, and she checked the bottom of several reports. They were all signed by Dr. Gerheiser, the physician who'd written the fabricated account of Steve's incarceration. "That's odd," she mused.

"What?"

"Dr. Gerheiser. He admitted you, so I assumed he was on the psychiatric staff. Now he's signing in a bunch of medical cases. I don't get it."

She watched as Steve rubbed his hand across his chest.

"Operations. Tissue typing. Dead patients," she mused. "Do you think they're into some kind of illegal medical research?"

Steve stared at her. "It could be."

"But how does Sharon fit in?"

"My brother Derrick is on the hospital board. Suppose he was in on whatever was going down and Sharon found out?"

"He'd have his own sister drugged and killed?"

Steve's face twisted. "Derrick's a lot like our father. Greenbacks are the only thing he really loves—except himself. If it came to a choice between his future or his sister's, which one do you think he'd pick?"

They weren't able to come to any further conclusions at the moment. To break the tension, Steve had gotten up and turned on the television set again. The station was in the middle of a series of commercials, and the sight of kids eating McDonald's hamburgers and satisfied customers singing the praise of Fox Chevrolet made Abby realize how isolated she and Steve were. They hadn't seen another human being since they'd passed the patrol after the bay bridge.

Abby glanced at her watch. "It's almost time for the midday news. Why don't you get Channel 11, and we'll see if anything interesting is happening."

Steve changed the channel and started toward the sofa.

"At the top of the news this noon," local anchorwoman Janet Cook began, "police are investigating the murder of Federal Hill resident Adam Goodwin."

"Adam Goodwin!" Steve whirled to face the screen.

"An insurance agent for Concord Life, Goodwin was found by a neighbor who came over to complain about a television set loudly blaring in the middle of the night," the newscaster continued. "Police have arrested Ezra Hornby, founder and director of the Lazarus Mission on Eastern Avenue in Highlandtown."

Steve looked thunderstruck.

"Adam Goodwin. Where have I heard that name?" Abby asked.

"From me. He was the one dating Sharon."

"Now he's dead."

On the television the picture had switched to a grimy-looking red brick building. Men with unkempt hair and dirty clothes milled about on the sidewalk. A reporter thrust a microphone in front of one. "How will the arrest of Mr. Hornby affect the mission?"

"Man, I don't know."

"Do you think he's guilty?"

"No way. He's the best. He always finds the dough to take care of us real good." The man wiped a hand across his mouth, showing ragged, dirty fingernails. "Ezra feeds us, gives us a place to sleep. Gives us hope. He knows what it's like, 'cause he was on the skids once hisself."

Abby stared at the picture. "How could they arrest a man like that?"

"They must have some kind of evidence."

"I'm going to call Jo." Abby crossed the room and dialed her friend's number.

"O'Malley and O'Malley. Can you hold for a minute?"

"It's me, Abby."

"Abby! Wait a minute."

A moment later Jo was back on the line. "I was hoping you'd call."

"I just turned on the TV and heard the news. I suppose you know a lot more than we do."

"I sure do. You know, I've done a bunch of insurance investigations for Concord, so I have some real good contacts down there. Guess what? Sharon Claiborne had an insurance policy with them. She switched agents and had Adam Goodwin change the beneficiary for her. Only there's some question about why he didn't turn the forms in promptly. The policy didn't pay out because the death was a suicide."

"That's very interesting."

"It's even more interesting when you know that the Lazarus Mission was the beneficiary."

"My God. How does this all fit together?" Abby wondered aloud.

Steve had gotten up and strode across the room, hovering over Abby. Sensing his need to join the conversation, she pointed to the stairs and mouthed, "There's a phone in the master bedroom."

A moment later Steve came on the line. "This is Steve Claiborne. Tell me what you've found out."

"Glad to hear you're feeling better," Jo said.

"Jo, when this is all over, we'll sit down for a nice get-acquainted chat."

Jo laughed. "You're right." Quickly she repeated the information she'd just related to Abby.

"Do you realize Hornby and Goodwin both stood to profit from Sharon's death—until the deal went rotten?" Steve spoke to both Abby and Jo. "Maybe Hornby did kill Goodwin when he found out what happened."

"Ezra Hornby? You've got to be kidding. He's one of Baltimore's most respected philanthropists," Jo objected.

"Maybe he wasn't too choosy about where he got his money," Steve muttered.

Abby sucked in a sharp breath. "Listen, Jo, thanks," she said to the detective. "We'll be back in touch with you."

"Wait—"

Abby hung up and Steve came pounding down the stairs. "What is it? What's wrong?"

"That man. That dead man at the Sterling Clinic with the incision down his chest. I just remembered what I was thinking when I saw him. He looked like he'd walked into the hospital from skid row."

"Yeah?"

"Well, he was a lot like those guys we just saw on TV milling around in front of the Lazarus Mission."

Steve blinked and gestured toward the records that were still spread out on the table. "God Almighty, do you think that's how all those indigent patients got to Sterling? Did Hornby cart them over there a few at a time?"

Abby slumped into one of the kitchen chairs. "He needed money. Maybe they were paying him so much a head to use them for their illegal research." It was hard to keep her voice steady.

"It would be perfect. Men off the street who'd already severed their connections with their homes and families. No one would miss them."

Abby wrapped her arms around her shoulders and rubbed her skin, trying to banish the bone-chilling cold that had settled over her. The more they found out about Sterling, the more diabolical the whole thing got.

Steve dropped to the floor beside her and covered her cold hands with his warm ones. There was a look of excitement mixed with the concern on his face.

"Sweetheart, something good came out of that TV newscast."

She raised her head, unable to summon much enthusiasm. "What?"

"Adam Goodwin was the man I was supposed to meet at the Blue Star. Hearing about him brought back the memory."

"Oh, Steve. What else do you remember?"

His brows knit together. Then his grip tightened on hers. "That son of a—"

"Who? Adam?"

"I've just remembered exactly what happened when Michelle and some bruiser dragged me out the door of the Blue Star. Someone was waiting in the back seat of a car. It was my brother, Derrick."

Chapter Thirteen

"I told you Derrick was in this up to his ears," Steve grated. "there was a woman in the car with him. She gave me an injection as soon as I tumbled into the back seat." He pressed his hand against his chest, and Abby knew he was thinking about the shaved skin. It had become a token of his own narrow escape from death. "Some more details are coming back now." His face contorted as he struggled to concentrate.

Abby twined her fingers with his, offering silent encouragement. But she didn't interrupt. This was too important to him. To both of them.

"The nurse was there in the psycho ward. She's the one who gave me more injections. Her and that George Napier character. And some other guy."

"Did you see Derrick again?"

"No. But I was out of it a good part of the time." He leaned toward Abby. "You don't know how much it means to be able to remember what happened."

"I'm so glad," Abby whispered. She sensed that some of the anxiety had left Steve, but she also knew he was eager to get on with things. "I guess we have to find some proof of what your brother's been up to and take it to the police. Wait a minute. With everything that's been going on, I forgot about the date. Derrick lied to me about when Sharon was admitted to the hospital. It was the morning she called. Maybe that's why I couldn't get in touch with him.''

"She phoned you for help the morning they were abducting her!''

"Oh, Steve. I didn't even realize what was happening. I should have called the police.''

"Abby, it wasn't your fault! What could you have told them?''

"I . . .''

"You've got to put that behind you. We've got to concentrate on what's happening now. The problem is, there's no proof of what Derrick told you. He could say that you misunderstood.''

"You're right. It's my word against his, and the police are going to believe him.''

"Unfortunately they're not going to believe me, either. I'm an escaped mental patient.'' Steve shuddered. "If we go to the police now, they'll contact Sterling. And the hospital will send someone to put me in a straitjacket and give me some more 'medicine' to calm me down.''

Abby saw that his teeth were clenched. Under his tan his face had gone pale. He'd been through a hideous experience. She understood very well why he wanted to avoid the tender mercies of the Sterling Clinic at all costs. "They're not going to get anywhere near you until we can prove our story,'' she promised.

When her hand found his, he clasped her tightly. "Abby, I'm sorry. I feel pretty stupid reacting like that.''

"I'd react the same way if it had happened to me,'' she assured him quietly.

Steve cleared his throat. "We'll find a way out of this mess,'' he vowed.

"Yes."

His expression turned thoughtful. "We've been talking about pinning something on Derrick, but I don't think my brother's the one running the show, even though he's on the hospital board."

"Why not?"

"Because he's too tied up with Claiborne Associates. Believe me, I know what kind of commitment that bloodsucker of a corporation takes. That's one of the reasons I bailed out instead of knuckling under to my father. I wasn't going to indenture myself to a bunch of companies the old man thought more of than he did his family."

"Derrick certainly was hostile to me when I wanted to help Sharon."

"I didn't say he wasn't in it up to his ears. I just said he wasn't the one in charge."

Abby thought for a moment. "Do you think a scam this size could go on at Sterling without Wyndham right in the middle of it? He's the chief of staff, after all."

"I think we have to assume, at least, that he's in on it. Who else could be involved?"

Mentally Abby began to run through a list of people she knew at the hospital. "Kellogg," she murmured.

"Who's he?"

"A doctor I once interviewed for a paper. I saw him at the hospital the first time I tried to have a look at Sharon's records. He called me yesterday."

"What?"

"I forgot all about it. But he left two messages on my answering machine. Maybe we ought to find out what he wants."

Steve looked uncertain. "That could be dangerous. He might very well be in the middle of things. But if we play it right, we could end up with some useful information."

"I'm going to have to be the one to talk to him."

"Yeah. Let's let him think I'll still too wigged out to hold a coherent conversation."

They both agreed that it was too risky to phone from the house. So for the first time since the fugitives arrived at Wayne's they ventured off his property. But neither one of them wanted to head into St. Michaels, particularly when Abby pointed out that the police station was right on Main Street.

So they drove to a country store on the outskirts of Easton and called from a booth across from the gas pumps. Abby held the receiver. Steve squeezed into the booth beside her and bent his head to listen. Although they'd agreed on what to say before leaving Wayne's house, Steve had brought along pencil and paper in case they needed to communicate without letting Kellogg know they were both evaluating his end of the conversation.

Abby's hand was shaky as she dropped coins into the proper slots and dialed the number. Steve slipped his arm around her waist, and she leaned her head against his shoulder as the number rang.

"May I speak to Dr. Kellogg?" she asked when a woman answered the phone.

"Whom should I say is calling?"

"Dr. Abby Franklin."

It was only a moment before Kellogg came on the line. "Thank God you called," he exclaimed. "I was just about to try your answering service again. Didn't they contact you?"

"Yes, I got a message that you wanted to talk to me."

"Dr. Franklin, Abby, I know this sounds crazy, but both of us are in grave danger."

Steve, who could hear the physician as clearly as Abby, rolled his eyes.

"What do you mean?" she questioned.

"I've just discovered what's going on at the clinic."

"Oh?"

"It's not something I'd want to discuss on the phone. But for months I've been looking the other way when questionable things happened."

"Like the men from the Lazarus Mission?" Abby fished.

"What better supply of used parts?"

Used parts? She and Steve exchanged glances.

"What really got me thinking was that business with Sharon and Steve Claiborne both ending up in the hospital," Kellogg was saying. "Their records were identical, and we both know that couldn't be possible. So I started doing some poking around."

"Do you happen to know why Derrick Claiborne lied to me about when his sister was admitted to the hospital?"

There was a pause on the other end of the line. "I heard Wyndham and Claiborne talking. When you started asking questions, Derrick panicked and thought it would sound better if he said she'd been in the hospital for weeks."

"And they had her killed because she discovered what they were up to?"

"Yes. They weren't going to jeopardize a multi-million-dollar business. These people are ruthless. I think the only option you and I have is to join forces and go to the police together. If there are two of us, I don't see how they can avoid an official investigation. But we have to talk first and get the facts straight. Neither one of us wants to end up being arrested."

This wasn't at all what Abby had expected, and she was thrown off balance. Kellogg sounded so sincere, and he did have a national reputation—which he would naturally want to protect. She looked questioningly at Steve and he wrote, "Ask him why he thinks you can help."

"This is all very interesting," she began. "But why are you contacting me?"

"I know you must be the one who got poor Claiborne out of that locked ward. How is he? Is he okay?"

Abby gave the answer they'd prepared. "He's in pretty bad shape. I'm worried about brain damage from the combination of drugs they gave him."

"Then there's even more reason why you can't stay in hiding. He needs medical attention."

"What are you suggesting?"

"Tell me where you are and I'll pick you up."

"Dr. Kellogg, I'd like to believe you. But after what's been happening, I'm sure you can understand why I can't afford to trust you."

"Quite right, my dear."

"So we're at a stalemate."

Kellogg was silent for a moment. "Would you agree to meet me in a public place?"

"Possibly."

"I've been stringing Wyndham along, so I know he's got you pinpointed somewhere on the Eastern Shore."

Despite her resolve to play it cool, Abby gasped.

"You were spotted by a police officer on the other side of the bay bridge, which means it's only a matter of time before Wyndham finds you."

Abby looked at Steve. He shook his head. Before he could write anything she said, "All right, I'll meet you."

"You've made the right decision."

"You said something about a public place."

"I've been thinking about the Oxford-Bellevue ferry."

"Why there?"

"I think you'll agree that no one can sneak up on us in the middle of the Tred Avon River."

Abby didn't have much experience with this sort of thing. "That makes sense," she told Kellogg.

"I could be in Oxford by six o'clock this afternoon."

Now that they'd agreed to meet, Abby didn't want to prolong the agony. "Make it five."

"All right. But I'll have to leave pretty soon."

"What does your car look like?"

"A silver Mercedes. What will you be driving?"

As Abby started to answer, Steve pressed his fingers urgently against her lips and shook his head violently.

"Dr. Franklin? Are you still there?" the question came through the phone line.

"Uh, sorry, I'm not sure what I'll be driving. I mean, if the police are looking for my car . . ." Her voice trailed off.

"Abby, don't you trust me?" the surgeon asked.

"Of course, or I wouldn't be meeting you. I'll see you at five." Abby hung up and pressed her head back against the cold glass of the phone booth, thankful that the ordeal was over.

"If you'd told him what car you were driving, a sniper with a high-powered rifle could pick you off while you waited for the ferry to dock," Steve said, his voice surprisingly mild.

"High-powered rifle?"

"You don't really trust the man, do you, Abigail? You have no idea what he might be going to pull. This could be a trick to put us out of the action for good."

"Don't call me Abigail. I didn't trust him, but I didn't think—"

"You've got to think. Your life depends on it."

She looked at him challengingly. "All right, give me a quick course in covert meetings. How do I make sure I'm prepared?"

"You're not going."

"Steve, I don't see what other option we have. We're cut off here. Isolated. And he said Wyndham knows where we are. A squad from the clinic could sweep down on us. Or maybe they've told the police we're armed and dangerous."

"I've got the picture. But, Abby, we just don't know if he's telling the truth. There sure hasn't been anything about us on the TV news. Maybe he's lying about Wyndham."

"Except he knew about the policeman stopping me just after the bay bridge. And he picked a meeting place within thirty miles of here."

Steve scuffed at the gravel in the parking area. "Okay, he knows our general location, but if we had picked the rendezvous point, we'd be in a better position."

"You're right. I'm not used to thinking on my feet when it comes to this cloak-and-dagger stuff."

He turned toward her, his eyes seeking hers. "Yes, you are, sweetheart. If you weren't, I'd be dead by now." He swallowed. "Abby, I'm sorry if I flew off the handle."

She grinned up at him. "Actually, the Steve Claiborne I used to know would have snatched the phone out of my hand and slammed it back on the hook."

He cocked his head to one side, his expression thoughtful. "You're right. I would."

Abby opened the door of her car and slid behind the wheel. "We're both learning something." If they'd had the time, she would have pursued the point.

"What do you think about the information Kellogg dropped?" Steve asked as he climbed into the passenger seat.

"You mean about the used parts and the multi-million-dollar business?"

"Yes."

"I don't know. It would take years to develop a research project into a marketable product. I got the feeling he was talking about money they were making now."

"That's what it sounded like."

Abby's brow wrinkled. "Kellogg was called away to surgery just after an ambulance came screaming up the driveway and almost knocked me down."

"What do you think he was doing?"

Her mind made a series of unconscious connections, and she spoke before she fully realized what she was saying. "Harvesting some used parts." A chill swept across her skin.

Steve's head whipped around. "My God! Do you mean, as in organ transplants?"

"It fits. Don't you see? It fits. Psychotics and indigent patients go into the clinic and only their vital organs leave." The words left a bitter taste in Abby's mouth, and she scrambled to backpedal. "But they're not doing transplants at Sterling, as far as I know."

"Maybe not in Baltimore. But they could be getting the organs here and using them somewhere else."

"That's right. Sterling is associated with an international hospital network."

Abby saw the look of shock that transformed Steve's face. "What?"

"God Almighty. About six months ago I was asked if I'd be willing to deliver transplant organs to hard-to-reach locations on an emergency basis. They gave me some story about cutting through red tape in order to save lives."

"Why you?"

"Probably a recommendation from my dear brother. Derrick had a pretty good idea about the kind of cargo business I've been running."

"You had no way of knowing what was happening at Sterling. And we're still not sure the whole thing is connected."

"At least we have a better idea about what to ask Kellogg," Steve muttered. "We've got a few hours to get ready for the meeting. We'd better make the most of them."

"Before we go back home, let me call Jo again."

"Why?"

"I want to tell her what we've come up with and see what she can find out."

"Ask her to check out that Dr. Gerheiser. The guy who signed those all admissions papers."

"That's a good idea."

Abby kept the phone call as brief as possible. As she drove back to their hideout, she kept sliding Steve little glances. He was deep in thought and didn't say anything until they were almost at Wayne's driveway.

"I've got an idea about how to work the meeting with Kellogg," he said. "The first thing we need to do is make sure you get to Oxford early. What's the ferry like, by the way?"

Abby thought for a moment. "Nothing fancy. Just a flat bargelike affair with railings. I think it holds about six or eight cars."

"No cabin?"

Abby shook her head.

"Good. Then there's no place for someone to hide—except in one of the cars."

THE MAN MONITORING Dr. Donald Kellogg's phone smiled. He had the number Abby Franklin was calling from. But when he put a trace through, it turned out to be a pay phone outside Easton. So she was playing it cagey. Probably her hideout wasn't in Easton or Oxford, either. But that didn't matter. She'd agreed to meet Kellogg at the Oxford-Bellevue ferry, which meant that they were going to be able to take care of several problems at one time. Hopefully she'd bring Steve with her. But even if she didn't, there wasn't much an escaped mental patient with brain damage was going to be able to do on his own.

Too bad she'd made it five o'clock. That didn't leave much time, and there was a lot to do. The first thing he'd better take care of was the Mercedes. Kellogg had brought the car in for service, but it would be dangerous to make any special preparations until they were actually needed. Now he'd have to call up and tell the mechanic to get on the stick.

Then there was George Nash. The man had been standing by for a couple of days. Now that the clock was ticking, he needed to be briefed.

"IF THE POLICE are looking for your car, you're better off driving Wayne's pickup," Steve told Abby as they pulled into the long drive that led to Bachelor's Cape.

"Our host didn't leave the key."

"Don't worry. I can take care of that." They parked by the garage and went in to have a look at the battered burgundy pickup. It had a wide silver racing stripe and an aluminum shell over the flatbed.

"This'll do," Steve pronounced after he'd given the vehicle a quick inspection. "How long will it take to get to the ferry from here?"

"About half an hour."

Steve rummaged in the garage, looking for equipment that might be useful. All he found was a hunting knife. "Not much good unless we get into hand-to-hand combat," he sighed.

Abby shivered. She hadn't been thinking in those terms.

Quickly they returned to the house. For the next two hours Steve briefed Abby on every contingency she might encounter. Quietly she admitted to herself that there were dozens of potential problems.

Steve took one of Wayne's duck hunting rifles out of the cabinet and checked the action. "Too bad you can't stick this sucker in your purse. Does he have a pistol in the house?"

"Forget it. I wouldn't know what to do with it, anyway."

His hands clenched the rifle barrel.

"I'll be fine."

While they were at the general store, Steve had insisted on picking up some fresh food. Now he opened the refrigerator and paced back and forth as he began to eat one of the pit beef sandwiches he'd bought. He stopped to take a sip of Dr. Pepper.

Abby's stomach gave a little lurch. She knew he was still catching up on the meals he'd missed in the hospital. But how could he even think about food at a time like this? The very thought of trying to choke down anything made her queasy.

"Let's go over some of the stuff again. Okay, so if you notice that you're being followed, what do you do?" he quizzed.

"Make a U-turn and head for downtown. Try to lose him on a side street."

"What if Kellogg's not alone?"

"Don't stop. Don't get on the ferry."

The quiz went on until she could recite the answers by heart. Finally it was time to leave. In the garage Steve gave Abby's hand a quick squeeze. Turning, she threw her arms around him. His own arms came up to clasp her tightly.

"I don't like the idea of your having to be the point man," he muttered. "But he'll be expecting to see you driving."

"I can do it."

"I know that, sweetheart."

She swallowed around the lump that threatened to block her windpipe. "I've only got one chance to get this right."

"You will."

They clung together for another long moment. Then Steve opened the driver's door of the truck and waited while she climbed inside and fastened her seat belt.

Forcing a grin, she gave him a thumbs-up sign and sat behind the wheel, taking several deep breaths. Finally there was nothing else to do but back out of the garage and head down the driveway.

After turning onto the highway, Abby glanced over her shoulder. Maybe all Steve's preparations were unnecessary. Kellogg would turn out to be a good guy. They'd go to the police who would immediately give them protection and arrest the unscrupulous doctors at Sterling. Then she and Steve could live happily ever after. It was a nice fairy tale, she told herself. But deep down Abby knew it wasn't going to be that easy. Particularly the part about her and Steve.

MELISSA WEXLER HAD a lot of experience working the system at the Parkland School. There was a substitute teacher in gym class, so the fourth-grader said she had a stomach ache and asked to go to the nurse's office. Instead of reporting to the infirmary, she went back to her locker, got the puzzle box she'd brought with her that morning and found a nice quiet table in the back of the library.

Of course, Mrs. Desmond wanted to know what she was doing there, so she showed her the box and said she was working on a report on Oriental art. After helping her find some books, Mrs. Desmond finally left Melissa alone so that she could work on the puzzle.

She had already figured out a sequence of eight moves. After finding one more, Melissa could hardly repress a squeal of triumph. As she watched with a mixture of excitement and satisfaction, a drawer near the bottom of the box slid open. Inside was a folded section of newspaper, a crumpled tissue with a lipstick smudge, a silver dollar, a three-inch computer disk and four acorn cups.

Melissa carefully smoothed out the tissue and put everything on the table. Then she unfolded the newspaper. It was a six-month-old article about someone named Dr. Donald Kellogg, a famous surgeon who had come from Denver to work at the Sterling Clinic. Someone had circled a number of the paragraphs with a red ballpoint pen and underlined some of the words.

The little girl spun one of the acorn cups around and made a face. If there was anything important on the disk, it would have to wait until she got home. Or maybe she'd better call Dr. Franklin and tell her. It would be neat if Abby let her keep the dollar.

TURNING ONTO ROUTE 333, Abby headed toward Oxford. Every couple of minutes she glanced in the rearview mirror, but no one seemed to be following the pickup. As she approached the outskirts of town, she felt her tension mounting. What if a police car stopped her again? If Kellogg was telling the truth, this time they'd have her description.

Her mouth was dry and she was having trouble swallowing as she began to encounter more traffic. But she forced herself to proceed at a steady pace. She took a gradual turn to the right around the Marine Basin and headed for the more populated area of town. West Division Street. High Street. City Hall. The Oxford Methodist Church. Abby tried to stay calm by ticking off familiar landmarks. Down near the ferry slip she could see the Robert Morris Inn, the eighteenth-century home of one of the signers of the Declaration of Independence that was now a small hotel.

On a Tuesday afternoon there were no cars lining up for the ferry, which was about halfway across the Tred Avon River on its way to Bellevue. It wouldn't be back on their side of the river for at least twenty minutes.

Instead of pulling up to the ferry slip, Abby turned into the parking lot beside the gray stone hotel and pulled around the corner where she couldn't be seen from the direction of town. Leaning back against the headrest, she closed her eyes for a moment. So far, so good, she congratulated herself. Yet her hands felt cold and clammy. For some reason she couldn't keep them from trembling now that she no longer needed to clutch the wheel. Slipping them between her hips and the seat warmed them a bit and stopped the shaking, but she knew this was going to be one of the longest half hours of her life. If only there was something to do besides sit here like a duck in hunting season.

JO O'MALLEY DRUMMED her fingers against one of the few patches on her desk where the wooden surface was visible through the scattered piles of paper. There was no way she was going to go near the Sterling Clinic, but she'd called and asked to speak to Dr. Louis Gerheiser. After a few moments of dead silence, the switchboard operator told her there was no extension for a physician of that name.

Next she'd called the welfare department. Since Gerheiser had signed in so many indigent patients, he ought to have some sort of listing with that agency. But there was no record of his having worked with welfare cases in the city of Baltimore.

Stranger and stranger, she thought. Perhaps she could track him down through the State Medical Accreditation Board.

ABBY STARED at the river, wishing the wait were over. The ferry seemed to move in slow motion, but finally it reached the far shore. After loading and unloading cars, it started back.

Now her heart began to slam against her ribs again as she craned her neck toward the street. Where was Kellogg? It was almost time for him to show up. What if he were coming across on the ferry? Nervously she worried her bottom lip between her teeth. Steve hadn't said anything about the surgeon's arriving from the other side of the river. What was she supposed to do then?

A moment later Abby sighed with relief as a silver Mercedes pulled up at the ferry slip. She peered at the man behind the wheel, unable to see much because he had a hat pulled down over his face. Didn't he want her to recognize him? Or was he worried about being spotted by someone else?

"He's here," she said aloud, and started the engine again.

The ferry docked and the gate opened. After the vehicles from the other side of the river drove off, the silver Mercedes and one other car pulled on.

She'd have to hurry now if she was going to make it, Abby thought as she shifted into first gear and headed for the entrance to the parking lot. As she paused to let a motorcycle pass, she saw a black car pull up along the water's edge about fifty yards downriver from the landing. Something made the hair on her neck twitch, and she peered at the windshield. She couldn't see the driver, but a glint of reflected sunlight flashed in her eye.

"What—?" Abby pointed toward the car.

"Somebody's watching the ferry with binoculars." The shout came from the man who had been hiding under the metal shell that covered the back of the truck. "Let's get the hell out of here!"

Chapter Fourteen

Steve climbed through the back window into the cab as Abby started the engine and circled out the other side of the parking lot. She longed to speed up. However, she knew she had to drive slowly so as not to call attention to the truck.

"What's going on?" she asked.

"It looks like your friend Kellogg double-crossed us. Or maybe he was followed. But we're not going to stay around and quiz him about it."

Abby turned back toward the center of town. In the rearview mirror she glanced at the ferry, wondering what Kellogg was going to do when he discovered hers wasn't one of the other cars that had gotten on. It was too late for him to get off. The barge had already pulled away from the dock.

Abby took another quick look at the silver Mercedes. It was now riding proudly on the flatbed of the ferry, standing out in contrast against the blue river.

Steve had just twisted around in his seat to see the ferry when a blinding flash of light lit the sky. Abby stamped on the brake and threw her arms over her head just as an earsplitting explosion shattered the air. Then a shock wave rocked the truck.

"What?" she croaked, clutching Steve's arm.

"The ferry. It blew up."

Abby swung the truck to the side of the road, pulled up the emergency brake and turned around to look at the conflagration. They both stared in stunned silence at the giant ball of flame floating in the river. As they watched, a gas tank caught fire with another rocking explosion.

ASSISTANT DISTRICT ATTORNEY Daniel Cassidy leaned back in his swivel chair and contemplated Jo O'Malley. Private detectives didn't usually play ball with the criminal justice system—which made her late-afternoon visit to his office more than a little unusual. "You say you have a hypothetical situation you want to discuss. In confidence," he clarified as he studied her face. He hadn't seen her looking so strung out since her husband, Skip, had been killed while investigating a case of industrial espionage at an electronics plant. Her redhead complexion was so pale that it was almost translucent. And the skin around her eyes was shadowed and drawn. He'd bet she hadn't gotten a good night's sleep in days. It looked like something big had her worried.

"Right, a hypothetical situation," Jo agreed. After yesterday's startling developments, she'd finally admitted to herself that she and Abby were in over their heads and needed help. When she'd decided to talk to someone in the district attorney's office, she'd singled out Cassidy. They'd been on opposite sides of a few cases, but she liked him. More than that, she knew he was ambitious. One good coup could advance his position within the department considerably. The only problem was he'd been busy all day. This afternoon was the earliest he could see her.

"Regarding a case you're working on?" he asked, trying to pin her down.

"Not exactly."

"Jo, if you want my help, you're going to have to be a bit more forthcoming."

She laughed. "Dan, that's against my nature. Besides, now that I'm sitting across your desk from you, I'm starting to wonder if you're going to believe the crazy situation I've stumbled into."

Dan thought for a moment. "So don't tell me what you've stumbled into. Give me a plot for one of those detective stories you've always said you were going to write."

"A story. Yeah. I'll tell you a story." Jo tapped a finger against her lip. "Well, it all begins when this psychologist discovers one of her former patients is being held captive in a mental hospital. The woman dies, and it's supposed to be a suicide. But when the psychologist and her detective friend start investigating, they find out there are some weird things going on at the hospital. Like they find the woman's brother has been kidnapped, drugged and slapped in the psychiatric ward—and scheduled for chest surgery in the morning."

Cassidy sat forward in his chair. "Kidnapped and drugged? Surgery? Are we talking about a Baltimore hospital?"

"Dan, remember this is just a story."

"Why are you telling it to me?"

"Because the plot keeps thickening." Jo gripped the arms of her chair. It was time to put up or shut up. "The psychologist and her detective friend spring the guy from the hospital in the middle of the night. Only nobody knows the detective is involved. But the doctor and the patient are on the run, and I'm pretty sure that if the hospital staff locates them, they're going to shoot first and ask questions later."

"Holy Mother. Maybe you'd better tell me everything you know."

"I can't do that. Not officially."

"How is the patient doing?"

"The doctor says he's recovering."

"Does this story have anything to do with the Hornby-Goodwin case?"

Jo blanched. "What makes you think so?"

"Some very peculiar stuff I've uncovered in Ezra Hornby's records."

"GOD ALMIGHTY" Steve exclaimed as the fireball ballooned over the river.

"Dr. Kellogg. He was in the middle of—" Abby's voice cracked. "Oh, Steve, you were right. I would...we would..." Abby began to shake violently as the realization of what might have happened slammed into her like a second shock wave from the explosion.

"I told you these guys played rough. But this surprises even me," he added under his breath.

Other motorists had pulled off the road and were still gawking at the burning ferry. In the distance a siren blared.

"Come on," Steve urged. "We'd better get out of here."

They were both too shaken to talk as they drove back through Oxford. Abby caught Steve glancing over his shoulder several times.

Then he swore under his breath.

"What's wrong?"

"A black car is following us. You've got to lose it."

Abby made a sharp turn onto a side street in the historic district. The black car took the curve behind them and speeded up as she stepped on the gas.

Fingers fused to the wheel, Abby sped past Edwardian mansions and Victorian cottages.

"Faster," Steve urged.

"If I drive any faster, I'll get us killed."

As she rounded a corner, Abby missed an old lady with a toy poodle by a hair's breadth. Teeth clamped together, she took another quick turn and then ducked down an alley that ran in back of the business district. Roaring out onto Route 333, she crossed the street and pulled in back of a bank. Out of the corner of her eye she saw the black car go streaking by down the Main Street.

"Great going. You lost him," Steve sighed with relief.

"Thank God."

"Better put a little more distance between us and the main road."

Abby drove several blocks deeper into the residential district before pulling up in front of a clapboard bungalow. Then she slumped against the wheel and cradled her head on her arms.

Steve stroked her back. "You were great."

"I almost mowed down a lady and a dog."

"But you didn't get a ticket."

Abby snorted.

"Want me to drive the rest of the way home?" Steve questioned.

"Yes." She was more than ready to change places.

"Is there any way to get back to Wayne's without taking the highway?" Steve asked as he released the emergency brake.

"No direct way."

"I don't care if it's direct. I just don't want to run into that car coming back the other way when the driver figures out we've lost him."

"Then turn left at the next street." Abby leaned back and closed her eyes. Now that she wasn't putting all her efforts into trying to outrun the black car, her mind was scrambling to make sense of what had just happened. "Poor Kellogg," she finally murmured. "They killed him, too."

"I'm afraid it looks that way."

"I guess he wasn't lying to me about not being involved in the dirty dealings."

"I guess he wasn't as careful as he should have been. Wyndham must have figured out what he was up to. But we're not going to let him get us."

Cautiously they made their way back to St. Michaels on a series of back roads, some of them gravel.

"Steve, I'm glad you didn't let me go alone," Abby breathed as she leaned back against the seat.

"There was no way I was going to just send you off into danger like that."

"You were right. I was about as prepared as Little Red Riding Hood."

He found her hand. "That's not true. Abby, I've never met anyone like you. You've got guts." He swallowed. "And loyalty. But sometimes I feel as if I'm taking advantage of you."

She laughed. "You're wrong. I haven't let a man take advantage of me since Brad Fairfax."

The personal conversation was interrupted as she directed him onto another side road. Once they were back on course, he glanced sideways at her. "Abby, it's been a long time since I put my trust in anyone but myself."

She turned her palm up and clasped his hand. "I know."

"It's hard to suddenly have to rethink all the assumptions you've made about life. Or to let down your guard with people."

"I know that, too. What I'm trying to tell you is that I've done a lot of rethinking in the past few days."

"Abby, I told you. I care about you. But don't make plans."

"It takes two people to make plans."

His eyes didn't leave the road. "Right now I want to get you out of the mess I dragged you into."

"I think I played a major role in getting myself into trouble. As for getting out of this, we'll do it together."

They were close to Wayne's property now, and there was no way to avoid driving on a short stretch of highway. Abby kept an eagle eye out for the black car, but it didn't reappear. When they turned through the gateposts of Bachelor's Cape, she sagged down into the seat.

After pulling into the garage, Steve came around and opened her door. Instead of helping Abby down, he turned her toward him and cradled her in his arms.

It felt warm and safe in his embrace. Closing her eyes, she burrowed closer. But when she felt his body tense, she looked up questioningly. "What is it?"

"I was thinking about that first time I held you. It was after the elevator."

"I was trying not to admit it then, but it was sexy—even if I was about as steady on my feet as a sailor on shore leave."

"Yeah." His tone changed. "Then it flashed into my mind—they asked me a lot of questions about you."

"Who?"

"The doctor who was running the show. Gerheiser, I guess. And that nurse. They wanted to know about our relationship."

"There wasn't much to tell."

"One very memorable kiss. I wonder if I described it in detail."

Abby brushed her lips against his jaw and felt his knuckles stroke against her cheek. He was remembering more and more of what had happened in the hospital. Maybe if she snuck up on him with a quick question, his mind would dredge up something else.

"What did they ask you about Sharon?"

"When I'd last seen her. If I'd sent her any presents." She could feel his smile against her face. "You're doing a good job of ambushing me, Dr. Franklin."

"I know how to make the right moves. What kind of presents?"

"Well, like the puzzle box."

Abby's eyes sought Steve's. "Puzzle box! Somebody sent me an Oriental puzzle box in the mail. Just after Sharon phoned me."

"Was it about twelve by ten—wood and inlaid ivory— with dragons and peacocks?"

"Yes!"

"I sent it to Sharon for her birthday about five years ago. It's got a trick drawer."

"So she must be the one who mailed it to me. There was no return address. I thought there was something inside. But I couldn't get it open. That's why I gave it to Melissa to see what she could do with it."

"That little girl we met at your building?"

Abby nodded. "Remember, she said she was working on the puzzle I'd given her."

"I didn't connect the conversation with the box," Steve muttered. "I can't believe a kid could get that thing open. Sharon couldn't even do it until I came back and showed her the sequence of moves."

"You don't know Melissa. We're talking genius IQ."

Steve's expression held a mixture of doubt and excitement. "Let's go give the kid a call. Even if she hasn't opened the box, I can tell her how to do it, and we'll find out if anything important is inside."

"Oh, Steve, maybe Sharon sent me some evidence we can use against Sterling—some proof that we're both not crazy."

Chapter Fifteen

Steve paced back and forth while Abby made the call. At first she thought no one was going to answer the phone in the Wexlers' apartment. Finally, after six rings, Melissa picked up the receiver.

"Hello?" The little girl sounded impatient.

"Melissa, this is Abby Franklin."

"Abby! Oh, Abby. Where are you? I've been trying to call you for a couple of days."

Abby realized she needed to start with some reassurances. "I'm away at the beach, honey. But you can't get in touch with me directly. If you need to leave a message, call my friend Jo O'Malley." She gave the little girl the number.

"I was just starting to look at the files on the disk." Melissa was bursting to tell her own news.

"What disk?"

Steve stopped pacing and turned to face the kitchen, his eyebrows raised.

"The little disk that was in the puzzle box."

"You got the box open?"

Steve stopped in midstride and turned to face Abby. "I'd like to talk to her."

She handed him the phone. "Melissa, this is Steve Claiborne. We met last week when I brought Abby home."

"I remember you. You spent the night at Abby's apartment because your car was still there in the morning."

"On the sofa, Melissa. I spent the night on the sofa."

The little girl giggled. "I think it's romantic."

"I want to talk to you about the puzzle box."

"Did Abby tell you about it?"

"It was a present I sent my sister from Hong Kong. And she mailed it to Abby. Can you tell me what was inside?"

"Well, there was a 1938 silver dollar. If you know anything about coins, I can tell you the designer's name is omitted and stars are added to the back. It's worth over ten thousand dollars, so I guess you're not going to let me keep it."

"We'll negotiate that point later."

"What else did you find?"

"A computer disk. It's got all these funny medical records. From someplace called the Laza—"

Abby and Steve were both so intent on the phone call that neither one of them heard the front door open or saw the two men step inside.

"Put down the phone, Steve, or I'll blow your girlfriend away."

Abby whirled around, her eyes wide with shock. Steve's gaze riveted to the man who'd issued the curt order. It was his brother, Derrick. Standing beside him was a very smug-looking Dr. Donald Kellogg.

"Hang up the phone," Derrick repeated as he leveled the gun at Abby's chest.

"What's wrong? What's going on?" Melissa was shouting as Steve hung up. Abby moved closer to him, and he pulled her protectively against his body.

"How touching," Derrick observed dryly. The two brothers glared at each other.

"You bastard!" Steve growled. "How could you kill your own sister?"

Derrick shrugged.

Abby continued to stare at Kellogg.

Steve's gaze swung to the other man. "I know you. You're Gerheiser."

"A perfectly natural mistake on your part. However, Dr. Gerheiser doesn't exist. He was just a convenient fiction we used for signing records."

"You were the one who interrogated me." Steve's expression twisted with remembered pain.

"Yes."

"But your car. On the ferry..." Abby broke in.

The surgeon made a dismissive gesture. "What a pity. I rather liked that sedan. But luckily for me I wasn't driving. George Napier, I believe you call him, was kind enough to bring the vehicle down to Oxford."

No. Stop. Unreal. Not happening, Abby's mind screamed. "You...lied...to me," she whispered.

"My apologies, my dear." Kellogg gestured toward Steve and Abby. "Both of you, step away from the phone. Stand over there by the window where I can see what you're doing. And no sudden moves."

She was viewing the scene through someone else's eyes, hearing through someone else's ears. That was the only way she could be here in this room and not sink to the floor in terror.

"Move!"

On someone else's legs she followed directions. She wasn't sure they would hold her up. She wanted to reach for Steve's hand. At least that would give her the illusion of reassurance. But his arms were stiff at his sides.

"How did you find us?" Abby managed.

"We started asking around about the pickup truck. Your friend Wayne got into an argument with one of the locals at a bar," Derrick explained. "There was a shouting match in the parking lot, and Wayne drove away before he got slugged. The guy who wanted to lay him out remembered the truck."

"Shut up," Kellogg snapped. "This isn't a briefing session."

Derrick's face seethed with suppressed anger, and he jerked the gun toward Steve and Abby. "Don't move a muscle," he ordered.

While Derrick kept his gun trained on the pair, the surgeon placed another call to Baltimore.

"This is Dr. Donald Kellogg. Is the Medevac helicopter standing by? Good. Let me give you the location..." As he hung up, he smiled pleasantly at Steve and Abby, but he didn't lower the gun. "All taken care of. Your transportation will be here shortly. Then both of you will be able to make yourselves useful around the clinic."

Slowly reality was seeping into Abby's brain, but she didn't ask for any more details. She was pretty sure she knew what Kellogg had in mind for both her and Steve now. Used parts. Just like the men from the Lazarus Mission.

"Until it's time to leave, I suggest we all sit down and make ourselves comfortable," the surgeon continued.

The captives were directed to the couch. They were going to let her sit down. She was almost grateful. She wouldn't have to stand on wobbly legs anymore.

As Abby started to sink down, she noticed that Steve was no longer at her side. Glancing quickly behind her, she saw he was edging around the sofa and backing up toward the corner of the room. His face was white, his upper lip beaded with sweat.

"Get over here, Claiborne," Kellogg growled. "Or you're really going to need medical attention."

"No," Steve shouted. His eyes were large and glazed and his movements were jerky. "You're not going to touch me again, you bastard."

Abby jumped up, the guns trained on them fading momentarily into the background. "Steve. Oh, God. It's all right. Please." She had been so sure he was getting better. The strain of being taken prisoner again must have been too much for him.

"What the hell's the matter with him?" Derrick snapped. As the gap widened between the pair of captives, he seemed uncertain whether to train his gun on Steve or Abby.

"Flashback," Abby breathed as she rounded the end table. "From all the damn drugs your doctor friend pumped into his body. It keeps happening to him." She was so intent on reaching Steve that she almost tripped over the electric cord to the lamp on the table.

"Sit down, Claiborne!" Kellogg bellowed.

Steve's eyes flicked wildly to Kellogg, then back to Abby. "Water." His voice was high-pitched, almost strangled. "Glass of water in my face."

"Steve, please," Abby tried again.

"What the hell's he talking about?" Derrick demanded.

Caught up in their own drama, the captives ignored him.

"Water in my face," he gibbered. "Cold water. Ł the river."

Kellogg made a disgusted noise. "What in hell are we going to do now?"

"You're the one who did this to him," Abby snapped, but she didn't turn to look at the surgeon or Derrick. She didn't dare face either one of them because she didn't want them to see the hope shining in her eyes. *Glass of water in my face.* After he'd gone off the end of the pier, Steve had said that the cold water had woken him up. Now, unless she was badly mistaken, he knew exactly what he was doing. He was trying to throw the enemy off balance so that they could escape. And he was doing a damn good job.

"What do you do for him when he's like this?" Kellogg demanded.

"Do you have any sedatives in your medical bag?" Abby questioned, as if the physician had suddenly become her best hope for bringing Steve around.

"Yes."

"He's going to need another injection to quiet him down."

Kellogg took an uncertain step toward the door.

"No, you're not going to give me any more shots." Steve backed away again, but his eyes bored into Abby now.

She nodded almost imperceptibly, hoping he would realize that she understood.

Abby's gaze was glued to Steve. His shoulders were almost against the wall. If only he could tell her what he wanted her to do. Cautiously she edged toward him, her whole body tense as she waited for further directions. The sofa was between her and the gunmen now.

In the distance she thought she heard the whir of a helicopter's propeller. No. Please, not yet, she prayed. If reinforcements came, it was all over.

Steve must have heard the noise, too. He glanced up, his face a mask of terror as he hunched his shoulders and cringed away. Then he was shouting. "Abby, down. Get down."

It was as if his words had triggered a series of reflexes in the people around the room. Abby dropped to the floor. Kellogg fired his gun, but his bullets plowed into the sofa cushions.

At the same time Steve reached down and pulled out the hunting knife that he'd found in Wayne's garage and strapped to his ankle before they'd left for the ferry. In one fluid motion he threw the knife at Derrick. It thunked into his brother's chest, and the older man folded.

Kellogg paused for a moment as he stared in stunned disbelief at his partner. Then he was dashing forward, his gun trained on Steve.

Abby couldn't see what was happening, but she heard the scuffle of feet. Was there *anything* she could do? Her finger closed around the electric cord, and she jerked it out of the outlet. She gave a hard yank, sending the ceramic lamp to the floor in a loud crash. The diversion stopped Kellogg for a few seconds, long enough for Steve to press his shoulders to the wall and give a mighty push with his legs against the sofa. The heavy piece of furniture flew forward across the floor and slammed into Kellogg's shins. He went down with a shout of pain. Even before he hit the floorboards, Steve was leaping across the sofa and twisting the gun from his hand.

Derrick's weapon had dropped out of his fingers. Abby scrambled around the sofa and scooped it up.

Holding it with both hands, she kept it trained on Derrick who had pulled the knife out of his chest and lay gasping in a growing pool of blood.

"Help. I need help," he moaned.

Steve stood staring down at the man on the floor. Despite everything it was hard to deal with the knowledge that he'd actually thrown the knife at his own brother. Yet Derrick had ordered Sharon killed. He and Abby would have been next.

Derrick looked up pleadingly, and Steve motioned to Kellogg. "See if you can do anything for him. But don't try any tricks." He turned away, pain and anger etched on his face.

"I think it's finally time to call the police," Abby added.

By the time two police cars arrived, Abby and Steve were holding four captives—Derrick, Kellogg and the two medics who had come to take them back to Sterling.

It took Dan Cassidy several days to sort out the details of the plot that had swirled around the Sterling Clinic. Some of the story came from Derrick. Recovered from a punctured lung, he realized the advantages of cooperating with the police, particularly after his wife Cecile had volunteered to testify against him and Kellogg, the man who had seduced her and then forced her to keep tabs on her husband for him. More information came from Ezra Hornby and Frances Backmann, Kellogg's other mistress.

Miss Backmann was picked up at Baltimore-Washington International Airport with a ticket to Hong Kong via Switzerland. In her possession were Sterling Clinic medical records and the number of a Swiss bank account Kellogg had earmarked for his private use.

Cassidy pieced a lot of the story together by comparing the different accounts from the principals. But he still wasn't ready to discuss the big picture until Steve forced the issue by refusing to give him any more cooperation.

As Steve stood up and leaned over the assistant district attorney's desk, Abby tried to put a restraining hand on his arm, but he wouldn't back down. "I think you're going to start giving us some answers now," he grated. "Or I'm going to walk out of here. And you're going to have a tough time sending a subpoena to Jamshedpur."

Cassidy studied the other man. Steve Claiborne had been through hell, and he was entitled to an explanation.

"A lot of the details are still confidential. We're not sure how far the network extends. Kellogg was planning to branch out with his own transplant practice here in Baltimore. But up till now the organs obtained at the clinic were being shipped around the country, even around the world."

"I have the feeling I delivered some of them myself," Steve admitted. "I thought I was working for an international health organization." When Cassidy started to open his mouth, Steve added, "I'm not going to sell an exposé to the *National Enquirer*. I just want to know what happened to my sister—and why."

The two men eyed each other. Finally Cassidy looked down. "Okay, I'll tell you everything we know. Cecile explained why the clinic decided it had to get your sister out of the way. Apparently Sharon was doing volunteer work in the kitchen at the Lazarus Mission and got to know some of the men. She was upset when a number of her friends disappeared and told Adam Goodwin."

"Her mistake," Steve said.

"Yes. From what I gather, he found out about Hornby's innovative source of income and told the clinic Sharon was on to them."

"So Wyndham gave the order to get rid of her?" Abby guessed.

Cassidy shook his head. "That's what we thought at first. But Wyndham wasn't running the show. Kellogg and Derrick had convinced him the scheme was a good idea, and at first he didn't object. Kellogg was the one in charge."

"So why did Ezra Hornby kill Adam?" Abby asked.

"He didn't. It only looked that way because he'd been at Adam's town house earlier demanding money. Kellogg had Goodwin murdered when he found out about the insurance scam he'd set up with Hornby."

"It's hard to picture all this intrigue going on in the middle of a respected hospital," Abby mused.

"They thought they could get away with it. Kellogg probably would have pulled the whole thing off if the two of you hadn't insisted on finding out why Sharon died," Cassidy said.

Steve and Abby exchanged glances. Then he turned back to Cassidy. "What can you tell us about George Napier? Was he really killed in the explosion?"

"Yes. By the way, his real name was George Nash. He was a small-time hood brought in to work at the hospital. After you began asking questions and showed up at the funeral, Wyndham got nervous and set him up to check you out—and 'fix' the elevator."

Abby felt a momentary chill sweep over her skin as she remembered the accident. George Nash or whatever the man's name really was had changed her feelings about elevators forever.

"Frances Backmann convinced him he was going down to meet the ferry and bring you back, but Kellogg's car was loaded with explosives."

"Why did they blow the ferry up? They must have realized I wasn't on it."

"It looks like Nash lost his touch. Probably because he was snitching samples from the hospital's drug supply. He botched the elevator job. Then on the ferry, either something was wrong with the controls or he pushed the wrong button."

Abby shuddered, remembering the explosion.

"Poetic justice," Steve murmured under his breath.

It was late in the afternoon before Steve and Abby finally escaped from the assistant D.A.'s office. From their questions to Cassidy they'd also learned that Kellogg had hired the woman named Michelle not only to drug Steve but also to strip Sharon's town house of incriminating evidence.

"We haven't found her yet," he'd said. "But we will."

Abby was surprised to discover that the sun was setting as they stepped out onto the street. Her body was stiff from having sat in Cassidy's office all day. As she stretched and rolled her shoulders, she saw that Steve was going through the same maneuver.

"How do you feel?" she asked.

"Tired but vindicated." Steve unlocked the car door, and they got in. "I guess you probably want to go home and get some rest," he added uncertainly.

"Aren't you hungry?" Abby grabbed for an excuse to keep them together.

"A little."

"We could go down to Harborplace and get something to take back to my apartment." Even as she made the suggestion, she felt a little self-conscious. Over the past few days her life had been intimately enmeshed with Steve's. Now she wasn't sure how to behave with him.

"I—" he began.

"We need to talk."

"All right."

Abby felt her tension mounting as they walked past stands selling everything from soft-shell crabs to buffalo wings and stir-fried vegetables. Somehow none of it looked appetizing. But she bought a fruit shake and a Hunan beef. Steve opted for French fries and a thick corned beef sandwich.

The silence between them seemed to stretch. "I'm glad we didn't really need all that crazy stuff in the puzzle box to figure out what was going on," Abby said as they made their way back to the car. "Hornby's computer disk was important as evidence, but I still don't understand the significance of the other things."

"I guess Sharon wasn't thinking straight by then because of the stuff Goodwin was feeding her." Steve's jaw clenched. Then he brought his emotions under control again. "Maybe she thought the tissue with lipstick was evidence of Cecile's affair. And I don't know about the acorn cups."

"There are oak trees all over the clinic grounds," Abby offered.

"That could be it. Anyway, I think I understand the silver dollar. Derrick had a collection of them. So I guess she was trying to tell you he was involved.'"

The conversation lapsed again. Silently they rode the elevator up to her apartment. Silently she opened the door and set the food on the table.

Steve pulled out a chair, sat down and unwrapped his sandwich. Since the hospital, his appetite had been voracious. Now, instead of eating, he just stared at the food. Abby took a few swallows of her fruit shake and realized she wasn't going to be able to choke her dinner down, either. It was time to stop dancing away from their emotions. Over the past few days she'd admitted to herself that she had fallen in love with Steve. But she wasn't sure how to break the news—or whether she even should.

"Are you planning to just walk out of my life?" Abby finally asked the question that had been haunting her.

Steve put down his drink and raised his eyes to her. "Abby, I care more about you than I would have believed possible. But it's all happened so fast. Like being caught in a whirlwind."

"I know." She was remembering the power and the intensity of her feelings the night they'd made love.

"I always expected to live my life a certain way—with no strings attached. Marriage and happily ever after weren't part of my vocabulary."

She dredged air from the bottom of her lungs. "You're leaving."

He raked a hand through his sun-streaked hair. "I don't even know how we'd work things out. Your life is here. I don't belong in Baltimore anymore."

She'd been trained to sit and listen. Now she wanted to interrupt, but he plowed ahead.

"We weren't exactly thrown together under normal circumstances. Now this pressure's building up inside me. I feel like I have to make the right decision or fly into a million pieces. But what I really have to do is get some perspective. You need that, too."

He could be right, although she was sure she'd come to the same conclusions no matter how long she had to think things over. All at once she couldn't simply watch him walk away without letting him know there was something to come back to.

"Steve, I expected to live my life a certain way, too. I told you that it was going to be safe and predictable. Then you practically accused me of malpractice, and I decided I was going to prove you were wrong."

"Sweetheart, I'm sorry. I was way off base about that. I was off base about a lot of things."

"Don't be sorry. I learned some important lessons from you. I found out that when you have strong feelings about something—or someone—you have to go with your instincts or die a little bit inside."

They stared at each other across the kitchen table the way they had once before. But now there was a different kind of tension between them. "My instincts tell me the two of us belong together. But if you can't come to that conclusion yourself, all the arguments in the world won't convince you. Go back to India if that's what you need to do. But remember that I love you."

"Abby, I'm not even sure what love is."

"You just have to decide that you're not afraid to learn."

"What if I can't be anything different than the man I made myself into?"

"You've already started to change."

"What do you mean?"

"The way you've opened yourself to me. I could point out a lot of little things. But think about how it was back at Wayne's when Kellogg and Derrick had their guns trained on us. You trusted me to do the right thing the way you've never trusted anyone before in your life. If I hadn't caught on to what you were doing when you pulled that flashback trick, we would have both been killed."

He stood up and came around the table. In one swift motion he pulled her out of her chair and into his arms.

For a moment suspended in time he hugged her tight against his body, and she knew that all the forces of nature couldn't tear them apart if he didn't want to let her go.

"Abby, I didn't have time to think about the consequences at Wayne's."

"That's what I mean."

There was more she wanted to say, but logic had no role here. Only emotion.

There was more he should say. But talking wasn't going to solve anything now.

Letting her go was the hardest thing he'd ever done in his life. But before she could see the moisture that threatened to brim out of his eyes and down his cheeks, he turned and strode toward the door.

Epilogue

It was a hot afternoon in August. Abby Franklin, Jo O'Malley and Laura Roswell had just come back from a late lunch in Little Italy.

"Thank God the air-conditioning's working again," Jo observed as they stepped into the lobby of 43 Light Street. "If we had to spend another week like the last one, I was planning to pack it in and go visit my mom up in Garrett County."

"At least you don't have to wear a suit to work," Laura said, lifting her blond hair so that the back of her neck could cool off.

"You've been awful quiet, Abby," Jo remarked.

"I'm just tired."

The two other women shot her sympathetic looks. They'd both tried to get Abby to talk about Steve Claiborne. But she'd made it clear that the topic was off-limits.

"Maybe you could come up to western Maryland with me this weekend," Jo suggested. "We could do some sailing on Deep Creek Lake. Or some hiking."

"Maybe." Abby didn't put a lot of enthusiasm into her response, and the three friends parted.

Her first afternoon session was with a young mother suffering a postpartum depression. At least she was still competent to deal with other people's problems, Abby thought with satisfaction after the woman had left. Her patient was feeling better. It was the therapist who needed some intensive counseling.

She closed her eyes for a moment and tried to will the tightness out of her chest. It had been almost three months. If Steve was coming back, he'd be here by now. She had to accept his decision and get on with her life.

Two other patients filled the afternoon. Then Abby was alone again. Unable to face going home to her empty apartment, she sat at the desk writing up some notes.

She wasn't sure what made her look up. Certainly not the sound of a footstep. But all at once the doorway between her inner and outer offices was filled with a tall male figure. He wore boots, faded slacks and a rumpled khaki shirt that looked as if they'd traveled halfway around the world in an airplane cockpit.

"I told you to get a better lock." The voice was gritty and edged with fatigue.

"I did."

"Not good enough."

Abby studied Steve's face. It was leaner than she remembered, and his cheeks and chin were covered with blond stubble. But the overall impression was the same as when she'd first seen him. He looked untamed, dangerous, aggressive. Yet there was a hint of something in the blue eyes that hadn't been there before. Something that made her heart turn over in her chest.

Neither one of them moved. But the air in the room was suddenly charged as if a summer storm were about to break. Heat lightning seemed to crackle in the atmosphere. Like the night they'd made love. But what was going to happen now?

She swallowed around the lump that blocked her throat. "How are you?"

"Tired. Out of sorts. Half crazy with wanting you. And yourself?"

"Tired. Half crazy with wanting you. And suddenly feeling a whole lot better than I have in months."

He was across the room then in two quick steps. Just as he had the last time they'd seen each other, he hauled her out of her chair and folded her into his arms.

She pressed her face against his chest, breathing in his familiar scent, giddy with joy. Yet even now she was hardly able to take in the reality of his return.

"It took you long enough to come back," she said through a smile.

"You're glad to see me." His voice held a note of relief—and wonder.

"Did you think I wouldn't be?"

"I wasn't sure." His Adam's apple bobbed. "You might have had second thoughts...."

"I've had second thoughts, all right. About telling you to go back to India." Abby's hands sifted through Steve's hair. "So what are you doing in Baltimore?"

"Groveling." There was a nervous edge to his laughter. "Actually it took me about thirty minutes to realize I was miserable without you. But I kept telling myself that you were better off without me."

"Never!"

"After a while I started thinking about what you told me that night at Wayne's."

"I told you a lot of things. I wasn't sure you wanted to listen."

"I must have been paying attention on some level. You said I had to ask for what I wanted. That's pretty simple, really. And pretty scary."

She waited, hardly daring to breathe.

"Abby, will you . . . would you consider some kind of permanent arrangement with a guy like me?"

"Only if it's very permanent."

"Thank the Lord."

He covered her lips with his, and for long moments there were only murmurs and small sighs of pleasure as they feasted on each other.

When he raised his head, his expression was fierce—yet still edged with uncertainty. "But, sweetheart, we will have a bunch of details to work out. I mean, I haven't had much practice with commitments."

She stroked a gentle finger against his cheek. "You weren't afraid to ask for my love. Even if you couldn't quite say the word."

His eyes met hers. The uncertainty was gone. "Abigail, I'm not afraid to tell you I love you."

"Steve, you can even call me Abigail. But only in private. The important thing is that you love me. The rest will work itself out."

He clung to her promise. But there was one thing he did know for sure. This time he wasn't going to let her go.

Harlequin Intrigue®

COMING NEXT MONTH

#145 SOUTHERN CROSS by Jenna Ryan
At NORStar Space Park, fantasy became reality.
There, dreams came true . . . but so did nightmares.
Especially for Kristian Ellis, who witnessed a murder
but couldn't prove it. Only one man could help her—
Tory Roberts, part-owner of the space park, the man
determined to become a permanent part of her life.

#146 DIAMOND OF DECEIT by M. L. Gamble
Bank exec Emma Kingston was vacationing when the
vault blew up. A man was killed—his identity
strangely obliterated—and a king's ransom littered
the floor but not a thing was stolen. Philip Rowlands
had an explanation: after years of hunting down
Coop, Emma's fiancé, Philip tracked him to the
bizarre break-in. Did Emma have something that
belonged to Coop? She claimed she had nothing but
memories that had turned bitter two years ago when
Coop was presumed dead. Was Philip the answer to
an imperiled woman's prayers? Or the deluded
prisoner of an obsession?

HARLEQUIN'S WISHBOOK
SWEEPSTAKES RULES & REGULATIONS
NO PURCHASE NECESSARY TO ENTER OR RECEIVE A PRIZE

1. To enter and join the Reader Service, affix the Four Free Books and Free Gifts sticker along with both of your other Sweepstakes stickers to the Sweepstakes Entry Form. If you do not wish to take advantage of our Reader Service, but wish to enter the Sweepstakes only, do not affix the Four Free Books and Free Gifts sticker to the Sweepstakes Entry Form. Incomplete and/or inaccurate entries are ineligible for that section or sections of prizes. Not responsible for mutilated or unreadable entries or inadvertent printing errors. Mechanically reproduced entries are null and void.

2. Whether you take advantage of this offer or not, your Sweepstakes numbers will be compared against a list of winning numbers generated at random by the computer. In the event that all prizes are not claimed by March 31, 1992, a random drawing will be held from all qualified entries received from March 30, 1990 to March 31, 1992, to award all unclaimed prizes. All cash prizes (Grand to Sixth), will be mailed to the winners and are payable by check in U.S. funds. Seventh prize to be shipped to winners via third-class mail. These prizes are in addition to any free, surprise or mystery gifts that might be offered. Versions of this sweepstakes with different prizes of approximate equal value may appear in other mailings or at retail outlets by Torstar Corp. and its affiliates.

3. The following prizes are awarded in this sweepstakes: ★ Grand Prize (1) $1,000,000; First Prize (1) $25,000; Second Prize (1) $10,000; Third Prize (5) $5,000; Fourth Prize (10) $1,000; Fifth Prize (100) $250; Sixth Prize (2500) $10; ★ ★ Seventh Prize (6000) $12.95 ARV.

   ★ This Sweepstakes contains a Grand Prize offering of $1,000,000 annuity. Winner will receive $33,333.33 a year for 30 years without interest totalling $1,000,000.

   ★ ★ Seventh Prize: A fully illustrated hardcover book published by Torstar Corp. Approximate value of the book is $12.95.

   Entrants may cancel the Reader Service at any time without cost or obligation to buy (see details in center insert card).

4. This promotion is being conducted under the supervision of Marden-Kane, Inc., an independent judging organization. By entering this Sweepstakes, each entrant accepts and agrees to be bound by these rules and the decisions of the judges, which shall be final and binding. Odds of winning in the random drawing are dependent upon the total number of entries received. Taxes, if any, are the sole responsibility of the winners. Prizes are nontransferable. All entries must be received by no later than 12:00 NOON, on March 31, 1992. The drawing for all unclaimed sweepstakes prizes will take place May 30, 1992, at 12:00 NOON, at the offices of Marden-Kane, Inc., Lake Success, New York.

5. This offer is open to residents of the U.S., the United Kingdom, France and Canada, 18 years or older except employees and their immediate family members of Torstar Corp., its affiliates, subsidiaries, Marden-Kane, Inc., and all other agencies and persons connected with conducting this Sweepstakes. All Federal, State and local laws apply. Void wherever prohibited or restricted by law. Any litigation respecting the conduct and awarding of a prize in this publicity contest may be submitted to the Régie des loteries et courses du Québec.

6. Winners will be notified by mail and may be required to execute an affidavit of eligibility and release which must be returned within 14 days after notification or an alternative winner will be selected. Canadian winners will be required to correctly answer an arithmetical skill-testing question administered by mail which must be returned within a limited time. Winners consent to the use of their names, photographs and/or likenesses for advertising and publicity in conjunction with this and similar promotions without additional compensation.

7 For a list of our major winners, send a stamped, self-addressed envelope to: WINNERS LIST c/o MARDEN-KANE, INC., P.O. BOX 701, SAYREVILLE, NJ 08871. Winners Lists will be fulfilled after the May 30, 1992 drawing date.

If Sweepstakes entry form is missing, please print your name and address on a 3"×5" piece of plain paper and send to:

In the U.S.
Harlequin's WISHBOOK Sweepstakes
P.O. Box 1867
Buffalo, NY 14269-1867

In Canada
Harlequin's WISHBOOK Sweepstakes
P.O. Box 609
Fort Erie, Ontario
L2A 5X3

Offer limited to one per household.

LTY-H890

COMING SOON...

For years Harlequin and Silhouette novels have been taking readers places—but only in their imaginations.

This fall look for PASSPORT TO ROMANCE, a promotion that could take you around the corner or around the world!

Watch for it in September!

★

Harlequin® / *Silhouette*®